T0266151

The Gospel in
Dorothy L. Sayers

Dorothy Sayers, 1928

The Gospel in Dorothy L. Sayers

Selections from Her Novels, Plays, Letters, and Essays

Edited by Carole Vanderhoof

PLOUGH PUBLISHING HOUSE

Published by Plough Publishing House
Walden, New York
Robertsbridge, England
Elsmore, Australia
www.plough.com

Plough produces books, a quarterly magazine, and Plough.com to encourage people and help them put their faith into action. We believe Jesus can transform the world and that his teachings and example apply to all aspects of life. At the same time, we seek common ground with all people regardless of their creed.

Plough is the publishing house of the Bruderhof, an international Christian community. The Bruderhof is a fellowship of families and singles practicing radical discipleship in the spirit of the first church in Jerusalem (Acts 2 and 4). Members devote their entire lives to serving God, one another, and their neighbors, renouncing private property and sharing everything. To learn more about the Bruderhof's faith, history, and daily life, see Bruderhof.com. (Views expressed by Plough authors are their own and do not necessarily reflect the position of the Bruderhof.)

Copyright © 2018 by Plough Publishing House
All rights reserved.

Excerpts from Dorothy L. Sayers are copyrighted and reprinted by permission of the estate of Dorothy Sayers, the Watkins/Loomis Agency, and the following publishers: HarperCollins, Houghton Mifflin Harcourt, Open Road Integrated Media, and Thomas Nelson. See acknowledgements page for details.

ISBN: 978-0-87486-181-5
22 21 20 19 18   1 2 3 4 5 6 7

Cover image: Pictorial Press Ltd / Alamy Stock Photo.
Image on page ii: Alpha Historica / Alamy Stock Photo
A catalog record for this book is available from the British Library.
Library of Congress Cataloging-in-Publication Data

Names: Sayers, Dorothy L. (Dorothy Leigh), 1893-1957, author. | Vanderhoof, Carole, editor. | Lewis, C. S. (Clive Staples), 1898-1963, contributor.
Title: The Gospel in Dorothy Sayers : selections from her novels, plays, letters, and essays / edited by Carole Vanderhoof, with an appreciation by C. S. Lewis.
Description: Walden, New York : Plough Publishing House, 2018. | Includes bibliographical references.
Identifiers: LCCN 2018027266 (print) | LCCN 2018034836 (ebook) | ISBN 9780874866582 (epub) | ISBN 9780874866599 (mobi) | ISBN 9780874866636 (pdf) | ISBN 9780874861815 (pbk.)
Classification: LCC PR6037.A95 (ebook) | LCC PR6037.A95 A6 2018 (print) | DDC 823/.912--dc23
LC record available at https://lccn.loc.gov/2018027266

Printed in the United States of America

Contents

Introduction

... Please realise that words are not just "talky-talk" – they are real and vital; they can change the face of the world. They are a form of action – "in the beginning was the Word . . . by Whom all things were made." Even the spate of futile words that pours out from the ephemeral press and the commercial-fiction-mongers has a real and terrible power; it can become a dope as dangerous as drugs or drink; it can rot the mind, sap the reason, send the will to sleep; it can pull down empires and set the neck of the people under the heel of tyranny. "For every idle word that ye speak ye shall render account at the day of judgment." I do not think that means that we shall have to pay a fine in a few million years' time for every occasion on which we said "dash it all" or indulged in a bit of harmless frivol; but I do think it was meant as an urgent warning against abusing or under-rating the power of words, and that the judgment is eternal – that is, it is here and now.[1]

For almost a century, the murder mysteries of Dorothy L. Sayers have kept enthusiasts hungrily turning pages. Many of these readers never guess how seriously Sayers took the business of wielding words, or realize that she is also known for her acumen

---

1 Dorothy L. Sayers, "A Note on Creative Reading," in *Begin Here: A Statement of Faith* (London: Victor Gollancz, 1940).

as an essayist, playwright, apologist, theologian, and translator. This anthology brings together the best of both worlds; the
selections uncover the gospel themes woven throughout Sayers's
popular fiction alongside related readings from her plays, letters,
talks, and essays.

It took a lifetime for Dorothy L. Sayers to explore the power
of words; her passion for expression grew with age and experience. Already something of a celebrity for her detective stories,
during the bombing of Britain in World War II she increasingly
deployed her words to address more pressing social issues and
matters of faith, which brought a deluge of demands on her time.
But attempts to divert her from practicing her art as a writer
were fruitless. As she once wrote, "To take novelists and play-
wrights away from doing good work in their own line . . . and
collar them for the purpose of preaching sermons or opening
Church bazaars is a spoiling of God's instrument and defeats its
own aims in the end." [2]

Often the unbeliever responded with interest, much to her
surprise. Perhaps this was because her approach was rarely
didactic, as she wrote in an exchange of letters with C. S. Lewis:

> You must not look at them from above, or outside, and say: "Poor
> creatures; they would obviously be the better for so-and-so – I
> must try and make up a dose for them." You've got to come gal-
> loping out shouting excitedly: "Look here! Look what I've found!
> Come and have a bit of it – it's grand – you'll love it – I can't keep
> it to myself, and anyhow, I want to know what you think of it." [3]

2   Sayers to Count Michael de la Bedoyere, editor of the *Catholic Herald,* October
    7, 1941, *The Letters of Dorothy L. Sayers: Volume Two: 1937–1943: From Novelist
    to Playwright,* ed. by Barbara Reynolds (Cambridge: Dorothy L. Sayers Society,
    1997), 308.

3   Sayers to Lewis, July 31, 1946, *The Letters of Dorothy L. Sayers: Volume Three: 1944–
    1950: A Noble Daring,* ed. by Barbara Reynolds (Cambridge: Dorothy L. Sayers
    Society, 1998), 253.

Her undiplomatic passion earned her a crusty and brash reputation. Lewis called her "gleefully ogreish."[4] But in her personal
correspondence she sometimes displays a humbler side, one that
isn't quite as assured as she was in print. Before we survey her
work it is worth reviewing the life of this engaging and forthright woman.

Sayers was born in Oxford in 1893. Her father was headmaster
at the Christ Church Cathedral School there, but within a year
the family moved to the fen country when he accepted a job as
rector of an Anglican church in Huntingdonshire. She was an
only child, educated by her parents and governesses at home and
steeped in the atmosphere of the church. At sixteen she entered
the Godolphin School in Salisbury, and reveled in the drama
and music programs. In 1915 Sayers received a certificate of first
class honors in medieval French literature from the all-women
Somerville College at Oxford. Almost immediately she published two books of poetry: *Op. I* in 1916 and *Catholic Tales and
Christian Songs* in 1918.

Sayers considered herself Anglo-Catholic, the High-Church
branch of Anglicanism. She used the word "Catholic" in her
writings to mean ecumenical, addressing her lectures and articles to Roman Catholics, Anglo-Catholics, and Greek Orthodox
alike. "I make it a rule never to make an attack on any one of
these three communions, and never, if I can help it, to exhibit
their disagreements but to emphasise their agreement."[5]

4   C. S. Lewis, "A Panegyric for Dorothy L. Sayers," in *On Stories and Other Essays
    on Literature,* ed. Walter Hooper (London: Harcourt Brace Jovanovich, 1966).
5   As quoted in Laura K. Simmons, *Creed without Chaos: Exploring Theology in the
    Writings of Dorothy I. Sayers* (Grand Rapids: Baker Academic, 2005), 16.

During the First World War women found more job opportunities open to them, although the *"Kinder, Küche, Kirche"* [6] debate over the role of women in the workplace raged. Sayers would address this conflict in essays and several of her later mystery novels. At the time, however, she was only able to secure short-lived jobs teaching, tutoring, and as an intern in a publishing house. It was only in 1920 that Oxford awarded degrees to women; she was one of the first to receive a retroactive master's degree. Eight years afterward, Parliament passed laws that gave women voting rights equal to those of men.

Following several years of unemployment, living on an allowance from her parents and doing odd translation jobs, she became an advertising copywriter for S. H. Benson's in London, a large and prosperous agency. By all accounts she was successful, coming up with jingles and tag lines for Coleman's Mustard and Guinness Beer (My goodness, My Guinness!). In her off hours she started working on her first mystery novel, *Whose Body?*, which was published in 1923.

After a series of unhappy relationships, Sayers bore a son out of wedlock in 1924. The father was a married man; he did not acknowledge the boy. A cousin who took in foster children provided a home for the child. For the rest of her life Sayers kept her son a secret from her parents and the public, although she was in constant contact with her cousin and provided the money for the boy's keep and education. Sayers knew that the situation would have shamed her father and caused gossip in his congregation. It is significant, in light of what must have been an unremitting guilt, that Sayers wrote with intensity of the role of the conscience, repentance, and salvation throughout her life, in her fiction and plays as well as her essays.

---

6   A German phrase translated "children, kitchen, church," the supposed sphere of women.

In 1926, Sayers married Captain Oswald Atherton "Mac" Fleming, a Scottish journalist and World War I veteran. Since he was divorced they could not have a church wedding; they were married in a registry office. Neighbors knew Sayers as Mrs. Fleming, although she continued to use "Dorothy L. Sayers" as a pen name. From her lively letters to her mother, it appears that hilarious jaunts in Sayers's old motorcycle and sidecar typified the early years of their marriage. Unfortunately, his health declined – perhaps due to being wounded and gassed in the war – and when he could no longer work, Mac drank heavily. Sayers continued to care for him until his death in 1950.

One of the founding members of the Detection Club, Sayers reigned as president from 1949 until her death. G.K. Chesterton preceded her, and Agatha Christie succeeded her in the role. When a new member joined, he or she had to take the club oath, with one hand on a skull: "Do you promise that your Detectives shall well and truly detect the Crimes presented to them, using those Wits which it shall please you to bestow upon them, and not placing reliance upon, nor making use of, Divine Revelation, Feminine Intuition, Mumbo-Jumbo, Jiggery-Pokery, Coincidence, or the Act of God?"[7] The club sometimes even wrote books collaboratively, with each author contributing a chapter.

Those who know Dorothy L. Sayers as a writer of religious essays often wonder how she could also write popular fiction. Of course, at the beginning the books were a way to make a living, cashing in on the detective story craze of the twenties. Agatha Christie was writing her Miss Marple mysteries, and

7   Alzina Stone Dale, *Maker and Craftsman: The Story of Dorothy L. Sayers* (Lincoln, NE: iUniverse, 2003), 77.

G. K. Chesterton his Father Brown tales. Sayers, like Chesterton, found murder mysteries a vehicle to explore the choices characters make between good and evil. But she never let that get in the way of spinning a captivating yarn. In the introduction to a collection of short stories that she edited, she admits the widespread attraction of the genre:

> Some prefer the intellectual cheerfulness of the detective story; some the uneasy emotions of the ghost story; but in either case, the tale must be about dead bodies or very wicked people, preferably both, before the Tired Business Man can feel really happy and at peace with the world. . . . [Such stories] make you feel that it is good to be alive, and that, while alive, it is better, on the whole, for you to be good. (Detective authors, by the way, are nearly all as good as gold, because it is part of their job to believe and to maintain that Your Sin Will Find You Out. That is why Detective Fiction is, or should be, such a good influence in a degenerate world, and that, no doubt, is why so many bishops, school masters, eminent statesmen and others with reputations to support, read detective stories to improve their morals, and keep themselves out of mischief.)[8]

The public devoured Sayers's mysteries with enthusiasm and she was able to quit her job at Benson's to write full-time in 1931. Three years later, when her son was ten, Sayers announced to her friends that she had "adopted" him – a prevarication, since legally she was already his mother. The boy assumed the surname Fleming, although he still lived with the cousin when not at boarding school.

As Sayers matures with the characters in her fiction, her themes become more subtle and perceptive. *Gaudy Night* (1935) and *Busman's Honeymoon* (1936), her last two published

---

8   Dorothy L. Sayers, *Great Short Stories of Detection, Mystery, and Horror, Third Series* (London: Victor Gollancz, 1934), 11–12.

mysteries, are Sayers best-known works today. In these books her characters have developed realistic human complexity, and Sayers has clearly drifted from the intellectual puzzle detective story into the realm of the novel. Indeed, *Busman's Honeymoon,* which was originally a stage play, is subtitled *A Love Story with Detective Interruptions.* In it, the formerly happy-go-lucky Lord Peter Wimsey agonizes over sending a criminal to face the death penalty. Wimsey visits the condemned man to ask his forgiveness on the night before the execution, and is met with curses. It takes hours of painful brooding before he returns to Harriet. Will he open himself to his new wife and admit his weakness? She knows she cannot force him, but waits to see if he will turn to her for comfort. In the pre-dawn hours he finally ascends the stairs. These scenes are more reminiscent of Jane Austen than Arthur Conan Doyle. Sayers has pushed the murder mystery as far as she could toward the tense interpersonal exploration of the modern novel.

It is not difficult to find gospel themes in Sayers's fiction. Wimsey never calls himself a Christian, but Sayers uses his ambivalence to present subtle questions of faith to the reader. At the end of this last book it is Lord Peter's conscience, heightened to excruciating sensitivity by tragic experiences as an officer in World War I, that turn his thoughts toward eternity as he waits for the hour of the criminal's execution. He asks Harriet:

"If there *is* a God or a judgment – what next? What have we done?"

"I don't know. But I don't suppose anything we could do would prejudice the defence."

"I suppose not. I wish we knew more about it."[9]

9 Dorothy L. Sayers, *Busman's Honeymoon: A Love Story with Detective Interruptions* (London: Victor Gollancz, 1937), 378–379.

Although Sayers would write and publish a few more detective short stories in the next years, she had come to the end of what she wanted to express in the genre. Instead she turned to writing plays with Christian themes, like *The Zeal of Thy House,* performed at the Canterbury Festival in 1937. An account of an architect who rebuilt part of Canterbury Cathedral after a twelfth-century fire forms the kernel of the play. His arrogance leads to his literal downfall – he injures himself falling from a lift that he had designed. Human fallibility destroys, but out of our weakness God can bring good – another gospel theme – as the architect learns humility and turns to repentance at the close of the scene.

As part of play's promotion Sayers wrote several pieces for newspapers insisting that the gospel is an exciting story. The most outstanding is "The Dogma Is the Drama," an article published in April 1938 in *St. Martin's Review.* It begins with the startling statement: "'Any stigma,' said a witty tongue, 'will do to beat a dogma'; and the flails of ridicule have been brandished with such energy of late on the threshing-floor of controversy that the true seed of the Word has become well-nigh lost amid the whirling of chaff." Her reputation as an apologist and theologian flourished, much to her chagrin. She called herself a playwright.

Reluctantly, Sayers agreed to radio broadcasts and lectures. She compiled the essays and articles into books such as *Unpopular Opinions* and *Creed or Chaos?* Another theologically innovative book-length essay, *The Mind of the Maker,* illuminates the nature of the Trinity using the analogy of the creative process. In her introduction to a 1979 edition, Madeleine L'Engle asserts that "the joy of this book is the vitality of the writer's mind, and her luminous understanding of human creativity."

In 1941 the BBC commissioned Sayers to write a series of radio plays on the life of Christ. Broadcast between Christmas 1941 and October 1942, they stirred up a storm of controversy. It was perhaps the first time that an actor had played the voice of Christ on the radio. In addition to that scandal, Sayers's characters spoke contemporary English, not the words of the King James Version of the Bible. She worked directly from the Greek sources, and this gave the broadcasts an immediacy that brought the gospel, in all its raw violence and beauty, into two million living rooms.[10] *The Man Born to Be King: A Play-Cycle on the Life of Our Lord and Saviour Jesus Christ* was then published in book form in 1943.

The director of religious broadcasting at the BBC, Dr. James Welch, wrote to the Archbishop of Canterbury, William Temple, regarding Sayers's dramas, "My serious judgment is that these plays have done more for the preaching of the Gospel to the unconverted than any other single effort of the churches or religious broadcasting since the last war – that is a big statement, but my experience forces me to make it."[11] In August 1943, Archbishop Temple nominated Sayers for a Lambeth Doctorate in Divinity, which she declined. Her reply to the archbishop is surprisingly humble:

> Thank you very much for the great honour you do me. I find it very difficult to reply as I ought, because I am extremely conscious that I don't deserve it. A Doctorate of Letters – yes; I have served Letters as faithfully as I knew how. But I have only served Divinity, as it were, accidentally, coming to it as a writer rather than as a Christian person. A Degree in Divinity is not, I suppose, intended as a certificate of sanctity, exactly; but I should feel better

---

10 Foreword by J. W. Welch to *The Man Born to Be King*, 12.

11 Welch to William Temple, June 1943, *Letters*, 2:429.

about it if I were a more convincing kind of Christian. I am never quite sure whether I really am one, or whether I have only fallen in love with an intellectual pattern.[12]

She goes on to say that her future output will not be on the "austere level" of the recent radio plays. "I can't promise not to break out into something thoroughly secular, frivolous or unbecoming. . . . I shouldn't like your first woman D. D. to create scandal, or give reviewers cause to blaspheme."

Perhaps she was protecting her privacy against notoriety that might have resulted in the exposure of her son. But this reply is also typical of her policy not to set forth her own personal beliefs, or promote herself, but explain the gospel as contained in the creeds of the church. Fan letters made her irritable. She enclosed this dry retort in a letter to a friend, "Why do you want a letter from me telling you about God? You will never bother to check up on it and find out whether I am giving you a personal opinion or the Church's doctrine, and your minds are so confused that you would rather hear the former than the latter. Go away and do some work, and let me get on with mine."[13]

One of the best examples of Sayers's humorous letters is the earliest extant from her long correspondence with C. S. Lewis. Writing as though she is one of the devils in Lewis's book, *The Screwtape Letters*, which had just come out the previous year, she enclosed an advance copy of *The Man Born to Be King*. In the letter she writes as "Sluckdrib," the devil personally responsible for Dorothy L. Sayers:

The effect of writing these plays upon the character of my patient is wholly satisfactory. I have already had the honour to report

12 Sayers to Temple, September 7, 1943, *Letters*, 2:430.

13 Satiric letter written by Sayers to Eric Fenn of the BBC, who had passed on to her a request for a letter "setting forth the Christian Faith and the Christian Way of Life." This "Letter Addressed to 'Average People'" was published in a church paper, *The City Temple Tidings*, July 1946.

intellectual and spiritual pride, vainglory, self-opinionated dog-matism, irreverence, blasphemous frivolity, frequentation of the company of theatricals, captiousness, impatience of correction, polemical fury, shortness of temper, neglect of domestic affairs, lack of charity, egotism, nostalgia for secular occupations, and a growing tendency to consider the Bible as Literature. . . .[but] the capture of one fifth-rate soul (which was already thoroughly worm-eaten and shaky owing to my assiduous attention) scarcely compensates for the fact that numbers of stout young souls in brand-new condition are opening up negotiations with the Enemy and receiving reinforcement of faith. *We* knew, of course, that the author is as corrupt as a rotten cheese; why has no care been taken to see that this corruption (which must, surely, permeate the whole work) has its proper effect upon the listeners? . . . Either the Enemy is really able to turn thorns into grapes and thistles into figs, or (as I prefer to believe) there is mismanagement somewhere.[14]

Not long afterward, hearing the missile attack siren, Sayers grabbed a handy book on her way to the air raid shelter in her backyard. This was the beginning of her last great love affair with words. The book was Dante's *Inferno*. This epic saga of sin, repentance, and salvation lit her imagination. She wrote, "I feel it is, as Tennyson observed, 'one clear call for me.'"[15] In a blaze of enthusiasm, she taught herself to read medieval Italian so that she could make her own translation of the *Divine Comedy*.

It is no wonder that her play *The Just Vengeance,* performed a year after the cataclysmic end of World War II, broods on Dantean themes of original sin, inherited guilt, and shared responsibility. Barbara Reynolds, Sayers's good friend and biog-rapher, holds that it is in this play that Sayers moves beyond just an intellectual assent to the creeds. The Christ figure's final

14 Sayers to Lewis, May 13, 1943, *Letters,* 2:410–411.

15 Sayers to the Dean of Chichester, March 7, 1947, *Letters,* 3:299.

speech, which Reynolds calls "one of the most moving things [Sayers] ever wrote," is "a profession of her own faith and hope."[16]

> Come then, and take again your own sweet will
> That once was buried in the spicy grave
> With Me, and now is risen with Me, more sweet
> Than myrrh and cassia; come, receive again
> All your desires, but better than your dreams,
> All your lost loves, but lovelier than you knew,
> All your fond hopes, but higher than your hearts
> Could dare to frame them; all your City of God
> Built by your faith, but nobler than you planned.[17]

As she worked on Dante's epic, Sayers's admiration for medieval scholarship grew, which resulted in a lecture given at an Oxford summer school for teachers. "The Lost Tools of Learning," like a pebble thrown into a pond, spawned a "classical education" movement that continues to cite Sayers as an inspiration. In the United States alone, the Association of Classical Christian Schools now boasts over two hundred member schools.

Sayers's goal is familiar: "For the sole true end of education is simply this: to teach men how to learn for themselves." But her surprising proposition is to call for a return to teaching grammar, logic, and rhetoric as the primary tools for achieving this purpose.

> For we let our young men and women go out unarmed, in a day when armour was never so necessary. By teaching them all to read, we have left them at the mercy of the printed word. By the invention of the film and the radio, we have made certain that no aversion to reading shall secure them from the incessant battery

---

16 *Letters*, 2:299.

17 Dorothy L. Sayers, "The Just Vengeance," *Four Sacred Plays* (London: Victor Gollancz, 1948).

of words, words, words. They do not know what the words mean; they do not know how to ward them off or blunt their edge or fling them back; they are a prey to words in their emotions instead of being the masters of them in their intellects.[18]

Sayers finished the first book of her *Divine Comedy* translation, *Hell*, in 1949, surprising reviewers with fearless poetry that used the original rhyme scheme and meter, a feat hitherto considered impossible. The second volume, *Purgatory,* was published in 1955, along with *Introductory Papers on Dante,* a collection of her lectures. These books, with her introductions and notes, are still in print today; more than a million readers have benefited from her work. Reynolds calls them "a literary and cultural phenomenon unprecedented in Dante studies."[19]

At this point Sayers took a break from Dante and reworked her translation of *The Song of Roland,* which she had begun forty years before. Of this epic poem she said, "It is not merely Christian in subject; it is Christian to its very bones. . . . And it is a Christianity as naïve and uncomplicated as might be found at any time in the simplest village church. These violent men of action are called on to do their valiant duty to the Faith and to the Emperor; and when they die, they will be taken to lie on beds of flowers among – strangely but somehow appropriately – the Holy Innocents, in a Paradise inhabited by God and His angels."[20]

18 Dorothy L. Sayers, *The Lost Tools of Learning* (London: Methuen, 1948).

19 *Letters,* 3:xiv.

20 Dorothy L. Sayers, introduction to *The Song of Roland,* trans. by Dorothy L. Sayers (New York: Penguin, 1957), 19.

As she began to translate Dante's *Paradise*,[21] Dorothy L. Sayers died of a sudden heart attack on December 17, 1957, at the age of sixty-four. She had completed twenty of the thirty-four cantos of Dante's allegory of the soul's ascent to God. It is difficult to imagine Sayers spending eternity lying on a bed of flowers, however. She sketched her idea of a blissful life after death in a letter to her producer during rehearsals for *The Man Born to Be King*. All she requests is uninterrupted time to revel in her God-given vocation: "When we go to heaven all I ask is that we shall be given some interesting job and allowed to get on with it. No management; no box-office; no dramatic critics; and an audience of cheerful angels who don't mind laughing."[22]

Carole Vanderhoof

---

21 Barbara Reynolds, a friend and fellow scholar, finished Sayers's translation of *Paradise* in 1962.

22 Sayers to Val Gielgud, January 13, 1942, *Letters*, 2:342.

Whose Body?

Conscience

Published in 1923, Whose Body? *is Dorothy L. Sayers's first foray into the writing of detective novels. The memory of the First World War is still fresh, especially to Lord Peter Wimsey, the protagonist of what will become twelve novels and many short stories. Some critics have objected to Wimsey's lighthearted babble, seeing nothing in it but a poor imitation of Bertie Wooster, a creation of Sayers's contemporary P. G. Wodehouse. But already in this first installment, Lord Peter's offhand remarks hint at a young author not only adept at religious and literary allusion but also taken with underlying themes of free will, responsibility, and the role of the conscience. For instance, in this fast-paced book full of slapstick humor there are at least thirteen references to Dante. Appropriately, the first words in the book are: "Oh, damn!"*

In this scene, Lord Peter Wimsey is in conversation with Detective Parker, who has asked his help with a case.

"D'you like your job?"

The detective considered the question, and replied·

"Yes – yes, I do. I know it to be useful, and I am fitted to it. I do it quite well – not with inspiration, perhaps, but sufficiently well to take a pride in it. It is full of variety and it forces one to keep up to the mark and not get slack. And there's a future to it. Yes, I like it. Why?"

"Oh, nothing," said Peter. "It's a hobby to me, you see. I took it up when the bottom of things was rather knocked out for me, because it was so damned exciting, and the worst of it is, I enjoy it – up to a point. If it was all on paper I'd enjoy every bit of it. I love the beginning of a job – when one doesn't know any of the people and it's just exciting and amusing. But if it comes to really running down a live person and getting him hanged, or even quodded, poor devil, there don't seem as if there was any excuse for me buttin' in, since I don't have to make my livin' by it. And I feel as if I oughtn't ever to find it amusin'. But I do."

Parker gave this speech his careful attention.

"I see what you mean," he said.

"There's old Milligan, f'r instance," said Lord Peter. "On paper, nothin' would be funnier than to catch old Milligan out. But he's rather a decent old bird to talk to. Mother likes him. He's taken a fancy to me. It's awfully entertainin' goin' and pumpin' him with stuff about a bazaar for church expenses, but when he's so jolly pleased about it and that, I feel a worm. S'pose old Milligan has cut Levy's throat and plugged him into the Thames. It ain't my business."

"It's as much yours as anybody's," said Parker; "it's no better to do it for money than to do it for nothing."

"Yes, it is," said Peter stubbornly. "Havin' to live is the only excuse there is for doin' that kind of thing."

"Well, but look here!" said Parker. "If Milligan has cut poor old Levy's throat for no reason except to make himself richer,

I don't see why he should buy himself off by giving £1,000 to Duke's Denver church roof, or why he should be forgiven just because he's childishly vain, or childishly snobbish."

"That's a nasty one," said Lord Peter.

"Well, if you like, even because he has taken a fancy to you."

"No, but – "

"Look here, Wimsey – do you think he *has* murdered Levy?"

"Well, he may have."

"But do you think he has?"

"I don't want to think so."

"Because he has taken a fancy to you?"

"Well, that biases me, of course – "

"I daresay it's quite a legitimate bias. You don't think a callous murderer would be likely to take a fancy to you?"

"Well – besides, I've taken rather a fancy to him."

"I daresay that's quite legitimate, too. You've observed him and made a subconscious deduction from your observations, and the result is, you don't think he did it. Well, why not? You're entitled to take that into account."

"But perhaps I'm wrong and he did do it."

"Then why let your vainglorious conceit in your own power of estimating character stand in the way of unmasking the singularly cold-blooded murder of an innocent and lovable man?"

"I know – but I don't feel I'm playing the game somehow."

"Look here, Peter," said the other with some earnestness, "suppose you get this playing-fields-of-Eton complex out of your system once and for all. There doesn't seem to be much doubt that something unpleasant has happened to Sir Reuben Levy. Call it murder, to strengthen the argument. If Sir Reuben has been murdered, is it a game? And is it fair to treat it as a game?"

"That's what I'm ashamed of, really," said Lord Peter. "It *is* a game to me, to begin with, and I go on cheerfully, and then I suddenly see that somebody is going to be hurt, and I want to get out of it."

"Yes, yes, I know," said the detective, "but that's because you're thinking about your attitude. You want to be consistent, you want to look pretty, you want to swagger debonairly through a comedy of puppets or else to stalk magnificently through a tragedy of human sorrows and things. But that's childish. If you've any duty to society in the way of finding out the truth about murders, you must do it in any attitude that comes handy. You want to be elegant and detached? That's all right, if you find the truth out that way, but it hasn't any value in itself, you know. You want to look dignified and consistent – what's that got to do with it? You want to hunt down a murderer for the sport of the thing and then shake hands with him and say, 'Well played – hard luck – you shall have your revenge tomorrow!' Well, you can't do it like that. Life's not a football match. You want to be a sportsman. You can't be a sportsman. You're a responsible person."

"I don't think you ought to read so much theology," said Lord Peter. "It has a brutalizing influence."

Lord Peter reached home about midnight, feeling extraordinarily wakeful and alert. Something was jigging and worrying in his brain; it felt like a hive of bees, stirred up by a stick. He felt as though he were looking at a complicated riddle, of which he had once been told the answer but had forgotten it and was always on the point of remembering. . . .

He roused himself, threw a log on the fire, and picked up a book which the indefatigable Bunter, carrying on his daily fatigues amid the excitements of special duty, had brought from the Times Book Club. It happened to be Sir Julian Freke's "Physiological Bases of the Conscience," which he had seen reviewed two days before.

"This ought to send one to sleep," said Lord Peter; "if I can't leave these problems to my subconscious I'll be as limp as a rag tomorrow. . . ."

Mind and matter were one thing, that was the theme of the physiologist. Matter could erupt, as it were, into ideas. You could carve passions in the brain with a knife. You could get rid of imagination with drugs and cure an outworn convention like a disease. "The knowledge of good and evil is an observed phenomenon, attendant upon a certain condition of the brain-cells, which is removable." That was one phrase; and again:

"Conscience in man may, in fact, be compared to the sting of a hive-bee, which, so far from conducing to the welfare of its possessor, cannot function, even in a single instance, without occasioning its death. The survival-value in each case is thus purely social; and if humanity ever passes from its present phase of social development into that of a higher individualism, as some of our philosophers have ventured to speculate, we may suppose that this interesting mental phenomenon may gradually cease to appear; just as the nerves and muscles which once controlled the movements of our ears and scalps have, in all save a few backward individuals, become atrophied and of interest only to the physiologist."

"By Jove!" thought Lord Peter, idly, "that's an ideal doctrine for the criminal. A man who believed that would never – "

And then it happened – the thing he had been half-unconsciously expecting. It happened suddenly, surely, as unmistakably as sunrise. He remembered – not one thing, nor another thing, nor a logical succession of things, but everything – the whole thing, perfect, complete, in all its dimensions as it were and instantaneously; as if he stood outside the world and saw it suspended in infinitely dimensional space. He no longer needed to reason about it, or even to think about it. He knew it. . . .

"He called on me, sir, with an anti-vivisectionist pamphlet" – all these things and many others rang together and made one sound, they swung together like bells in a steeple, with the deep tenor booming through the clamour:

"The knowledge of good and evil is a phenomenon of the brain, and is removable, removable, removable. The knowledge of good and evil is removable."

Lord Peter Wimsey was not a young man who habitually took himself very seriously, but this time he was frankly appalled. "It's impossible," said his reason, feebly; *"credo quia impossibile,"*[1] said his interior certainty with impervious self-satisfaction. "All right," said conscience, instantly allying itself with blind faith, "what are you going to do about it?"

Lord Peter realizes that the doctor must have perpetrated the crime, but the horror of the deed and the duty that now rests on his shoulders trigger a flashback – memories of tragedy and heavy responsibility from the war. It is only after a few days of rest that he is able to return to his work and pass on his intuition to Inspector Sugg of Scotland Yard. The amoral doctor, who at one time was

---

1   *"Credo quia impossibile"* (I believe it because it is impossible) attributed to Tertullian, *De Carne Christi.*

in love with the wife of Sir Reuben Levy, must have switched the
murdered body of the financier with that of a medical cadaver.

Parker and Lord Peter were at 110 Piccadilly. Lord Peter was
playing Bach and Parker was reading Origen when Sugg was
announced.

"We've got our man, sir," said he.

"Good God!" said Peter. "Alive?"

"We were just in time, my lord. We rang the bell and marched
straight up past his man to the library. He was sitting there doing
some writing. When we came in, he made a grab for his hypo-
dermic, but we were too quick for him, my lord. We didn't mean
to let him slip through our hands, having got so far. We searched
him thoroughly and marched him off." . . .

"He was writing a full confession when we got hold of him,
addressed to your lordship. The police will have to have it, of
course, but seeing it's written for you, I brought it along for you
to see first. Here it is."

He handed Lord Peter a bulky document.

"Thanks," said Peter. "Like to hear it, Charles?"

"Rather."

Accordingly Lord Peter read it aloud.

Dear Lord Peter – When I was a young man I used to play chess
with an old friend of my father's. He was a very bad, and a very
slow, player, and he could never see when a checkmate was inevitable, but insisted on playing every move out. I never had any
patience with that kind of attitude, and I will freely admit now
that the game is yours. I must either stay at home and be hanged
or escape abroad and live in an idle and insecure obscurity. I
prefer to acknowledge defeat.

If you have read my book on "Criminal Lunacy," you will remember that I wrote: "In the majority of cases, the criminal betrays himself by some abnormality attendant upon this pathological condition of the nervous tissues. His mental instability shows itself in various forms: an overweening vanity, leading him to brag of his achievement; a disproportionate sense of the importance of the offence, resulting from the hallucination of religion, and driving him to confession; egomania, producing the sense of horror or conviction of sin, and driving him to headlong flight without covering his tracks; a reckless confidence, resulting in the neglect of the most ordinary precautions, as in the case of Henry Wainwright, who left a boy in charge of the murdered woman's remains while he went to call a cab, or on the other hand, a nervous distrust of apperceptions in the past, causing him to revisit the scene of the crime to assure himself that all traces have been as safely removed as *his own judgment knows them to be.*" I will not hesitate to assert that a perfectly sane man, not intimidated by religious or other delusions, could always render himself perfectly secure from detection, provided, that is, that the crime were sufficiently premeditated and that he were not pressed for time or thrown out in his calculations by purely fortuitous coincidence. . . .

Of all human emotions, except perhaps those of hunger and fear, the sexual appetite produces the most violent and, under some circumstances, the most persistent reactions; I think, however, I am right in saying that at the time when I wrote my book, my original sensual impulse to kill Sir Reuben Levy had already become profoundly modified by my habits of thought. To the animal lust to slay and the primitive human desire for revenge, there was added the rational intention of substantiating my own theories for the satisfaction of myself and the world.

If all had turned out as I had planned, I should have deposited a sealed account of my experiment with the Bank of England, instructing my executors to publish it after my death. Now that accident has spoiled the completeness of my demonstration, I entrust the account to you, whom it cannot fail to interest, with the request that you will make it known among scientific men, in justice to my professional reputation. . . .

Meanwhile, I carefully studied criminology in fiction and fact – my work on "Criminal Lunacy" was a side-product of this activity – and saw how, in every murder, the real crux of the problem was the disposal of the body. As a doctor, the means of death were always ready to my hand, and I was not likely to make any error in that connection. Nor was I likely to betray myself on account of any illusory sense of wrongdoing. The sole difficulty would be that of destroying all connection between my personality and that of the corpse. You will remember that Michael Finsbury, in Stevenson's entertaining romance, observes: "What hangs people is the unfortunate circumstance of guilt." It became clear to me that the mere leaving about of a superfluous corpse could convict nobody, provided that nobody was guilty in connection *with that particular corpse.* Thus the idea of substituting the one body for the other was early arrived at, though it was not till I obtained the practical direction of St. Luke's Hospital that I found myself perfectly unfettered in the choice and handling of dead bodies. From this period on, I kept a careful watch on all the material brought in for dissection.

My opportunity did not present itself until the week before Sir Reuben's disappearance, when the medical officer at the Chelsea workhouse sent word to me that an unknown vagrant had been injured that morning by the fall of a piece of scaffolding, and was exhibiting some very interesting nervous and cerebral reactions.

I went round and saw the case, and was immediately struck by the man's strong superficial resemblance to Sir Reuben. He had been heavily struck on the back of the neck, dislocating the fourth and fifth cervical vertebræ and heavily bruising the spinal cord. It seemed highly unlikely that he could ever recover, either mentally or physically, and in any case there appeared to me to be no object in indefinitely prolonging so unprofitable an existence. He had obviously been able to support life until recently, as he was fairly well nourished, but the state of his feet and clothing showed that he was unemployed, and under present conditions he was likely to remain so. I decided that he would suit my purpose very well, and immediately put in train certain transactions in the City which I had already sketched out in my own mind. In the meantime, the reactions mentioned by the workhouse doctor were interesting, and I made careful studies of them, and arranged for the delivery of the body to the hospital when I should have completed my preparations. . . .

The rest was simple. I carried my pauper along the flat roofs, intending to leave him, like the hunchback in the story, on someone's staircase or down a chimney. I had got about half way along when I suddenly thought, "Why, this must be about little Thipps's place," and I remembered his silly face, and his silly chatter about vivisection. It occurred to me pleasantly how delightful it would be to deposit my parcel with him and see what he made of it. I lay down and peered over the parapet at the back. It was pitch-dark and pouring with rain again by this time, and I risked using my torch. That was the only incautious thing I did, and the odds against being seen from the houses opposite were long enough. One second's flash showed me what I had hardly dared to hope – an open window just below me.

I knew those flats well enough to be sure it was either the bathroom or the kitchen. I made a noose in a third bandage that I had brought with me, and made it fast under the arms of the corpse. I twisted it into a double rope, and secured the end to the iron stanchion of a chimney-stack. Then I dangled our friend over. I went down after him myself with the aid of a drain-pipe and was soon hauling him in by Thipps's bathroom window. . . .

First, however, I had to go over to the hospital and make all safe there. I took off Levy's head, and started to open up the face. In twenty minutes his own wife could not have recognized him. I returned, leaving my wet galoshes and mackintosh by the garden door. My trousers I dried by the gas stove in my bedroom, and brushed away all traces of mud and brick-dust. My pauper's beard I burned in the library.

I got a good two hours' sleep from five to seven, when my man called me as usual. I apologized for having kept the water running so long and so late, and added that I thought I would have the cistern seen to.

I was interested to note that I was rather extra hungry at breakfast, showing that my night's work had caused a certain wear-and-tear of tissue. I went over afterwards to continue my dissection. During the morning a peculiarly thickheaded police inspector came to inquire whether a body had escaped from the hospital. I had him brought to me where I was, and had the pleasure of showing him the work I was doing on Sir Reuben Levy's head. Afterwards I went round with him to Thipps's and was able to satisfy myself that my pauper looked very convincing.

As soon as the Stock Exchange opened I telephoned my various brokers, and by exercising a little care, was able to sell out the greater part of my Peruvian stock on a rising market.

Towards the end of the day, however, buyers became rather unsettled as a result of Levy's death, and in the end I did not make more than a few hundreds by the transaction.

Trusting I have now made clear to you any point which you may have found obscure, and with congratulations on the good fortune and perspicacity which have enabled you to defeat me, I remain, with kind remembrances to your mother,

Yours very truly,

JULIAN FREKE

POST-SCRIPTUM: My will is made, leaving my money to St. Luke's Hospital, and bequeathing my body to the same institution for dissection. I feel sure that my brain will be of interest to the scientific world. As I shall die by my own hand, I imagine that there may be a little difficulty about this. Will you do me the favour, if you can, of seeing the persons concerned in the inquest, and obtaining that the brain is not damaged by an unskillful practitioner at the post-mortem, and that the body is disposed of according to my wish?[2]

From an address Sayers delivered in May 1940 titled "Creed or Chaos?":

The final tendency of the modern philosophies – hailed in their day as a release from the burden of sinfulness – has been to bind man hard and fast in the chains of an iron determinism. The influences of heredity and environment, of glandular make-up and the control exercised by the unconscious, of economic necessity and the mechanics of biological development, have all been invoked to assure man that he is not responsible for his

---

2   Dorothy L. Sayers, *Whose Body?* (London: T. Fisher Unwin, 1923), ch. 7–8.

misfortunes and therefore not to be held guilty. Evil has been represented as something imposed upon him from without, not made by him from within.

The dreadful conclusion follows inevitably, that as he is not responsible for evil, he cannot alter it; even though evolution and progress may offer some alleviation in the future, there is no hope for you and me, here and now. I well remember how an aunt of mine, brought up in an old-fashioned liberalism, protested angrily against having continually to call herself a "miserable sinner" when reciting the Litany. To-day, if we could really be persuaded that we are miserable sinners – that the trouble is not outside us but inside us, and that therefore, by the grace of God, we can do something to put it right – we should receive that message as the most hopeful and heartening thing that can be imagined.[3]

Here Sayers tries her hand at satire, with a parody of liberal religious thought:

Creed of St. Euthanasia

I believe in Man, Maker of himself and inventor of all Science. And in Myself, his Manifestation, and Captain of my Psyche; and that I should not suffer anything painful or unpleasant.

And in a vague Evolving Deity, the future-begotten Child of Man; conceived by the Spirit of Progress, born of Emergent Variants: who shall kick down the ladder by which he rose, and tell history to go to hell;

---

3 "Creed or Chaos?," an address delivered at the Biennial Festival of the Church Tutorial Classes Association in Derby, May 4, 1940, published in Dorothy L. Sayers, *Creed or Chaos?* (London: Methuen, 1947).

Who shall some day take off from earth and be jet-propelled into the heavens; and sit exalted above all worlds, Man the Master Almighty.

And I believe in the Spirit of Progress, who spake by Shaw and the Fabians; and in a modern, administrative, ethical and social Organization; in the Isolation of Saints, the Treatment of Complexes, Joy through Health, the Destruction of the Body by Cremation (with music while it burns), and then I've had it.[4]

From the introduction to her translation of Dante:

Whether in Hell or in Purgatory, you get what you want – if that is what you really do want. If you insist on having your own way, you will get it: Hell is the enjoyment of your own way for ever. If you really want God's way for you, you will get it in Heaven, and the pains of Purgatory will not deter you, they will be welcomed as the means to that end. It must always be remembered that for Dante, as for all Catholic Christians, man is a responsible being. The dishonouring notion that he is the helpless puppet of circumstance or temperament, and therefore not justly liable to punishment or reward, is one which the poet over and over again goes out of his way to refute. That is why so many of the "sermons" in the *Purgatory* deal with the subject of Free Will. When every allowance is made (and Dante makes generous allowance), when mercy and pity and grace have done all they can, the consequences of sin are the sinner's – to be borne, at his own choice, in a spirit of sullen rebellion or of ready acquiescence.[5]

---

4   "More Pantheon Papers," originally published in *Punch,* January 13, 1954, 84.

5   Dorothy L. Sayers, introduction to Dante Alighieri, *Purgatory,* trans. by Dorothy L. Sayers (London: Penguin, 1955), 16–17.

2

Unnatural Death

Sin and Grace

In this selection from Unnatural Death, *Lord Peter steps into a church in search of Miss Climpson. Not seeing her in the dim sanctuary, he turns to leave, then stops and comes back, approaching a friendly-looking priest.*

"I say," he said, "you give advice on moral problems and all that sort of thing, don't you?"

"Well, we're supposed to try," said the priest. "Is anything bothering you in particular?"

"Ye-es," said Wimsey, "nothing religious, I don't mean – nothing about infallibility or the Virgin Mary or anything of that sort. Just something I'm not comfortable about."

The priest – who was, in fact, the vicar, Mr. Tredgold – indicated that he was quite at Lord Peter's service.

"It's very good of you. Could we come somewhere where I didn't have to whisper so much. I never can explain things in a whisper. Sort of paralyses one, don't you know."

"Let's go outside," said Mr. Tredgold.

So they went out and sat on a flat tombstone.

"It's like this," said Wimsey. "Hypothetical case, you see, and so on. S'posin' one knows somebody who's very, very ill and can't last long anyhow. And they're in awful pain and all that, and kept under morphia – practically dead to the world, you know. And suppose that by dyin' straight away they could make something happen which they really wanted to happen and which couldn't happen if they lived on a little longer (I can't explain exactly how, because I don't want to give personal details and so on) – you get the idea? Well, supposin' somebody who knew all that was just to give 'em a little push off so to speak – hurry matters on – why should that be a very dreadful crime?"

"The law – " began Mr. Tredgold.

"Oh, the law says it's a crime, fast enough," said Wimsey. "But do you honestly think it's very bad? I know you'd call it a sin, of course, but why is it so very dreadful? It doesn't do the person any harm, does it?"

"We can't answer that," said Mr. Tredgold, "without knowing the ways of God with the soul. In those last weeks or hours of pain and unconsciousness, the soul may be undergoing some necessary part of its pilgrimage on earth. It isn't our business to cut it short. Who are we to take life and death into our hands?"

"Well, we do it all day, one way and another. Juries – soldiers – doctors – all that. And yet I do feel, somehow, that it isn't a right thing in this case. And yet, by interfering – finding things out and so on – one may do far worse harm. Start all kinds of things."

"I think," said Mr. Tredgold, "that the sin – I won't use that word – the damage to Society, the wrongness of the thing lies much more in the harm it does the killer than in anything it can do to the person who is killed. Especially, of course, if the killing is to the killer's own advantage. The consequence you mention – this thing which the sick person wants done – does the other person stand to benefit by it, may I ask?"

"Yes. That's just it. He – she – they do."

"That puts it at once on a different plane from just hastening a person's death out of pity. Sin is in the intention, not the deed. That is the difference between divine law and human law. It is bad for a human being to get to feel that he has any right whatever to dispose of another person's life to his own advantage. It leads him on to think himself above all laws – Society is never safe from the man who has deliberately committed murder with impunity. That is why – or one reason why – God forbids private vengeance."

"You mean that one murder leads to another."

"Very often. In any case it leads to a readiness to commit others."

"It has. That's the trouble. But it wouldn't have if I hadn't started trying to find things out. Ought I to have left it alone?"

"I see. That is very difficult. Terrible, too, for you. You feel responsible."

"Yes."

"You yourself are not serving a private vengeance?"

"Oh, no. Nothing really to do with me. Started in like a fool to help somebody who'd got into trouble about the thing through having suspicions himself. And my beastly interference started the crimes all over again."

"I shouldn't be too troubled. Probably the murderer's own guilty fears would have led him into fresh crimes even without your interference."

"That's true," said Wimsey, remembering Mr. Trigg.

"My advice to you is to do what you think is right, according to the laws which we have been brought up to respect. Leave the consequences to God. And try to think charitably, even of wicked people. You know what I mean. Bring the offender to justice, but remember that if we all got justice, you and I wouldn't escape either."

"I know. Knock the man down but don't dance on the body. Quite. Forgive my troublin' you – and excuse my bargin' off, because I've got a date with a friend. Thanks so much. I don't feel quite so rotten about it now. But I was gettin' worried."

Mr. Tredgold watched him as he trotted away between the graves. "Dear, dear," he said, "how nice they are. So kindly and scrupulous and so vague outside their public-school code. And much more nervous and sensitive than people think. A very difficult class to reach. I must make a special intention for him at Mass to-morrow."

Being a practical man, Mr. Tredgold made a knot in his handkerchief to remind himself of this pious resolve.

"The problem – to interfere or not to interfere – God's law and Cæsar's. Policemen, now – it's no problem to them. But for the ordinary man – how hard to disentangle his own motives. I wonder what brought him here. Could it possibly be – No!" said the vicar, checking himself, "I have no right to speculate." He drew out his handkerchief again and made another mnemonic knot as a reminder against his next confession that he had fallen into the sin of inquisitiveness.[1]

From a radio broadcast:

We have seen, too, what happens to reason divorced from theology. Encouraged by its success in subduing the material universe, it refuses to admit the validity of anything that is not capable of scientific *proof*. Its next step is to try to justify the natural virtues by their material results – whence we get the ugly and egotistical

---

1   Dorothy L. Sayers, *Unnatural Death* (London: Collins, 1927), ch. 19.

doctrine of enlightened self-interest and the hideous tyranny of economics. The *last* achievement of reason is always to cast doubt on its own validity, so that the final result of rationalism is the appearance of a wholly irrational universe.

Thus, human ethics, left to themselves, become helpless and self-contradictory – exactly as they did in pagan times.

The men who now rule Germany [the Nazis], having thrown over the Christian theology, see clearly enough that the Christian ethics will not work without it. Therefore, they have jettisoned the ethics as well. We are greatly shocked by this. But have we the right to be surprised? If Christ is the only guarantee that reason is rational and goodness is good, then, the logical result of repudiating Christianity is the repudiation of reason and virtue.[2]

In her play The Devil to Pay, *Sayers puts these words in the mouth of the pope:*

. . . Hard it is, very hard,
To travel up the slow and stony road
To Calvary, to redeem mankind; far better
To make but one resplendent miracle,
Lean through the cloud, lift the right hand of power
And with a sudden lightning smite the world perfect.
Yet this was not God's way, Who had the power,
But set it by, choosing the cross, the thorn,
The sorrowful wounds. Something there is, perhaps,
That power destroys in passing, something supreme,
To whose great value in the eyes of God
That cross, that thorn, and those five wounds bear witness.
Son, go in peace; for thou hast sinned through love;

---

2 "The Religions Behind the Nation," radio broadcast March 5, 1941, as printed in Dorothy L. Sayers, *The Christ of the Creeds* (West Sussex: Dorothy L. Sayers Society, 2008), 47.

To such sin God is merciful. Not yet
Has thy familiar devil persuaded thee
To that last sin against the Holy Ghost
Which is, to call good evil, evil good.
Only for that is no forgiveness – Not
That God would not forgive all sins there are,
Being what He is; but that this sin destroys
The power to feel His pardon, so that damnation
Is consequence, not vengeance; and indeed
So all damnation is. I will pray for thee.
And you, my children, go home, gird your loins
And light your lamps, beseeching God to bring
His kingdom nearer, in what way He will. [3]

From the lecture "Creed or Chaos?":

A young and intelligent priest remarked to me the other day that he thought one of the greatest sources of strength in Christianity today lay in the profoundly pessimistic view it took of human nature. There is a great deal in what he says. The people who are most discouraged and made despondent by the barbarity and stupidity of human behaviour at this time are those who think highly of *Homo sapiens* as a product of evolution, and who still cling to an optimistic belief in the civilising influence of progress and enlightenment. To them, the appalling outbursts of bestial ferocity in the Totalitarian States, and the obstinate selfishness and stupid greed of Capitalist Society, are not merely shocking and alarming. For them, these things are the utter negation of everything in which they have believed. It is as though the bottom had dropped out of their universe. The whole

---

3   Dorothy L. Sayers, Scene II, *The Devil to Pay,* 1939, published in *Four Sacred Plays* (London: Victor Gollancz, 1948).

thing looks like a denial of all reason, and they feel as if they and the world had gone mad together.

Now for the Christian, this is not so. He is as deeply shocked and grieved as anybody else, but he is not astonished. He has never thought very highly of human nature left to itself. He has been accustomed to the idea that there is a deep interior dislocation in the very centre of human personality, and that you can never, as they say, "make people good by act of parliament," just because laws are man-made and therefore partake of the imperfect and self-contradictory nature of man. Humanly speaking, it is not true at all that "truly to know the good is to do the good"; it is far truer to say with St. Paul that "the evil that I would not, that I do" [Rom. 7:19]; so that the mere increase of knowledge is of very little help in the struggle to outlaw evil. The delusion of the mechanical perfectibility of mankind through a combined process of scientific knowledge and unconscious evolution has been responsible for a great deal of heartbreak. It is, at bottom, far more pessimistic than Christian pessimism, because, if science and progress break down, there is nothing to fall back upon. Humanism is self-contained – it provides for man no resources outside himself. . . .

The one point to which I should like to draw attention is the Christian doctrine of the moral law. The attempt to abolish wars and wickedness by the moral law is doomed to failure, because of the fact of sinfulness. Law, like every other product of human activity, shares the integral human imperfection; it is, in the old Calvinistic phrase, "of the nature of sin." That is to say: all legality, if erected into an absolute value, contains within itself the seeds of judgment and catastrophe. The law is necessary, but only, as it were, as a protective fence against the forces of evil, behind which the divine activity of grace may do its redeeming work. We can, for example, never make a positive peace or a positive righteousness by enactments against offenders; law is always prohibitive, negative, and corrupted by the interior contradictions of man's divided nature; it belongs to the category of judgment. That is why an intelligent understanding about sin is necessary to preserve the world from putting an unjustified confidence in the efficacy of the moral law taken by itself. It will never drive out Beelzebub; it cannot, because it is only human and not divine.

Nevertheless, the law must be rightly understood or it is not possible to make the world understand the meaning of grace. There is only one real law – the law of the universe; it may be fulfilled either by way of judgment or by the way of grace, but it must be fulfilled one way or the other. If men will not understand the meaning of judgment, they will never come to understand the meaning of grace. "If they hear not Moses or the Prophets, neither will they be persuaded, though one rose from the dead." [Luke 16:31] [4]

---

4   "Creed or Chaos?," published in *Creed or Chaos?*, 1949.

3

The Unpleasantness at the Bellona Club

Covetousness

The Unpleasantness at the Bellona Club opens with elderly Colonel Fentiman found dead in an armchair at his club. His son George, a veteran of World War I, confesses to the murder of his father, but Lord Peter soon realizes that this is a figment of George's troubled imagination, and the real murderer is Dr. Penberthy, who gave Colonel Fentiman a lethal dose of heart medicine. The doctor was engaged to marry Miss Dorland, Fentiman's niece. He was counting on her inheriting the money so that he could open a private clinic.

There was nobody in the library at the Bellona Club; there never is. Wimsey led Penberthy into the farthest bay and sent a waiter for two double whiskies.

"Here's luck!" he said.

"Good luck," replied Penberthy. "What is it?"

"Look here," said Wimsey. "You've been a soldier. I think you're a decent fellow. You've seen George Fentiman. It's a pity, isn't it?"

"What about it?"

"If George Fentiman hadn't turned up with that delusion of his," said Wimsey, "you would have been arrested for the murder this evening. Now the point is this. When you are arrested, nothing, as things are, can prevent Miss Dorland's being arrested on the same charge. She's quite a decent girl, and you haven't treated her any too well, have you? Don't you think you might make things right for her by telling the truth straight away?"

Penberthy sat with a white face and said nothing.

"You see," went on Wimsey, "if once they get her into the dock, she'll always be a suspected person. Even if the jury believe her story – and they may not, because juries are often rather stupid – people will always think there was "something in it." They'll say she was a very lucky woman to get off. That's damning for a girl, isn't it? They might even bring her in guilty. You and I know she isn't – but – you don't want the girl hanged, Penberthy, do you?"

Penberthy drummed on the table.

"What do you want me to do?" he said at last.

"Write a clear account of what actually happened," said Wimsey. "Make a clean job of it for these other people. Make it clear that Miss Dorland had nothing to do with it."

"And then?"

"Then do as you like. In your place I know what I should do."

Penberthy propped his chin on his hands and sat for some minutes staring at the works of Dickens in the leather-and-gold binding.

"Very well," he said at last. "You're quite right. I ought to have done it before. But – damn it! – if ever a man had rotten luck . . .

"If only Robert Fentiman hadn't been a rogue. It's funny, isn't it? That's your wonderful poetic justice, isn't it? If Robert

Fentiman had been an honest man, I should have got my half-million, and Ann Dorland would have got a perfectly good husband, and the world would have gained a fine clinic, incidentally. But as Robert was a rogue – here we are. . . .

"It was so hideously easy, you see . . . that was the devil of it. The old man came along and put himself into my hands. Told me with one breath that I hadn't a dog's chance of the money, and in the next, asked me for a dose. I just had to put the stuff into a couple of capsules and tell him to take them at 7 o'clock. He put them in his spectacle-case, to make sure he wouldn't forget them. Not even a bit of paper to give me away. And the next day I'd only to get a fresh supply of the stuff and fill up the bottle. I'll give you the address of the chemist who sold it. Easy? – it was laughable . . . people put such power in our hands. . . .

"I never meant to get led into all this rotten way of doing things – it was just self-defence. I still don't care a damn about having killed the old man. I could have made better use of the money than Robert Fentiman. He hasn't got two ideas in his head, and he's perfectly happy where he is. Though I suppose he'll be leaving the Army now. . . . As for Ann, she ought to be grateful to me in a way. I've secured her the money, anyhow."

"Not unless you make it clear that she had no part in the crime," Wimsey reminded him.

"That's true. All right. I'll put it all on paper for you. Give me half an hour, will you?"

"Right you are," said Wimsey.

He left the library and wandered into the smoking-room. Colonel Marchbanks was there, and greeted him with a friendly smile.

"Glad you're here, Colonel. Mind if I come and chat to you for a moment?"

"By all means, my dear boy. I'm in no hurry to get home. My wife's away. What can I do for you?"

Wimsey told him, in a lowered voice. The Colonel was distressed.

"Ah, well," he said, "you've done the best thing, to my mind. I look at these matters from a soldier's point of view, of course. Much better to make a clean job of it all. Dear, dear!

"Sometimes, Lord Peter, I think that the War has had a bad effect on some of our young men. But then, of course, all are not soldiers by training, and that makes a great difference. I certainly notice a less fine sense of honour in these days than we had when I was a boy. There were not so many excuses made then for people; there were things that were done and things that were not done. Nowadays men – and, I am sorry to say, women too – let themselves go in a way that is to me quite incomprehensible. I can understand a man's committing murder in hot blood – but poisoning – and then putting a good, lady-like girl into such an equivocal position – no! I fail to understand it. Still, as you say, the right course is being taken at last."

"Yes," said Wimsey.

"Excuse me for a moment," said the Colonel, and went out.

When he returned, he went with Wimsey into the library. Penberthy had finished writing and was reading his statement through.

"Will that do?" he asked.

Wimsey read it, Colonel Marchbanks looking over the pages with him.

"That is quite all right," he said. "Colonel Marchbanks will witness it with me."

This was done. Wimsey gathered the sheets together and put them in his breast pocket. Then he turned silently to the Colonel, as though passing the word to him.

"Dr. Penberthy," said the old man, "now that that paper is in Lord Peter Wimsey's hands, you understand that he can only take the course of communicating with the police. But as that would cause a great deal of unpleasantness to yourself and to other people, you may wish to take another way out of the situation. As a doctor, you will perhaps prefer to make your own arrangements. If not – "

He drew out from his jacket pocket the thing which he had fetched.

"If not, I happen to have brought this with me from my private locker. I am placing it here, in the table drawer, preparatory to taking it down into the country tomorrow. It is loaded."

"Thank you," said Penberthy.

The Colonel closed the drawer slowly, stepped back a couple of paces, and bowed gravely. Wimsey put his hand on Penberthy's shoulder for a moment, then took the Colonel's arm. Their shadows moved, lengthened, shortened, doubled and crossed as they passed the seven lights in the seven bays of the library. The door shut after them.[1]

From a talk titled "The Other Six Deadly Sins":

It was left for the present age to endow Covetousness with glamour on a big scale, and to give it a title which it could carry like a flag. It occurred to somebody to call it Enterprise. From the moment of that happy inspiration, Covetousness has gone forward and never looked back. It has become a swaggering, swashbuckling, piratical sin, going about with its hat cocked over its eye, and with pistols tucked into the tops of its jack-boots. Its war-cries are "Business Efficiency!" "Free Competition!" "Get

---

1   Dorothy L. Sayers, *The Unpleasantness at the Bellona Club* (London: Ernest Benn, 1928), ch. 22.

Out or Get Under!" and "There's Always Room at the Top!" It no longer screws and saves – it launches out into new enterprises; it gambles and speculates; it thinks in a big way; it takes risks. It can no longer be troubled to deal in real wealth, and so remain attached to Work and the Soil. It has set money free from all such hampering ties; it has interests in every continent; it is impossible to pin it down to any one place or any concrete commodity – it is an adventurer, a roving, rollicking free-lance.

It looks so jolly and jovial, and has such a twinkle in its cunning eye, that nobody can believe that its heart is as cold and calculating as ever. Besides, where is its heart? Covetousness is not incarnated in individual people, but in business corporations, joint-stock companies, amalgamations, trusts, which have neither bodies to be kicked, nor souls to be damned – nor hearts to be appealed to, either: it is very difficult to fasten on anybody the responsibility for the things that are done with money. Of course, if Covetousness miscalculates and some big financier comes crashing down, bringing all the small speculators down with him, we wag self-righteous heads, and feel that we see clearly where the fault lies. But we do not punish the fraudulent businessman for his frauds, but for his failure.

The Church says Covetousness is a deadly sin – but does She really think so? Is She ready to found Welfare Societies to deal with financial immorality as She does with sexual immorality? Do the officials stationed at church doors in Italy to exclude women with bare arms turn anybody away on the grounds that they are too well dressed to be honest? Do the vigilance committees who complain of "suggestive" books and plays make any attempt to suppress the literature which "suggests" that getting on in the world is the chief object in life? Is Dives,[2] like

---

2 Dives: Latin for "wealthy man" in the Vulgate. She is referring to the parable of the beggar Lazarus and the rich man (Luke 16:19–31).

Magdalen, ever refused the sacraments on the grounds that he, like her, is an "open and notorious evil-liver"? Does the Church arrange services with bright congregational singing, for Total Abstainers from Usury?

The Church's record is not, in these matters, quite as good as it might be. But it is perhaps rather better than that of those who denounce Her for Her neglect. The Church is not the Vatican, nor the Metropolitans, nor the Bench of Bishops; it is not even the Vicar or the Curate or the Churchwardens: the Church is you and I. And are you and I in the least sincere in our pretence that we disapprove of Covetousness?

Let us ask ourselves one or two questions. Do we admire and envy rich people because they are rich, or because the work by which they made their money is good work? If we hear that Old So-and-so has pulled off a pretty smart deal with the Town Council, are we shocked by the revelation of the cunning graft involved, or do we say admiringly: "Old So-and-so's hot stuff – you won't find many flies on him"? When we go to the cinema and see a picture about empty-headed people in luxurious surroundings, do we say: "What drivel!" or do we sit in a misty dream, wishing we could give up our daily work and marry into surroundings like that? When we invest our money, do we ask ourselves whether the enterprise represents anything useful, or merely whether it is a safe thing that returns a good dividend? Do we regularly put money into football pools or dog racing? When we read the newspaper, are our eyes immediately arrested by anything which says "millions" in large capitals, preceded by the £ or $ sign? Have we ever refused money on the grounds that the work that we had to do for it was something that we could not do honestly or do well? Do we *never* choose our acquaintances with the idea that they are useful people to know, or keep in with people in the hope that there is something to be got out of them? And do we – this is important – when we blame the mess that the economical world has got into, do we always lay the blame on wicked financiers, wicked profiteers, wicked capitalists, wicked employers, wicked bankers – or do we sometimes ask ourselves how far *we* have contributed to make the mess?[3]

---

3   "The Other Six Deadly Sins," an address given to the Public Morality Council at Caxton Hall, Westminster, October 23, 1941, published in *Creed or Chaos?*, 1949.

4

Strong Poison

Forgiveness

In Sayers's book Strong Poison, *the murdered man's father is a minor character, but she uses him to express a Christian perspective. The father could have been full of vindictive anger but instead displays a willingness to forgive.*

The clergyman was a tall, faded man, with lines of worry deeply engraved upon his face, and mild blue eyes a little bewildered by the disappointing difficulty of things in general. His black coat was old, and hung in depressed folds from his stooping, narrow shoulders. He gave Wimsey a thin hand and begged him to be seated.

Lord Peter found it a little difficult to explain his errand. His name evidently aroused no associations in the mind of this gentle and unworldly parson. He decided not to mention his hobby of criminal investigation, but to represent himself, with equal truth, as a friend of the prisoner's. That might be painful, but it would be at least intelligible. Accordingly, he began, with some hesitation:

"I'm fearfully sorry to trouble you, especially as it's all so very distressin' and all that, but it's about the death of your son, and the trial and so on. Please don't think I'm wanting to make an interfering nuisance of myself, but I'm deeply interested – personally interested. You see, I know Miss Vane – I – in fact I like her very much, don't you know, and I can't help thinking there's a mistake somewhere and – and I should like to get it put right if possible."

"Oh – oh, yes!" said Mr. Boyes. He carefully polished a pair of pince-nez and balanced them on his nose, where they sat crookedly. He peered at Wimsey and seemed not to dislike what he saw, for he went on:

"Poor misguided girl! I assure you, I have no vindictive feelings – that is to say, nobody would be more happy than myself to know that she was innocent of this dreadful thing. Indeed, Lord Peter, even if she were guilty, it would give me great pain to see her suffer the penalty. Whatever we do, we cannot bring back the dead to life, and one would infinitely prefer to leave all vengeance in the hand of Him to whom it belongs. Certainly, nothing could be more terrible than to take the life of an innocent person. It would haunt me to the end of my days if I thought there were the least likelihood of it. And I confess that, when I saw Miss Vane in court, I had grievous doubts whether the police had done rightly in accusing her."

"Thank you," said Wimsey, "it is very kind of you to say that. It makes the job much easier. Excuse me, you say, 'when you saw her in court.' You hadn't met her previously?"

"No. I knew, of course, that my unhappy son had formed an illicit connection with a young woman, but – I could not bring myself to see her – and indeed, I believe that she, with very proper feeling, refused to allow Philip to bring her into contact with any of his relations. Lord Peter, you are a younger man than I am, you belong to my son's generation, and you will perhaps understand that – though he was not bad, not depraved, I will never think that – yet somehow there was not that full confidence between us which there should be between father and son. No doubt I was much to blame. If only his mother had lived – "

"My dear sir," mumbled Wimsey, "I perfectly understand. It often happens. In fact, it's continually happening. The post-war generation and so on. Lots of people go off the rails a bit – no real harm in 'em at all. Just can't see eye to eye with the older people. It generally wears off in time. Nobody really to blame. Wild oats and, er, all that sort of thing."

"I could not approve," said Mr. Boyes, sadly, "of ideas so opposed to religion and morality – perhaps I spoke my mind too openly. If I had sympathised more – "

"It can't be done," said Wimsey. "People have to work it out for themselves. And, when they write books and so on, and get into that set of people, they tend to express themselves rather noisily, if you see what I mean."

"Maybe, maybe. But I reproach myself. Still, this does not help you at all. Forgive me. If there is any mistake and the jury were evidently not satisfied, we must use all our endeavours to put it right. How can I assist?"

"Well, first of all," said Wimsey, "and I'm afraid this is rather a hateful question, did your son ever say anything, or write anything to you which might lead you to think that he – was tired of his life or anything of that kind? I'm sorry."

"No, no – not at all. I was, of course, asked the same question by the police and by the counsel for the defence. I can truly say that such an idea never occurred to me. There was nothing at all to suggest it."

"Not even when he parted company with Miss Vane?"

"Not even then. In fact, I gathered that he was rather more angry than despondent. I must say that it was a surprise to me to hear that, after all that had passed between them, she was unwilling to marry him. I still fail to comprehend it. Her refusal must have come as a great shock to him. He wrote so cheerfully to me about it beforehand. Perhaps you remember the letter?" He fumbled in an untidy drawer. "I have it here, if you would like to look at it."

"If you would just read the passage, sir," suggested Wimsey.

"Yes, oh, certainly. Let me see. Yes. 'Your morality will be pleased to hear, Dad, that I have determined to regularise the situation, as the good people say.' He had a careless way of speaking and writing sometimes, poor boy, which doesn't do justice to his good heart. Dear me. Yes. 'My young woman is a good little soul, and I have made up my mind to do the thing properly. She really deserves it, and I hope that when everything is made respectable, you will extend your paternal recognition to her. I won't ask you to officiate – as you know, the registrar's office is more in my line, and though she was brought up in the odour of sanctity, like myself, I don't think she will insist on the Voice that Breathed o'er Eden. I will let you know when it's to be, so that you can come and give us your blessing (quâ father if not quâ parson) if you should feel so disposed.' You see, Lord Peter, he quite meant to do the right thing, and I was touched that he should wish for my presence."

"Quite so," said Lord Peter, and thought, "If only that young man were alive, how dearly I should love to kick his bottom for him."[1]

---

1   Dorothy L. Sayers, *Strong Poison* (London: Victor Gollancz Ltd., 1930), ch. 6.

From "Justus Judex," an early Sayers poem illustrating the boundless mercy of Christ:

> I walk in the world in judgment,
>   to sunder and not condemn;
> There be none so sunk and sodden
>   but I lay My hand on them,
> And if yet in the palsied body
>   one answering pulse can leap,
> Whether to love or hatred,
>   they are not dead but sleep.
>
> Therefore I swear, O Father and God,
>   I swear by Thy mighty throne,
> With the blood that was shed on Calvary
>   I bought them for Mine own;
> It shall dye them with shame and scarlet,
>   it shall sear them as burning coals,
> For they spilt and trampled it into the mire,
>   and it shall save their souls.
>
> Unbar the gates, good Peter,
>   and for twice a thousand years
> Let them writhe 'neath the rod of My pity
>   and the insult of My tears,
> Till hate is bound to the wheels of love,
>   and sin is made My slave,
> And I bring Mine own from the deep again,
>   My dead back from the grave.[2]

---

2   Dorothy L. Sayers, "Justus Judex," *Catholic Tales and Christian Songs* (Oxford: B H. Blackwell, 1918).

A magazine article, "Forgiveness and the Enemy":

Forgiveness is a very difficult matter. Many varieties of behaviour go by that name, and not all of them are admirable. There is the kind that says: "I forgive her as a Christian, but I shall never speak to her again." This is adequately dealt with by the caustic definition: "Christian forgiveness, which is no forgiveness at all," and need not be discussed, any more than the self-interest of those who –

> *Drink the champagne that she sends them,*
> *But they never can forget.*[3]

There is also the priggish variety, which greets persecution with the ostentatious announcement, "I forgive you, Jones, and I will pray for you." This, though it can base itself strongly on ethical and Scriptural sanction, shares with pacifism the serious practical disadvantage of so inflaming the evil passions of Jones that if the injured party had malignantly determined to drive Jones to the devil he could scarcely have hit upon a surer way. There is the conditional: "I will forgive you on condition you say you are sorry and never do it again." That has about it something which smacks too much of a legal bargain, and we are forced to remember that no man is so free from trespass himself that he can afford to insist on conditions. Only God is in a position to do that; and we recall the Catholic teaching that confession, contrition and amendment are the necessary conditions of absolution. But if we assert that Divine forgiveness is of this bargaining kind, we meet with a thundering denial from poet and prophet and from God Himself:

---

3 From an English folksong, "It's the Same the Whole World Over."

Doth Jehovah forgive a debt only on condition that it shall
Be payed? Doth he forgive Pollution only on conditions of
  Purity?
That Debt is not forgiven! That Pollution is not forgiven!
Such is the forgiveness of the gods, the moral virtues of the
Heathen, whose tender mercies are cruelty. But Jehovah's
  salvation
Is without money and without price, in the continual
  forgiveness of sins,
In the perpetual mutual sacrifice in great eternity. For behold!
There is none that liveth and sinneth not! And this is the
  covenant
Of Jehovah. "If you forgive one another, so shall Jehovah
  forgive you;
That He Himself may dwell among you."[4]

God's conditions, it appears, are of another kind. There is
nothing about demanding repentance and restitution or prom-
ises not to offend again: we must forgive unconditionally if we
hope to be forgiven ourselves: "as we forgive our debtors" – "unto
seventy times seven."

The whole teaching of the New Testament about forgiveness
is haunted by paradox and enigma, and cannot be summed up
in any phrase about simple kindliness. "Whether is easier: to
say *Thy sins be forgiven thee* or to say *Arise and walk?* But that ye
may know that the Son of Man hath power on earth to forgive
sins (then saith He to the sick of the palsy) Arise, take up thy
bed and go" [Luke 5:23]. The irony is so profound that we are
not certain which way to take it. "Do you think forgiveness is
something glib and simple? To be sure – it is just as simple as
this. Does it seem to you formidably difficult? To be sure, so is

4 William Blake, *Jerusalem*, 72.

this – but you see it can be done." Whereat, according to St. Luke, everybody, though pleased, was a little alarmed and thought it a very odd business.

It may be easier to understand what forgiveness is, if we first clear away misconceptions about what it does. It does not wipe out the consequences of the sin. The words and images used for forgiveness in the New Testament frequently have to do with the cancellation of a debt: and it is scarcely necessary to point out that when a debt is cancelled, this does not mean that the money is miraculously restored from nowhere. It means only that the obligation originally due from the borrower is voluntarily discharged by the lender. If I injure you and you mulct me in damages, then I bear the consequences; if you forbear to prosecute, then you bear the consequences. If the injury is irreparable, and you are vindictive, injury is added to injury; if you are forgiving and I am repentant, then we share the consequences and gain a friendship. But in every case the consequences are borne by somebody. The Parable of the Unmerciful Servant [Matt. 18:23–35] adds a further illuminating suggestion: that forgiveness is not merely a mutual act, but a social act. If injuries are not forgiven all round, the grace of pardon is made ineffective, and the inexorable judgment of the Law is forced into operation.

One thing emerges from all this: that forgiveness is not a doing-away of consequences; nor is it primarily a remission of punishment. A child may be forgiven and "let off" punishment, or punished and then forgiven; either way may bring good results. But no good will come of leaving him unpunished and unforgiven. Forgiveness is the re-establishment of a right relationship, in which the parties can genuinely feel and behave as freely with one another as though the unhappy incident had never taken place. But it is impossible to enjoy a right relationship with an offender who, when pardoned, continues to behave in an obdurate and unsocial manner to the injured party and to those whom he has injured, because there is something in him that obstructs the relationship. So that, while God does not, and man dare not, demand repentance as a condition for *bestowing* pardon, repentance remains an essential condition for *receiving* it. Hence the Church's twofold insistence – first that repentance is necessary, and secondly that all sin is pardoned instantly in the mere fact of the sinner's repentance. Nobody has to sit about being humiliated in the outer office while God despatches important business, before condescending to issue a stamped official discharge accompanied by an improving lecture. Like the Father of the Prodigal Son, God can see repentance coming a great way off and is there to meet it, and the repentance *is* the reconciliation.

If God does not stand upon His dignity with penitent sinners, still less, one would suppose, should we. But then, God is not inhibited, as we are, by unrepented sins of His own. It is when the injuries have been mutual that forgiveness becomes so complicated, since, as La Rochefoucauld[5] truly observes, it is very difficult to forgive those whom we have injured. The only fruitful line of thought to follow is, I think, to bear in mind that forgiveness has no necessary concern with payment or non-payment of reparations; its aim is the establishment of a free relationship. This aim is in no way advanced by mutual recrimination, or by the drawing-up of a detailed account to ascertain which side, on balance, is the more aggrieved party. If both were equally and immediately repentant, forgiveness – mutual and instantaneous – would *be* the right relationship.

5 François VI, Duc de La Rochefoucauld (1613–1680), known for maxims and epigrams. "We often forgive those that have injured us, but we can never pardon those that we have injured." As translated in *Moral Maxims and Reflections* (London: Methuen & Co., 1912).

But are there not crimes which are unforgivable or which we, at any rate, find we cannot bring ourselves to forgive? At the present moment, that is a question which we are bound to ask ourselves. And it is here, especially, that we must make a great effort to clear our minds of clutter. The issue is not really affected by arguments about who began first, or whether bombs or blockade are the more legitimate weapon to use against women and children, or whether a civilian is a military objective; nor need we object that no amount of forgiveness will do away with the consequences of the crimes – since we have already seen that forgiveness is not incompatible with consequence. The real question is this: When the war comes to an end, is there going to be anything in our minds, or in the minds of the enemy, that will prevent the re-establishment of a right relationship? That relationship need not necessarily be one of equal power on either side, and it need not exclude proper preventive measures against a renewal of the conflict – those considerations are again irrelevant. Are there any crimes that in themselves make forgiveness and right relations impossible?

If we again look at the New Testament, we shall find that what some people, with unconscious sarcasm, persist in calling "the simple Gospel" presents us, as usual, with a monstrous and shattering paradox. The most spectacular sin recorded there is the deliberate murder of God; and it is forgiven on the grounds that "they know not what they do" [Luke 23:34]. Is ignorance, then, an excuse? Can a man qualify for Heaven by pleading that he cannot tell right from wrong? Is not that the most damning of all disabilities – the final blasphemy that "shall not be forgiven, neither in this world, nor in the world to come" [Matt. 12:32]? Here is a distinction drawn like a sword at a point which we can scarcely see on the map.

Or perhaps the dividing line is clear enough, after all. The soldiers who crucified God had not, it is true, the heroic imagination that could see beyond their plain military duty to the eternal verities. But there was nothing in their ignorant hearts impenetrable to light. To such dim glimpses as they had, they seem to have responded. One ran for the hyssop; another said: "Indeed, there was something divine about this criminal." Forgiveness might work here and find no obstruction. But those others – all of them highly respectable people – had seen the healing power of God blaze in their eyes like the sun; they looked it full in the face, and said that it was the devil. This is the ultimate corruption that leaves no place for pardon; "I have so hardened my heart" (said the man in the iron cage) "that I *cannot* repent."[6]

I do not know that we are in any position to judge our neighbours. But let us suppose that we ourselves are free from this corruption (are we?) and that we are ready to greet repentance with open arms and re-establish with our enemies a relationship in which old wrongs are as though they had never been. What are we to do with those who cannot accept pardon when it is offered? And with those who have been corrupted from the cradle? Here, if anywhere, is the unforgivable – not in murdered citizens, ruined homes, broken churches, fire, sword, famine, pestilence, tortures, concentration camps, but in the corruption of a whole generation, brought up to take a devil of destruction for the God of creation and to dedicate their noblest powers to the worship of that savage altar. If for the guilty there remains only the judgment of the millstone and the deep sea, we still have to ask ourselves: What are we to do with these innocents?

---

6 "I sinned against the light of the Word and the goodness of God, I have grieved the Spirit, and He is gone. I tempted the devil, and he is come to me. I have provoked God to anger, and he has left me. I have so hardened my heart that I cannot repent." John Bunyan, "A Man in an Iron Cage," ch. 28 in *The Pilgrim's Progress* (1678).

For whether is easier: To say, *Thy sins be forgiven thee?*, or to say, *Arise and walk?* But that ye may know that the Son of Man hath power on earth to forgive sins (then saith He to the warped mind, the frozen brain, the starved heart, the stunted and paralysed soul) *Arise, take up thy bed and go to thy home.*

No: forgiveness is a difficult matter, and no man living is wholly innocent or wholly guilty. We, as a nation, are not very ready to harbour resentment, and sometimes this means that we forget without forgiving – that is, without ever really understanding either our enemy or ourselves. This time, we feel, forgetfulness will not be possible. If that is so and we make up our minds that no right relationship will ever be possible either, I do not quite see to what end we can look forward.[7]

7   "Forgiveness and the Enemy," *Fortnightly* 149 (April 1941), published in Dorothy L. Sayers, *Unpopular Opinions* (London: Victor Gollancz, 1946).

5

The Documents in the Case

Judgment

In Sayers's 1930 mystery The Documents in the Case, *the impulsive Mrs. Harrison writes to her lover about her husband, and what the local priest, Mr. Perry, would think of their extramarital relationship. It is with derision that she refers to her husband as the "Gorgon."*

. . . Do you know, there was a moment when I was frightened. I thought, for a horrible minute, that he had suspected something after all, and had only pretended to go out, and would come slinking back on purpose to catch us. Did that occur to you? And were *you* afraid to say anything, lest *I* should be frightened? I was. And then, quite suddenly, I felt certain, absolutely *certain* that it was all right. We were being watched over, Petra. We had been given that great hour – a little bit of eternity, just for you and me. God must be sorry for us. I can't believe it was sin – no one could commit a sin and be so happy. Sin doesn't exist, the conventional kind of sin, I mean – only lovingness and unlovingness – people like you and me, and people like him. I wonder what Mr. Perry would say to that. He is just crossing the road now to Benediction, as he calls it. He thinks he knows all about what is right and what is wrong, but lots of people think his candles and incense wicked, and call him a papist and idolater and things like that. And yet, out of his little, cold, parish experience, he would set himself up to make silly laws for you, darling, who are big and free and splendid. How absurd it all is! He preached such a funny sermon the other day, about the Law and the Gospel. He said, if we wouldn't do as the Gospel said, and keep good for the love of God, then we should be punished by the Law. And he said that didn't mean that God was vindictive, only that the Laws of Nature had their way, and worked out the punishment quite impartially, just as fire burns you if you touch it, not to punish you, but because that is the natural law of fire.

I am wandering on, darling, am I not? I only wondered what kind of natural revenge Mr. Perry thought God would take for what he would call our sin. It does seem so ridiculous, doesn't it? As if God or Nature would trouble about us, with all those millions and millions of worlds to see to. Besides, our love is the natural thing – it's the Gorgon who is unnatural and abnormal. Probably that's *his* punishment. He denies me love, and our love is Nature's revenge on him. But, of course, he wouldn't see it that way.

Oh, darling, what a wonderful time these last weeks have been. I enjoyed every minute. I have been so happy, I didn't know how to keep from shouting my happiness out loud in the streets. I wanted to run and tell the people who passed by, and the birds and the flowers and the stray cats how happy I was. Even the Gorgon being there couldn't spoil it altogether. Do you remember how angry he was about *The Sacred Flame*?[1] And you

---

1   William Somerset Maugham, *The Sacred Flame* (1928). A crippled World War I soldier is killed by his mother to save him the pain of knowing that his wife is pregnant by another man.

were holding my hand, and your hand was telling mine how true and right it was that the useless husband should be got out of the way of the living, splendid wife and her lover and child. Darling, I think that play is the most wonderful and courageous thing that's ever been written. What right have the useless people to get in the way of love and youth? Of course, in the play, it wasn't the husband's fault, because he was injured and couldn't help himself – but that's Nature's law again, isn't it? Get rid of the ugly and sick and weak and worn-out things, and let youth and love and happiness have their chance. It was a brave thing to write that, because it's what we all know in our hearts, and yet we are afraid to say it.

Petra, darling, my lover, my dearest one, how can we wait and do nothing, while life slips by? The time of love is so short – what can we do? Think of a way, Petra. Even – yes, I'm almost coming to that – even if the way leads through shame and disgrace – I believe I could face it, if there is no other. I know so certainly that I was made for you and that you are all my life, as I am yours. Kiss me, kiss me, Petra. I kiss my own arms and hands and try to think it's you. Ever, my darling, your own

LOLO

. . . Oh, Petra, I am so frightened. Darling, something dreadful has happened. I'm sure – I'm almost quite sure. Do you remember when I said Nature couldn't revenge herself? Oh, but she can and *has,* Petra. What shall I do? I've tried things, but it's no good. Petra, you've *got* to help me. I never thought of this – we were so careful – but something must have gone wrong. Petra, darling, I can't face it. I shall kill myself. He'll find out – he must find out, and he'll be so cruel, and it will all be too terrible. . . .

Darling, darling, do *something* – anything! I can't think of any way, but there must be one, somehow. Everybody will know, and there will be a frightful fuss and scandal. And even if we got a divorce, it wouldn't be in time – they are so slow in those dreadful courts. But I don't expect he would divorce me. He would just smother it all up and be cruel to me. I don't know. I feel so ill, and I can't sleep. He asked me what was the matter with me to-day. I'd been crying and I look simply awful. Petra, my dearest, what *can* we do. How cruel God is! He must be on the conventional people's side after all. Do write quickly and tell me what to do. And don't, don't be angry with me, darling, for getting you into this trouble. I couldn't help it. Write to me or come to me – I shall go mad with worry. If you love me at all, Petra, you must help me now.

Lolo[2]

From "Creed or Chaos?":

The word "punishment" for sin has become so corrupted that it ought never to be used. But once we have established the true doctrine of man's nature, the true nature of judgment becomes startlingly clear and rational. It is the inevitable consequence of man's attempt to regulate life and society on a system that runs counter to the facts of his own nature.

In the physical sphere, typhus and cholera are a judgment on dirty living; not because God shows an arbitrary favouritism to nice, clean people, but because of an essential element in the physical structure of the universe. In the state, the brutal denial of freedom to the individual will issue in a judgment of blood,

---

2   Dorothy L. Sayers and Robert Eustace, *The Documents in the Case* (London: Ernest Benn, 1930), "Section One: Synthesis."

because man is so made that oppression is more intolerable to him than death. The avaricious greed that prompts men to cut down forests for the speedy making of money brings down a judgment of flood and famine, because that sin of avarice in the spiritual sphere runs counter to the physical law of nature. We must not say that such behaviour is wrong because it does not pay; but rather that it does not pay because it is wrong. As T. S. Eliot says: "a wrong attitude towards nature implies, somewhere, a wrong attitude towards God, and the consequence is an inevitable doom."[3]

From the book The Mind of the Maker:

When the laws regulating human society are so formed as to come into collision with the nature of things, and in particular with the fundamental realities of human nature, they will end by producing an impossible situation which, unless the laws are altered, will issue in such catastrophes as war, pestilence and famine. Catastrophes thus caused are the execution of universal law upon arbitrary enactments which contravene the facts; they are thus properly called by theologians, judgments of God.

Much confusion is caused in human affairs by the use of the same word "law" to describe these two very different things: an arbitrary code of behaviour based on a consensus of human opinion and a statement of unalterable fact about the nature of the universe. . . .

There is a universal moral law, as distinct from a moral code, which consists of certain statements of fact about the nature of man; and by behaving in conformity with which, man enjoys

---

3   T. S. Eliot, *The Idea of a Christian Society* (New York: Harcourt, Brace, 1940), 61–62.

his true freedom. This is what the Christian Church calls "the natural law."[4] The more closely the moral code agrees with the natural law, the more it makes for freedom in human behaviour; the more widely it departs from the natural law, the more it tends to enslave mankind and to produce the catastrophes called "judgments of God."

The universal moral *law* (or natural law of humanity) is discoverable, like any other law of nature, by experience. It cannot be promulgated, it can only be ascertained, because it is a question not of opinion but of fact. When it has been ascertained, a moral *code* can be drawn up to direct human behaviour and prevent men, as far as possible, from doing violence to their own nature. No code is necessary to control the behaviour of matter, since matter is apparently not tempted to contradict its own nature, but obeys the law of its being in perfect freedom. Man, however, does continually suffer this temptation and frequently yields to it. This contradiction within his own nature is peculiar to man, and is called by the Church "sinfulness"; other psychologists have other names for it.

The moral *code* depends for its validity upon a consensus of human opinion about what man's nature really is, and what it ought to be, when freed from this mysterious self-contradiction and enabled to run true to itself. If there is no agreement about these things, then it is useless to talk of enforcing the moral code. It is idle to complain that a society is infringing a moral code intended to make people behave like St. Francis of Assisi if the society retorts that it does not wish to behave like St. Francis, and considers it more natural and right to behave like the Emperor Caligula. When there is a genuine conflict of

---

4 "The natural law may be described briefly as a force working in history which tends to keep human beings human" J. V. Langmead Casserley, *The Fate of Modern Culture* (London: Dacre, 1940).

opinion, it is necessary to go behind the moral code and appeal to the natural law – to prove, that is, at the bar of experience, that St. Francis does in fact enjoy a freer truth to essential human nature than Caligula, and that a society of Caligulas is more likely to end in catastrophe than a society of Franciscans. . . .

At the back of the Christian moral *code* we find a number of pronouncements about the moral *law,* which are not regulations at all, but which purport to be statements of fact about man and the universe, and upon which the whole moral code depends for its authority and its validity in practice. These statements do not rest on human consent; they are either true or false. If they are true, man runs counter to them at his own peril. He may, of course, defy them, as he may defy the law of gravitation by jumping off the Eiffel Tower, but he cannot abolish them by edict. Nor yet can God abolish them, except by breaking up the structure of the universe, so that in this sense they are not arbitrary laws. We may of course argue that the making of this kind of universe, or indeed of any kind of universe, is an arbitrary act; but, given the universe as it stands, the rules that govern it are not freaks of momentary caprice. There is a difference between saying: "If you hold your finger in the fire you will get burned" and saying, "If you whistle at your work I shall beat you, because the noise gets on my nerves."

The God of the Christians is too often looked upon as an old gentleman of irritable nerves who beats people for whistling. This is the result of a confusion between arbitrary "law" and the "laws" which are statements of fact. Breach of the first is "punished" by edict; but breach of the second, by judgment. . . .

In a similar way, volumes of angry controversy have been poured out about the Christian creeds, under the impression that they represent, not statements of fact, but arbitrary edicts.

The conditions of salvation, for instance, are discussed as though they were conditions for membership of some fantastic club like the Red-Headed League.[5] They do not purport to be anything of the kind. Rightly or wrongly, they purport to be necessary conditions based on the facts of human nature. We are accustomed to find conditions attached to human undertakings, some of which are arbitrary and some not. A regulation that allowed a cook to make omelettes only on condition of first putting on a top hat might conceivably be given the force of law, and penalties might be inflicted for disobedience; but the condition would remain arbitrary and irrational. The law that omelettes can be made only on condition that there shall be a preliminary breaking of eggs is one with which we are sadly familiar. The efforts of idealists to make omelettes without observing that condition are foredoomed to failure by the nature of things. The Christian creeds are too frequently assumed to be in the top-hat category; this is an error; they belong to the category of egg-breaking. Even that most notorious of damnatory clauses which provokes sensitive ecclesiastics to defy the rubric and banish the Athanasian Creed from public recitation does not say that God will refuse to save unbelievers; it is at once less arbitrary and more alarming: "which except a man believe faithfully, he *cannot* be saved." It purports to be a statement of fact. The proper question to be asked about any creed is not, "Is it pleasant?" but, "is it true?" "Christianity has compelled the mind of man not because it is the most cheering view of man's existence but because it is truest to the facts."[6] It is unpleasant to be called sinners, and much nicer to think that we all have hearts of gold – but have we? It is agreeable to suppose that the more scientific knowledge

5   Sir Arthur Conan Doyle, "The Red-Headed League," *The Strand Magazine*, (August, 1891).

6   Lord David Cecil, "True and False Values," *The Fortnightly* (March, 1940).

we acquire the happier we shall be – but does it look like it? It is encouraging to feel that progress is making us automatically every day and in every way better, and better, and better – but does history support that view? "We hold these truths to be self-evident: that all men were created equal"[7] – but does the external evidence support this *a priori* assertion? Or does experience rather suggest that man is "very far gone from original righteousness and is of his own nature inclined to evil"?[8, 9]

---

7   Thomas Jefferson: Declaration of Independence (1776).

8   Church of England: "Thirty-Nine Articles of Religion," Ninth Article, *Book of Common Prayer.*

9   Dorothy L. Sayers, *The Mind of the Maker* (New York: Harper & Row, 1941), ch. 1.

6

The Dogma Is the Drama

Belief

At the end of The Documents in the Case, *a group of gentlemen gathered for supper discuss whether contemporary scientific discoveries have dislodged faith.*

Perry's shabby little sitting-room seemed crowded with men and smoke when I arrived. Professor Hoskyns, long, thin, bald, and much more human-looking than his Press photographs, was installed in a broken-springed leather arm-chair and called Perry "Jim." There was also a swarthy little man in spectacles, whom they both called "Stingo," and who turned out to be Professor Matthews, the biologist, the man who has done so much work on heredity. A large, stout, red-faced person with a boisterous manner was introduced as Waters. He was younger than the rest, but they all treated him with deference, and it presently appeared that he was the coming man in chemistry. Desultory conversation made it clear that Matthews, Hoskyns and Perry had been contemporaries at Oxford, and that Waters had been brought by Matthews, with whom he was on terms of the heartiest friendship and disagreement. A thin youth, with an eager manner and an irrepressible forelock, completed the party. He sported a clerical collar and informed me that he was the new curate, and that it was "a wonderful opportunity" to start his ministry under a man like Mr. Perry. The dinner was satisfying. A vast beef-steak pudding, and apple-pie of corresponding size, and tankards of beer, quaffed from Perry's old rowing-cups, put us all into a mellow humour. Perry's asceticism did not, I am thankful to say, take the form of tough hash and lemonade, in spite of the presence on his walls of a series of melancholy Arundel prints, portraying brown and skinny anchorites, apparently nourished on cabbage-water. It rather tended to the idea of: "Beef, noise, the Church, vulgarity and beer,"[1] and I judged that in their younger days, my fellow-guests had kept the progs busy. However, the somewhat wearisome flood of undergraduate reminiscence was stemmed after a time, with suitable apologies, and Matthews said, a little provocatively:

"So here we all are. I never thought you'd stick to it, Perry. Which has made your job hardest – the War or people like us?"

"The War," said Perry, immediately. "It has taken the heart out of people."

"Yes. It showed things up a bit," said Matthews. "Made it hard to believe in anything."

"No," replied the priest. "Made it easy to believe and difficult not to believe – in anything. Just anything. They believe in everything in a languid sort of way – in you, in me, in Waters, in Hoskyns, in mascots, in spiritualism, in education, in the daily papers – why not? It's easier, and the various things cancel out and so make it unnecessary to take any definite steps in any direction."

---

1   "Chestertonian youths who five things revere – Beef, noise, the Church, vulgarity and beer." Anonymous quote describing Oxford in the 1920s.

"Damn the daily papers," said Hoskyns. "And damn education. All these get-clever-quick articles and sixpenny text-books. Before one has time to verify an experiment, they're all at you, shrieking to have it formulated into a theory. And if you do formulate it, they misunderstand it, or misapply it. If anybody says there are vitamins in tomatoes, they rush out with a tomato-theory. If somebody says that gamma-rays are found to have an action on cancer-cells in mice, they proclaim gamma-rays as a cure-all for everything from old age to a cold in the head. And if anybody goes quietly away into a corner to experiment with high-voltage electric currents, they start a lot of ill-informed rubbish about splitting the atom."

"Yes," said Matthews, "I thought I saw some odd remarks attributed to you the other day about that."

"Wasting my time," said Hoskyns. "I told them exactly what they put into my mouth. You're right, Jim, they'd believe anything. "The elixir of life – that's what they really want to get hold of. It would look well in a headline. If you can't give 'em a simple formula to cure all human ills and explain creation, they say you don't know your business."

"Ah!" said Perry, with a twinkle of the eye, "but if the Church gives them a set of formulæ for the same purpose, they say they don't want formulæ or dogmas, but just a loving wistfulness."[2]

A magazine article, "The Dogma is in the Drama," published in April 1938:

"Any stigma," said a witty tongue, "will do to beat a dogma"; and the flails of ridicule have been brandished with such energy of late on the threshing-floor of controversy that the true seed of

---

2 *The Documents in the Case*, 1930, "Section Two: Analysis."

the Word has become well-nigh lost amid the whirling of chaff. Christ, in His Divine innocence, said to the Woman of Samaria, "Ye worship ye know not what" [John 4:22] – being apparently under the impression that it might be desirable, on the whole, to know what one was worshipping. He thus showed Himself sadly out of touch with the twentieth-century mind, for the cry to-day is: "Away with the tedious complexities of dogma – let us have the simple spirit of worship; just worship, no matter of what!" The only drawback to this demand for a generalised and undirected worship is the practical difficulty of arousing any sort of enthusiasm for the worship of nothing in particular.

It would not perhaps be altogether surprising if, in this nominally Christian country, where the Creeds are daily recited, there were a number of people who knew all about Christian doctrine and disliked it. It is more startling to discover how many people there are who heartily dislike and despise Christianity without having the faintest notion what it is. If you tell them, they cannot believe you. I do not mean that they cannot believe the doctrine: that would be understandable enough, since it takes some believing. I mean that they simply cannot believe that anything so interesting, so exciting and so dramatic can be the orthodox Creed of the Church.

That this is really the case was made plain to me by the questions asked me, mostly by young men, about my Canterbury play, *The Zeal of Thy House*.[3] The action of the play involves a dramatic presentation of a few fundamental Christian dogmas – in particular, the application to human affairs of the doctrine of the Incarnation. That the Church believed Christ to be in any *real* sense God, or that the Eternal Word was supposed to be associated in any way with the work of Creation; that Christ was

---

3 Commissioned for the Canterbury Festival of 1937.

held to be at the same time Man in any *real* sense of the word; that the doctrine of the Trinity could be considered to have any relation to fact or any bearing on psychological truth; that the Church considered Pride to be sinful, or indeed took notice of any sin beyond the more disreputable sins of the flesh: – all these things were looked upon as astonishing and revolutionary novelties, imported into the Faith by the feverish imagination of a playwright. I protested in vain against this flattering tribute to my powers of invention, referring my inquirers to the Creeds, to the Gospels and to the offices of the Church; I insisted that if my play was dramatic it was so, not in spite of the dogma but because of it – that, in short, the dogma *was* the drama. The explanation was, however, not well received; it was felt that if there was anything attractive in Christian philosophy I must have put it there myself.

Judging by what my young friends tell me and also by what is said on the subject in anti-Christian literature written by people who ought to have taken a little trouble to find out what they are attacking before attacking it, I have come to the conclusion that a short examination paper on the Christian religion might be very generally answered as follows:

Q: What does the Church think of God the Father?

A: He is omnipotent and holy. He created the world and imposed on man conditions impossible of fulfilment; He is very angry if these are not carried out. He sometimes interferes by means of arbitrary judgments and miracles, distributed with a good deal of favouritism. He likes to be truckled to and is always ready to pounce on anybody who trips up over a difficulty in the Law, or is having a bit of fun. He is rather like a Dictator, only larger and more arbitrary.

Q: What does the Church think of God the Son?

A: He is in some way to be identified with Jesus of Nazareth. It was not His fault that the world was made like this, and, unlike God the Father, He is friendly to man and did His best to reconcile man to God (see *Atonement*). He has a good deal of influence with God, and if you want anything done, it is best to apply to Him.

Q: What does the Church think of God the Holy Ghost?

A: I don't know exactly. He was never seen or heard of till Whit-Sunday. There is a sin against Him which damns you for ever, but nobody knows what it is.

Q: What is the doctrine of the Trinity?

A: "The Father incomprehensible, the Son incomprehensible, and the whole thing incomprehensible." Something put in by theologians to make it more difficult – nothing to do with daily life or ethics.

Q: What was Jesus Christ like in real life?

A: He was a good man – so good as to be called the Son of God. He is to be identified in some way with God the Son (q.v.). He was meek and mild and preached a simple religion of love and pacifism. He had no sense of humour. Anything in the Bible that suggests another side to His character must be an interpolation, or a paradox invented by G. K. Chesterton. If we try to live like Him, God the Father will let us off being damned hereafter and only have us tortured in this life instead.

Q: What is meant by the Atonement?

A: God wanted to damn everybody, but His vindictive sadism was sated by the crucifixion of His own Son, who was quite innocent, and therefore a particularly attractive victim. He now only damns people who don't follow Christ or who never heard of Him.

Q: What does the Church think of sex?

A: God made it necessary to the machinery of the world, and tolerates it, provided the parties (a) are married, and (b) get no pleasure out of it.

Q: What does the Church call Sin?

A: Sex (otherwise than as excepted above); getting drunk; saying "damn"; murder, and cruelty to dumb animals; not going to church; most kinds of amusement. "Original sin" means that anything we enjoy doing is wrong.

Q: What is faith?

A: Resolutely shutting your eyes to scientific fact.

Q: What is the human intellect?

A: A barrier to faith.

Q: What are the seven Christian virtues?

A: Respectability; childishness; mental timidity; dulness; sentimentality; censoriousness; and depression of spirits.

Q: Wilt thou be baptised in this faith?

A: No fear!

I cannot help feeling that as a statement of Christian orthodoxy, these replies are inadequate, if not misleading. But I also cannot help feeling that they do fairly accurately represent what many people take Christian orthodoxy to be, and for this state of affairs I am inclined to blame the orthodox. Whenever an average Christian is represented in a novel or a play, he is pretty sure to be shown practising one or all of the Seven Deadly Virtues enumerated above, and I am afraid that this is the impression made by the average Christian upon the world at large.

Perhaps we are not following Christ all the way or in quite the right spirit. We are apt, for example, to be a little sparing of the palms and the hosannas. We are chary of wielding the scourge of small cords, lest we should offend somebody or interfere with trade. We do not furbish up our wits to disentangle knotty questions about Sunday observance and tribute-money, nor hasten to sit at the feet of the doctors, both hearing them and asking them questions. We pass hastily over disquieting jests about making friends with the mammon of unrighteousness and alarming observations about bringing not peace but a sword; nor do we distinguish ourselves by the graciousness with which we sit at meat with publicans and sinners. Somehow or other, and with the best intentions, we have shown the world the typical Christian in the likeness of a crashing and rather ill-natured bore – and this in the Name of One Who assuredly never bored a soul in those thirty-three years during which He passed through the world like a flame.

Let us, in Heaven's name, drag out the Divine Drama from under the dreadful accumulation of slip-shod thinking and trashy sentiment heaped upon it, and set it on an open stage to startle the world into some sort of vigorous reaction. If the pious are the first to be shocked, so much the worse for the pious – others will pass into the Kingdom of Heaven before them. If all men are offended because of Christ, let them be offended; but where is the sense of their being offended at something that is not Christ and is nothing like Him? We do Him singularly little honour by watering down His personality till it could not offend a fly. Surely it is not the business of the Church to adapt Christ to men, but to adapt men to Christ.

It is the dogma that is the drama – not beautiful phrases, nor comforting sentiments, nor vague aspirations to loving-kindness and uplift, nor the promise of something nice after death – but the terrifying assertion that the same God Who made the world lived in the world and passed through the grave and gate of death. Show that to the heathen, and they may not believe it; but at least they may realise that here is something that a man might be glad to believe.[4]

---

4   "The Dogma Is the Drama," *St. Martin's Review*, April 1938, published in *Creed or Chaos?*, 1949.

7

The Five Red Herrings

Pride

The Five Red Herrings *is a murder mystery published in 1931 and set in Galloway, Scotland. One of the suspects, Farren, disappears early in the investigation. Lord Peter tries to get information on his whereabouts from his wife, an elegant, and very proud, woman.*

To her, the beauty of an ordered life was more than a mere phrase; it was a dogma to be preached, a cult to be practised with passion and concentration. . . . And Mrs. Farren was a very beautiful woman, if you liked that style of thing, with her oval face and large grey eyes and those thick masses of copper-coloured hair, parted in the middle and rolled in a great knot on the nape of the neck. . . .

But she was the kind of woman who, if once she set out to radiate sweetness and light, would be obstinate in her mission. He studied the rather full, sulky mouth and narrow, determined forehead. It was the face of a woman who would see only what she wished to see – who would think that one could abolish evils from the world by pretending that they were not there. Such things, for instance, as jealousy or criticism of herself. . . .

[Wimsey] looked at her.

"Ah!" he said. "Stupid of me. It is your own pride that you are sheltering now." He came back into the room, treading gently, and laid his hat on the table. "My dear Mrs. Farren, will you believe me when I say that all men – the best and the worst alike – have these moments of rebellion and distaste? It is nothing. It is a case for understanding and – if I may say so – response."

"I am ready," said Gilda Farren, "to forgive – "

"Never do that," said Wimsey. "Forgiveness is the one unpardonable sin. It is almost better to make a scene – though," he added, thoughtfully, "that depends on the bloke's temperament."

"I should certainly not make a scene," said Mrs. Farren.

"No," said Wimsey. "I see that."

"I shall not do anything," said Mrs. Farren. "To be insulted was enough. To be deserted as well – " Her eyes were hard and angry. "If he chooses to come back, I shall receive him, naturally. But it is nothing to me what he chooses to do with himself. There seems to be no end to what women have to endure. I should not say as much as this to you, if – "

"If I didn't know it already," put in Wimsey.

"I have tried to look as though nothing was the matter," said Mrs. Farren, "and to put a good face on it. I do not want to show my husband up before his friends."

"Quite so," said Wimsey. "Besides," he added, rather brutally, "it might look as though you yourself had failed in some way."

"I have always done my duty as his wife."

"Too true," said Wimsey. "He put you up on a pedestal, and you have sat on it ever since. What more could you do?"

"I have been faithful to him," said Mrs. Farren, with rising temper. "I have worked to keep the house beautiful and – and to make it a place of refreshment and inspiration. I have done all I could to further his ambitions. I have borne my share of the household expenses – " Here she seemed suddenly to become aware of a tinge of bathos and went on hurriedly, "You may think all this is nothing, but it means sacrifice and hard work."

"I know that," replied Wimsey, quietly. . . .

Farren had returned to Kirkcudbright. His dream of escape had vanished. His wife had forgiven him. His absence was explained as a trifling and whimsical eccentricity. Gilda Farren sat, upright and serene, spinning the loose white flock into a strong thread that wound itself ineluctably to smother the twirling spindle. . . . So Farren sat sulkily in his studio and Mrs. Farren span – not a rope, perhaps, but fetters at any rate – in the sitting-room with the cool blue curtains.[1]

Sayers was asked to write a play in verse for the 1937 Canterbury Festival. The theme for that year was "artists and craftsmen," and her drama tells the story of William of Sens, an architect who led the rebuilding after a major part of the cathedral was destroyed by fire in 1174. The title comes from Psalm 69:9, "For the zeal of thine house hath eaten me up," a reference to the architect's arrogance that causes his crippling plunge from a scaffold. Although bedridden, he refuses to give up the work to another architect until confronted by the archangel Michael in a dream.

> WILLIAM: What, in my work? The sin was in my work?
> Thou liest. Though thou speak with God's own voice
> Thou liest. In my work? That cannot be.
> I grant the work not perfect; no man's work

---

1   Dorothy L. Sayers, *The Five Red Herrings* (Victor Gollancz, 1931), ch. 20.

Is perfect; but what hand and brain could do,
Such as God made them, that I did. Doth God
Demand the impossible? Then blame God, not me,
That I am man, not God. He hath broken me,
Hath sought to snatch the work out of my hand——
Wherefore? . . . O now, now I begin to see.
This was well said, He is a jealous God;
The work was not ill done – 'twas done too well;
He will not have men creep so near His throne
To steal applause from Him. Is *this* my fault?
Why, this needs no repentance, and shall have none.
Let Him destroy me, since He has the power
To slay the thing He envies – but while I have breath
My work is mine; He shall not take it from me.

MICHAEL: No; thou shalt lay it down of thine own will.

WILLIAM: Never. Let Him heap on more torments yet——

MICHAEL: He can heap none on thee, He hath not borne——

WILLIAM: Let Him strike helpless hands as well as feet——

MICHAEL: Whose Feet and Hands were helpless stricken through——

WILLIAM: Scourge me and smite me and make blind mine eyes——

MICHAEL: As He was blindfolded and scourged and smitten——

WILLIAM: Dry up my voice in my throat and make me dumb——

MICHAEL: As He was dumb and opened not His mouth——

WILLIAM: Cramp me with pains——

MICHAEL: As He was cramped with pains,
Racked limb from limb upon the stubborn Cross——

WILLIAM: Parch me with fever——

MICHAEL: He that cried, "I thirst"——

WILLIAM: Wring out my blood and sweat——

MICHAEL: Whose sweat, like blood,
Watered the garden in Gethsemane——

WILLIAM: For all that He can do I will not yield,
Nor leave to other men that which is mine,
To botch – to alter – turn to something else,
Not mine.

MICHAEL: Thou wilt not? Yet God bore this too,
The last, the bitterest, worst humiliation,
Bowing His neck under the galling yoke
Frustrate, defeated, half His life unlived,
Nothing achieved.

WILLIAM: Could God, being God, do this?

MICHAEL: Christ, being man, did this; but still, through faith
Knew what He did. As gold and diamond,
Weighed in the chemist's balance, are but earth
Like tin or iron, albeit within them still
The purchase of the world lie implicit:
So, when God came to test of mortal time
In nature of a man whom time supplants,
He made no reservation of Himself
Nor of the godlike stamp that franked His gold,
But in good time let time supplant Him too.
The earth was rent, the sun's face turned to blood,
But He, unshaken, with exultant voice
Cried, "It is finished!" and gave up the ghost.
"Finished" – when men had thought it scarce begun.
Then His disciples with blind faces mourned,

Weeping: "We trusted that He should redeem
Israel; but now we know not. What said He
Behind the shut doors in Jerusalem,
At Emmaus, and in the bitter dawn
By Galilee? "I go; but feed My sheep;
For Me the Sabbath at the long week's close –
For you the task, for you the tongues of fire."
Thus shalt thou know the Master Architect,
Who plans so well, He may depart and leave
The work to others. Art thou more than God?
Not God Himself was indispensable,
For lo! God died – and still His work goes on. . . .

WILLIAM: O, I have sinned. The eldest sin of all,
Pride, that struck down the morning star from Heaven
Hath struck down me from where I sat and shone
Smiling on my new world. All other sins
God will forgive but that. I am damned, damned,
Justly. Yet, O most just and merciful God,
Hear me but once, Thou that didst make the world
And wilt not let one thing that Thou hast made,
No, not one sparrow, perish without Thy Will
(Since what we make, we love) – for that love's sake
Smite only me and spare my handiwork.
Jesu, the carpenter's Son, the Master-builder,
Architect, poet, maker – by those hands
That Thine own nails have wounded – by the wood
Whence Thou didst carve Thy Cross – let not the Church
Be lost through me. Let me lie deep in hell,
Death gnaw upon me, purge my bones with fire,
But let my work, all that was good in me,
All that was God, stand up and live and grow.
The work is sound, Lord God, no rottenness there –
Only in me. Wipe out my name from men

But not my work; to other men the glory
And to Thy Name alone. But if to the damned
Be any mercy at all, O, send Thy spirit
To blow apart the sundering flames, that I,
After a thousand years of hell, may catch
One glimpse, one only, of the Church of Christ,
The perfect work, finished, though not by me. . . .

MICHAEL: How hardly shall the rich man enter in
To the Kingdom of Heaven! By what sharp, thorny ways,
By what strait gate at last! But when he is come,
The angelic trumpets split their golden throats
Triumphant, to the stars singing together
And all the sons of God shouting for joy.
Be comforted, thou that wast rich in gifts;
For thou art broken on the self-same rack
That broke the richest Prince of all the world,
The Master-man. Thou shalt not surely die,
Save as He died; nor suffer, save with Him;
Nor lie in hell, for He hath conquered hell
And flung the gates wide open. They that bear
The cross with Him, with Him shall wear a crown
Such as the angels know not. Then be still,
And know that He is God, and God alone.[2]

From Sayers's 1941 talk "The Other Six Deadly Sins":

But the head and origin of all sin is the basic sin of *Superbia* or
Pride. In one way there is so much to say about Pride that one
might speak of it for a week and not have done. Yet in another
way, all there is to be said about it can be said in a single sen-
tence. It is the sin of trying to be as God. It is the sin which

---

2 Scene IV, *The Zeal of Thy House*, 1937, published in *Four Sacred Plays*, 1948.

proclaims that Man can produce out of his own wits, and his own impulses and his own imagination the standards by which he lives: that Man is fitted to be his own judge. It is Pride which turns man's virtues into deadly sins, by causing each self-sufficient virtue to issue in its own opposite, and as a grotesque and horrible travesty of itself. The name under which Pride walks the world at this moment is the *Perfectibility of Man,* or the *Doctrine of Progress;* and its specialty is the making of blueprints for Utopia and establishing the Kingdom of Man on earth.

For the devilish strategy of Pride is that it attacks us, not on our weak points, but on our strong. It is preeminently the sin of the noble mind – that *corruptio optimi* which works more evil in the world than all the deliberate vices. Because we do not recognise pride when we see it, we stand aghast to see the havoc wrought by the triumphs of human idealism. We meant so well, we thought we were succeeding – and look what has come of our efforts! There is a proverb that says that the way to Hell is paved with good intentions. We usually take it as referring to intentions that have been weakly abandoned; but it has a deeper and much subtler meaning. For that road is paved with good intentions strongly and obstinately pursued, until they become self-sufficing ends in themselves and deified.

> Sin grows with doing good . . .
> Servant of God has chance of greater sin
> And sorrow; than the man who serves a king.
> For those who serve the greater cause may make the cause
>   serve them,
> Still doing right.[3]

The Greeks feared above all things the state of mind they called *hubris* – the inflated spirits that come with too much success.

---

3   T. S. Eliot, *Murder in the Cathedral,* commissioned for the Canterbury Festival, 1935.

Overweening in men called forth, they thought, the envy of the gods. Their theology may seem to us a little unworthy, but with the phenomenon itself and its effects they were only too well acquainted. Christianity, with a more rational theology, traces *hubris* back to the root-sin of Pride, which places man instead of God at the centre of gravity and so throws the whole structure of things into the ruin called Judgment. Whenever we say, whether in the personal, political or social sphere, *"I am the master of my fate, I am the captain of my soul"*[4] we are committing the sin of Pride; and the higher the goal at which we aim; the more far-reaching will be the subsequent disaster. That is why we ought to distrust all those high ambitions and lofty ideals which make the well-being of humanity their ultimate end. Man cannot make himself happy by serving himself – not even when he calls self-service the service of the community; for "the community" in that context is only an extension of his own ego. Happiness is a by-product, thrown off in man's service of God. And incidentally, let us be very careful how we preach that "Christianity is necessary for the building of a free and prosperous post-war world." The proposition is strictly true, but to put it that way may be misleading, for it sounds as though we proposed to make God an instrument in the service of man. But God is nobody's instrument. If we say that the denial of God was the cause of our present disasters, well and good; it is of the essence of Pride to suppose that we can do without God.

But it will not do to let the same sin creep back in a subtler and more virtuous-seeming form by suggesting that the service of God is necessary as a means to the service of man. That is a blasphemous hypocrisy, which would end by degrading God to the status of a heathen fetish, bound to the service of a tribe,

---

4   William Ernest Henley, "Invictus," *Book of Verses* (London: D. Nutt. 1888), 56–57.

and liable to be dumped head-downwards in the water-butt if He failed to produce good harvest-weather in return for services rendered.

"Cursed be he that trusteth in man," says Reinhold Niebuhr, "even if he be pious man or, perhaps, particularly if he be pious man."[5] For the besetting temptation of the pious man is to become the proud man: "He spake this parable unto certain which trusted in themselves that they were righteous" [Luke 18:9].[6]

From a letter to a certain Patricia Flavel, December 14, 1948:

Dear Miss Flavel,

The answer to your question is, I believe, that you should love yourself as much as is just. You must be precious to yourself because you are precious to God, remembering that in His sight your neighbour is equally precious, and precious in the same way. You must not do damage to your own soul, or your neighbour's; you must respect and take all reasonable care of your body and his, because it is God's property, and should not be treated with careless irreverence. You must not love yourself more than God – and neither must you love your neighbour more than God, nor think that your love for him is any excuse for offending God. You may rightly put your neighbour's interests before your own, because that is charity; but you must not put them before God's interests, because that is idolatry. Your love for your neighbour must not be possessive, or jealous, or degrading, or sloppily sentimental, because that kind of love is good neither for him nor for you. If he is an unlovable person, you must remember that God (however odd it may seem to you)

---

5   Reinhold Niebuhr, *Beyond Tragedy: Essays on the Christian Interpretation of History* (Charles Scribner's Sons, 1937).

6   "The Other Six Deadly Sins," published in *Creed or Chaos?*, 1949.

loves him, just as He loves you (however odd *that* may seem to other people or even to yourself). If your neighbour is wicked, you must contrive to love him while hating his wickedness; just as you manage to have a continual friendly concern for yourself, even in the moments when you do not think very highly of your own behaviour. And if you are ever tempted to despair of yourself or despise and hate yourself, you must resist that temptation, since it is not for you to treat any of God's creatures like that; and so also with your neighbour. . . .

These are of course counsels of perfection, and difficult to carry out in practice. It was (so to speak) shrewd of Our Lord to use the word "neighbour." It is much easier to feel warmly charitable towards some notorious villain in Kamschatka or Japan than to have patience with one's own relations or the tiresome woman next door. As the late Charles Williams once said to me, "Most of us are not very good at loving people, and that's the whole trouble." Still, we can but do our best; and it is easier, I think if we don't try to pump up a *liking* which we don't feel, but just concentrate on being in charity with people for God's sake.

Yours sincerely,

Dorothy L. Sayers[7]

---

7   *Letters*, 3:411–412.

8

Have His Carcase

Despair and Hope

In Have His Carcase, *Lord Peter Wimsey has fallen in love with a writer named Harriet Vane. Although she is still traumatized by her last romantic episode and repeatedly refuses to marry him, together they solve the murder of a taxi dancer at a seaside resort. Harriet asks for advice from a handsome friend of the murdered man, also employed to dance with lonely women.*

"Tell me, M. Antoine," said Harriet, as their taxi rolled along the Esplanade. "You who are a person of great experience, is love, in your opinion, a matter of the first importance?"

"It is, alas! Of a great importance, mademoiselle, but of the first importance, no!"

"What is of the first importance?"

"Mademoiselle, I tell you frankly that to have a healthy mind in a healthy body is the greatest gift of *le bon Dieu,* and when I see so many people who have clean blood and strong bodies spoiling themselves and distorting their brains with drugs and drink and foolishness, it makes me angry. They should leave that to the people who cannot help themselves because to them life is without hope."

Harriet hardly knew what to reply; the words were spoken with such personal and tragic significance. Rather fortunately, Antoine did not wait.

"*L'amour!* These ladies come and dance and excite themselves and want love and think it is happiness. And they tell me about their sorrows – me – and they have no sorrows at all, only that they are silly and selfish and lazy. Their husbands are unfaithful and their lovers run away and what do they say? Do they say, I have two hands, two feet, all my faculties, I will make a life for myself? No. They say, Give me cocaine, give me the cocktail, give me the thrill, give me my gigolo, give me *l'amo-o-ur!* Like a *mouton* bleating in a field. If they knew!"

Harriet laughed.

"You're right, M. Antoine. I don't believe *l'amour* matters so terribly, after all."

"But understand me," said Antoine who, like most Frenchmen, was fundamentally serious and domestic, "I do not say that love is not important. It is no doubt agreeable to love, and to marry an amiable person who will give you fine, healthy children. This Lord Peter Wimsey, *par exemple,* who is obviously a gentleman of the most perfect integrity – "

"Oh, never mind about *him!*" broke in Harriet, hastily. "I wasn't thinking about him. I was thinking about Paul Alexis and these people we are going to see."

"Ah! *C'est différent.* Mademoiselle, I think you know very well the difference between love which is important and love which is not important. But you must remember that one may have an important love for an unimportant person. And you must remember also that where people are sick in their minds or their bodies it does not need even love to make them do foolish things.[1]

---

1   Dorothy L. Sayers, *Have His Carcase* (New York: Harper & Row, 1932), ch. 15.

From an essay, "Christian Morality":

In the list of those Seven Deadly Sins which the Church offi-cially recognizes there is the sin which is sometimes called *Sloth,* and sometimes *Accidie.* The one name is obscure to us; the other is a little misleading. It does not mean lack of hustle: it means the slow sapping of all the faculties by indifference, and by the sensation that life is pointless and meaningless, and not-worth-while. It is, in fact, the very thing which has been called the Disease of Democracy. It is the child of Covetousness, and the parent of those other two sins which the Church calls Lust and Gluttony. Covetousness breaks down the standards by which we assess our spiritual values, and causes us to look for satisfac-tions in this world. The next step is the sloth of mind and body, the emptiness of heart, which destroy energy and purpose and issue in that general attitude to the universe which the inter-war jazz musicians aptly named "the Blues." For the cure of the Blues, Cæsar [2] (who has his own axe to grind) prescribes the dreary frivolling which the Churches and respectable people have agreed to call "immorality," and which, in these days, is as far as possible from the rollicking enjoyment of bodily pleasures which, rightly considered, are sinful only by their excess. The mournful and medical aspect assumed by "immorality" in the present age is a sure sign that in trying to cure these particular sins we are patching up the symptoms instead of tackling the disease at its roots. [3]

In The Light and the Life, *play seven of* The Man Born to Be King, *Sayers portrays Lazarus as a man haunted by depression.*

2   Cæsar: Her word for the world's attitudes.

3   "Christian Morality," *Unpopular Opinions,* 1946.

His sister, Mary of Bethany, Mary Magdalen, and the unnamed woman who anointed Jesus' feet (Luke 7:37–50) are combined into one character. She and Jesus are conversing with Lazarus in this scene from the radio play.

MARY: Even as a boy you were quiet and melancholy – my grave elder brother. You tried to tame my wild spirits. If I had listened to you I should never have sinned so deeply. But there was so much – so much to enjoy. I loved the beauty of the world. I loved the lights and the laughter, the jewels and the perfumes and the gold, and the applause of the people when I danced and delighted them all, with garlands of lilies in red braids of my hair.

LAZARUS: You were always in love with life.

MARY: I loved the wrong things in the wrong way – yet it *was* love of a sort . . . until I found a better.

JESUS: Because the love was so great, the sin is all forgiven.

MARY: Kind Rabbi, you told me so, when I fell at your feet in the house of Simon the Pharisee. . . Did you know? My companions and I came there that day to mock you. We thought you would be sour and grim, hating all beauty and treating life as an enemy. But when I saw you, I was amazed. You were the only person there that was really alive. The rest of us were going about half-dead – making the gestures of life, pretending to be real people. The life was not with us but with you – intense and shining, like the strong sun when it rises and turns the flames of our candles to pale smoke. And I wept and was ashamed, seeing myself such a thing of trash and tawdry. But when you spoke to me, I felt the flame of the sun in my heart. I came alive for the first time. And I love life all the more since I have learnt its meaning.

JESUS: That is what I am here for. I came that men should lay hold of life and possess it to the full.

LAZARUS: Rabbi, it is true. I feel it in you too – that immense vitality at which a man may warm himself as at a fire. In your presence, I think, no one could easily yield to death – not even I. Yet I am not like Mary. I hold to life only with one hand, and not with a very strong clasp. If death came to me quietly one day when you were not beside me, I should not struggle, but slip away with him in silence and be glad to go.

JESUS: Do you love me so little, Lazarus?

LAZARUS: I love you dearly. To say that I would die for you is nothing. I would almost be ready to live for you if you asked me.

JOHN: Oh, Master, hold him to that promise. Look, Lazarus, you have made your sister cry.

LAZARUS: I'm sorry. I'm afraid I'm rather a depressing companion. Pay no attention. Dry your eyes, Mary – here's Martha coming. She'll scold me if she sees you in tears. . . .

Lazarus has been dead for four days when Jesus and his disciples finally arrive again in Bethany. Mary and Martha go to meet him.

MARY: Oh, Rabbi! Oh, dear Master! You are welcome to our sad hearts. Alas! If you had come earlier, our brother would never have died.

JESUS: Are you sure of that, Mary?

MARY: Oh yes, I am sure. For I heard him tell you so. And indeed I believe that death itself could never abide your presence.

JESUS *(troubled):* O my sisters! O my children! If only the world had faith enough, that would be true indeed. . . . Where have you laid Lazarus?

MARY: He lies in a cave a little way from here.

JESUS: Show me the place.

1ST MOURNER: The prophet is troubled.

2ND MOURNER: He is weeping.

3RD MOURNER: He must have loved Lazarus very much.

4TH MOURNER: He opened the eyes of the blind – couldn't he have prevented his friend from dying?

1ST MOURNER: Alas! No man is strong enough to deliver the world from death. . . .

At Lazarus's grave:

MARTHA: Here is the place, dear Master. He lies in that quiet tomb, hewn out of the rock, with the great stone laid across it.

MARY: Lazarus, our brother, who had no love for life, let the burden slip from his shoulders, and now is troubled no longer.

MARTHA: He carried his life as a condemned man carries his cross. But now he has laid it down.

JESUS: If any man love me, let him take up his cross and follow me. . . . Roll away the stone from the tomb.

MOURNERS: Roll away the stone?

MARTHA *(horrified):* Master . . . he has been four days dead! The stench of corruption is on his flesh.

JESUS: Did I not tell you that if you believed you should see the glory of God? Roll back the stone.

MARY: Will none of you men do as the Rabbi says? . . . Oh, John, they are afraid.

JOHN: We will do it for you, Mary. Peter and James, come – set your hands to the stone.

1ST MOURNER: Here is a crowbar.

PETER: Lift all together.

(The stone is heaved off with a crash)

1ST MOURNER: The grave is open.

2ND MOURNER: What will he do?

3RD MOURNER: Something fearful is going to happen.

4TH MOURNER: Look! He is praying.

JESUS: Father, I thank Thee that Thou hast heard me. And I know that Thou hearest me always. But I give Thee thanks aloud, that these people that stand by may hear it and believe that Thou hast sent me. . . . *(loudly)* Lazarus!

1ST MOURNER: Oh, God! He is calling to the dead.

JESUS: Lazarus, come forth! *(A fearful pause)*

JEWESS *(in a thin, strangled gasp)*: Listen! . . . Listen! . . . A-ah-ah!

2ND MOURNER *(in a quick babble of terror)*: Oh, look! Oh, look! . . . out into the daylight . . . blind and bound . . . *moving* – with its feet still fast in the grave bands!

JESUS: Unbind him. Take the cloth from his face.

3RD MOURNER: No – no! What will it look like? The face of the four-days-dead?

MARY: Oh, Martha come and help me. . . . Lazarus – dear brother – speak if you can!

LAZARUS: Lord Jesus!

MARY: You are smiling – you are laughing – you are alive!

LAZARUS *(joyfully)*: Yes, I am alive!

MARTHA: Where have you been?

LAZARUS: With life.

MARY: Do you know who called you back?

LAZARUS: Life. He is here and he has never left me.

JESUS: Loose him and lead him home.[4]

From a lecture:

The Church names the sixth Deadly Sin *Acedia* or Sloth. In the world it calls itself *Tolerance;* but in Hell it is called *Despair.* It is the accomplice of the other sins and their worst punishment. It is the sin which believes in nothing, cares for nothing, seeks to know nothing, interferes with nothing, enjoys nothing, loves nothing, hates nothing, finds purpose in nothing, lives for nothing, and only remains alive because there is nothing it would die for. We have known it far too well for many years. The only thing perhaps that we have not known about it is that it is mortal sin.

---

4   Dorothy L. Sayers, Scenes I and IV, *The Light and the Life,* in *The Man Born To Be King: A Play-Cycle on the Life of Our Lord and Saviour Jesus Christ* (London: Victor Gollancz, 1943).

The War has jerked us pretty sharply into consciousness about this slugabed sin of Sloth, and perhaps we say too much about it. But two warnings are rather necessary.

First, it is one of the favourite tricks of this Sin to dissemble itself under cover of a whiffling activity of body. We think that if we are busily rushing about and doing things, we cannot be suffering from Sloth. And besides, violent activity seems to offer an escape from the horrors of Sloth. So the other sins hasten to provide a cloak for Sloth: Gluttony offers a whirl of dancing, dining, sports, and dashing very fast from place to place to gape at beauty-spots; which when we get to them, we defile with vulgarity and waste. Covetousness rakes us out of bed at an early hour, in order that we may put pep and hustle into our business; Envy sets us to gossip and scandal, to writing cantankerous letters to the papers, and to the unearthing of secrets and the scavenging of dustbins; Wrath provides (very ingeniously) the argument that the only fitting activity in a world so full of evil-doers and evil demons is to curse loudly and incessantly "Whatever brute and blackguard made the world";[5] while Lust provides that round of dreary promiscuity that passes for bodily vigour. But these are all disguises for the empty heart and the empty brain and the empty soul of *Acedia*.

Let us take particular notice of the empty brain. Here Sloth is in a conspiracy with Envy to prevent people from thinking. Sloth persuades us that stupidity is not our sin, but our misfortune: while Envy at the same time persuades us that intelligence is despicable – a dusty, highbrow, and commercially useless thing.

And secondly, the War has jerked us out of Sloth; but wars, if they go on very long, induce Sloth in the shape of war-weariness

---

5   "We for a certainty are not the first / Have sat in taverns while the tempest hurled / Their hopeful plans to emptiness, and cursed / Whatever brute and blackguard made the world." A. E. Housman, "IX," *Last Poems* (New York: Henry Holt and Company, 1922).

and despair of any purpose. We saw its effects in the last peace, when it brought all the sins in its train. There are times when one is tempted to say that the great, sprawling, lethargic sin of Sloth is the oldest and greatest of the sins and the parent of all the rest.[6]

A letter written to Eric Fenn of the BBC, who had passed on to Sayers a request for a letter "setting forth the Christian Faith and the Christian Way of Life," which she declines:

The only letter I ever want to address to "average people" is one that says "I do not care whether you believe in Christianity or not, but I do resent your being so ignorant, lazy, and unintelligent. Why don't you take the trouble to find out what is Christianity and what isn't? Why, when you can bestir yourselves to mug up technical terms about electricity, won't you do as much for theology before you begin to argue about it? Why do you never read either the ancient or the modern authorities in the subject, but take your information for the most part from biologists and physicists, who have picked it up as inaccurately as yourselves? (You wouldn't take the Bishop of Rum-ti-foo's opinion on biology, or be content with the Rev. Mr. Pulpit's exposition of atomic physics). Why do you accept mildewed old heresies as bold and constructive contributions to modern Christian thought, when any handbook on Church history would tell you where they come from? Why do you complain that the proposition 'God is Three-in-One' is obscure and mystical, and yet acquiesce meekly in the physicist's fundamental formula, $QP-PQ=ih/2\pi$ where $i=\sqrt{-1}$, when you know quite well that $\sqrt{-1}$ is paradoxical

---

6   "The Other Six Deadly Sins," published in *Creed or Chaos?*, 1949.

and π incalculatable?[7] What makes you suppose that the expression 'God ordains' is a narrow and bigoted anthropomorphism, whereas the expressions 'Nature provides' or 'science demands' are objective statements of fact? (Who are these abstractions that we should personify them?) Why, when you insist on the importance of being modern and progressive, do you never read any textual criticism of the Bible that is not fifty years out of date; and why, on the other hand, when you insist on going back to the 'pre-Pauline simplicity of the Gospels,' does it never occur to you to verify your dates and discover which came first, the Gospels or St. Paul? Why don't you do a hand's turn for yourselves, confound you? You would be ashamed to know as little about internal combustion as you do about the Nicene Creed. I admit that you can practise Christianity without knowing much about theology, just as you can drive a car without understanding internal combustion – but if something breaks down in the car, you go humbly to the man who understands the works, whereas if something goes wrong with your religion you merely throw the creed away and tell the theologian he's a liar. Why do you want a letter from me telling you about God? You will never bother to check up on it and find out whether I am giving you a personal opinion or the Church's doctrine, and your minds are so confused that you would rather hear the former than the latter. Go away and do some work, and let me get on with mine."

But this would scarcely suit your friend, and indeed I have work to do, which is always sadly behindhand. Besides, instruction is not my job, and I have already meddled in it for more than is healthy.[8]

---

7 Physicist Max Born's expression of Werner Heisenberg's uncertainty principle in quantum mechanics.

8 Dorothy L. Sayers, "Letter Addressed to 'Average People,'" *The City Temple Tidings*, July 1946, 166.

9

Murder Must Advertise

Greed

Sayers worked from 1921 to 1929 at an advertising agency in London, coining slogans and writing ad copy for clients such as Coleman's Mustard and Guinness Beer. So when she wrote Murder Must Advertise *in 1933, she had an insider's perspective on the way commerce plays on the greed of the consumer, as a drug pusher plays on the cravings of the addict. The book provides a vehicle for her rage against this exploitation. Lord Peter Wimsey gets a job at Pym's Publicity disguised as "Death Bredon," a lowly copyeditor, in order to investigate the death of one of the employees, who was found at the bottom of an iron staircase. At night, in the costume of a harlequin, he haunts the jazz-age parties of wealthy drug addicts, "symbolically opposing two cardboard worlds."* [1]

"Now, [said Peter,] Mr. Pym is a man of rigid morality – except, of course, as regards his profession, whose essence is to tell plausible lies for money – "

---

1   A comment made by Sayers about *Murder Must Advertise*, quoted by Ralph E. Hone in *Dorothy L. Sayers: A Literary Biography* (Kent State University, 1979), 66.

"How about truth in advertising?"

"Of course, there is *some* truth in advertising. There's yeast in bread, but you can't make bread with yeast alone. Truth in advertising," announced Lord Peter sententiously, "is like leaven, which a woman hid in three measures of meal. It provides a suitable quantity of gas, with which to blow out a mass of crude misrepresentation into a form that the public can swallow. . . ."

All over London the lights flickered in and out, calling on the public to save its body and purse: SOPO SAVES SCRUBBING – NUTRAX FOR NERVES – CRUNCHLETS ARE CRISPER – EAT PIPER PARRITCH – DRINK POMPAYNE – ONE WHOOSH AND IT'S CLEAN – OH, BOY! IT'S TOMBOY TOFFEE – NOURISH NERVES WITH NUTRAX – FARLEY'S FOOTWEAR TAKES YOU FURTHER – IT ISN'T DEAR, IT'S DARLING – DARLING'S FOR HOUSEHOLD APPLIANCES – MAKE ALL SAFE WITH SANFECT – WHIFFLETS FASCINATE. The presses, thundering and growling, ground out the same appeals by the million: ASK YOUR GROCER – ASK YOUR DOCTOR – ASK THE MAN WHO'S TRIED IT – MOTHERS! GIVE IT TO YOUR CHILDREN – HOUSEWIVES! SAVE MONEY – HUSBANDS! INSURE YOUR LIVES – WOMEN! DO YOU REALIZE? – DON'T SAY SOAP, SAY SOPO! Whatever you're doing, stop it and do something else! Whatever you're buying, pause and buy something different! Be hectored into health and prosperity! Never let up! Never go to sleep! Never be satisfied. If once you are satisfied, all our wheels will run down. Keep going – and if you can't, Try Nutrax for Nerves! . . .

To Lord Peter Wimsey, the few weeks of his life spent in unravelling the Problem of the Iron Staircase possessed an odd dreamlike quality, noticeable at the time and still more insistent in retrospect. The very work that engaged him – or rather, the shadowy simulacrum of himself that signed itself on every morning in the name of Death Bredon – wafted him into a sphere of dim platonic archetypes, bearing a scarcely recognizable relationship to anything in the living world. Here those strange entities, the Thrifty Housewife, the Man of Discrimination, the Keen Buyer and the Good Judge, forever young, forever handsome, forever virtuous, economical and inquisitive, moved to and fro upon their complicated orbits, comparing prices and values, making tests of purity, asking indiscreet questions about each other's ailments, household expenses, bed-springs, shaving cream, diet, laundry work and boots, perpetually spending to save and saving to spend, cutting out coupons and collecting cartons, surprising husbands with margarine and wives with patent washers and vacuum cleaners, occupied from morning to night in washing, cooking, dusting, filing, saving their children from germs, their complexions from wind and weather, their teeth from decay and their stomachs from indigestion, and yet adding so many hours to the day by labour-saving appliances that they had always leisure for visiting the talkies, sprawling on the beach to picnic upon Potted Meats and Tinned Fruit, and (when adorned by So-and-so's Silks, Blank's Gloves, Dash's Footwear, Whatnot's Weatherproof Complexion Cream and Thingummy's Beautifying Shampoos), even attending Ranelagh, Cowes, the Grand Stand at Ascot, Monte Carlo and the Queen's Drawing-Rooms. Where, Bredon asked himself, did the money come from that was to be spent so variously and so lavishly? If this hell's-dance of spending and saving were to stop for a moment, what would happen? If all the advertising in the world were to shut down tomorrow, would people still go on buying more soap, eating more apples, giving their children more vitamins, roughage, milk, olive oil, scooters and laxatives, learning more languages by gramophone, hearing more virtuosos by radio, re-decorating their houses, refreshing themselves with more non-alcoholic thirst-quenchers, cooking more new, appetizing dishes, affording themselves that little extra touch which means so much? Or would the whole desperate whirligig slow down, and the exhausted public relapse upon plain grub and elbow-grease? He did not know. Like all rich men, he had never before paid any attention to advertisements. He had never realized the enormous commercial importance of the comparatively poor. Not on the wealthy, who buy only what they want when they want it, was the vast superstructure of industry founded and built up, but on those who, aching for a luxury beyond their reach and for a leisure forever denied them, could be bullied or wheedled into spending their few hardly won shillings on whatever might give them, if only for a moment, a leisured and luxurious illusion. Phantasmagoria – a city of dreadful day, of crude shapes and colours piled Babel-like in a heaven of harsh cobalt and rocking over a void of bankruptcy – a Cloud Cuckooland, peopled by pitiful ghosts, from the Thrifty Housewife providing a Grand Family Meal for Fourpence with the aid of Dairyfields Butter Beans in Margarine, to the Typist capturing the affections of Prince Charming by a liberal use of Muggins's Magnolia Face Cream.

Among these phantasms, Death Bredon, driving his pen across reams of office foolscap, was a phantasm too, emerging from this nightmare toil to a still more fantastical existence amid people whose aspirations, rivalries and modes of thought were alien, and earnest beyond anything in his waking experience. Nor, when the Greenwich-driven clocks had jerked on to half-past five, had he any world of reality to which to return; for then the illusionary Mr. Bredon dislimned and became the still more illusionary Harlequin of a dope-addict's dream; an advertising figure more crude and fanciful than any that postured in the columns of the *Morning Star;* a thing bodiless and absurd, a mouthpiece of stale clichés shouting in dull ears without a brain. From this abominable impersonation he could not now free himself, since at the sound of his name or the sight of his unmasked face, all the doors in that other dream-city – the city of dreadful night – would be closed to him. . . .

"Do you really believe [said Detective Charles Parker to Wimsey] that the head of this particular dope-gang is on Pym's staff? It sounds quite incredible."

"That's an excellent reason for believing it. I don't mean in a *credo quia impossible* sense, but merely because the staff of a respectable advertising agency would be such an excellent hiding-place for a big crook. The particular crookedness of advertising is so very far removed from the crookedness of dope-trafficking."

"Why? As far as I can make out, all advertisers are dope-merchants."

"So they are. Yes, now I come to think of it, there is a subtle symmetry about the thing which is extremely artistic. All the same, Charles, I must admit that I find it difficult to go the whole way with Milligan. I have carefully reviewed the staff of Pym's, and I have so far failed to find any one who looks in the least like a Napoleon of crime. . . . I dare say I could spot [the murderer] without much difficulty – but that's not what you want, is it? You'd rather have the Napoleon of the dope-traffic, wouldn't you? If he exists, that is."

"Certainly I should," said Parker, emphatically.

"That's what I thought. What, if you come to think of it, is a trifle like an odd murder or assault, compared with a method of dope-running that baffles Scotland Yard? Nothing at all."

"It isn't, really," replied Parker, seriously. "Dope-runners are murderers, fifty times over. They slay hundreds of people, soul and body, besides indirectly causing all sorts of crimes among the victims. Compared with that, slugging one inconsiderable pip-squeak over the head is almost meritorious."

"Really, Charles! for a man of your religious upbringing, your outlook is positively enlightened."

"Not so irreligious, either. 'Fear not him that killeth, but him that hath power to cast into hell' [Luke 12:5]. How about it?"

"How indeed? Hang the one and give the other a few weeks in jail – or, if of good social position, bind him over or put him on remand for six months under promise of good behaviour."

Parker made a wry mouth.

"I know, old man, I know. But where would be the good of hanging the wretched victims or the smaller fry? There would always be others. We want the top people. Take even this man, Milligan, who's a pest of the first water – with no excuse for it, because he isn't an addict himself – but suppose we punish him here and now. They'd only start again, with a new distributor and a new house for him to run his show in, and what would anybody gain by that?"

"Exactly," said Wimsey. "And how much better off will you be, even if you catch the man above Milligan? The same thing will apply."

Parker made a hopeless gesture.

"I don't know, Peter. It's no good worrying about it. My job is to catch the heads of the gangs if I can, and, after that, as many as possible of the little people. I can't overthrow cities and burn the population."

"'Tis the Last Judgment's fire must cure this place,"[2] said Wimsey, "calcine its clods and set its prisoners free."[3]

From a magazine article, "The Psychology of Advertising," in the Spectator, *November 1937:*

I suppose that if happiness could be mailed direct to the public at half a crown a packet, there would still be many people too lazy, too indifferent or too cautious to purchase a postal-order and sign on the dotted line. As it is, though "a man's life consisteth not in the abundance of the things which he possessed" [Luke 12:15], the life of commerce does; and manufacturers are under the necessity of disposing of such comparatively unattractive commodities as boot-polish, butter beans, steel filing-cabinets, purgatives, laundry-soaps, vacuum-cleaners, tinned fish, sock-suspenders, clarified fats, sponge-rubber, saucepans, scouring-powders and gadgets for slicing raw carrots into patterns, in order to keep going the monstrous perpetual-motion machine that maintains the fabric of modern civilisation. It is the advertisement writer's job to persuade the world that these things are, in fact, happiness, temporarily disguised under protean and slightly unexpected forms.

---

2   " 'Tis the Last Judgment's fire must cure this place, / Calcine its clods and set my prisoners free." Robert Browning, "Childe Roland to the Dark Tower Came," *A Victorian Anthology, 1837–1895* (Cambridge: Riverside Press, 1895)

3   Dorothy L. Sayers, *Murder Must Advertise* (London: Victor Gollancz, 1933), ch. 5, 9, 15.

Inertia (technically known as sales-resistance) is strongly entrenched in the citadel of the soul, and it would be idle to expect the advertiser – faced by this colossal task – to be idealistic or over-scrupulous in his methods of attack. Like any other strategist, he assaults the weak places. Fear-gate, Sloth-gate, Greed-gate and Snob-gate are the four cardinal points at which the city of Mansoul can most effectively be besieged; and by these approaches he leads in his storm-troopers, marching handsomely under the banners of Health, Wealth, Leisure and Beauty.

By Fear-gate go in his formidable Death's-Head Hussars: Are you Suffering from Halitosis, Body-Odour, Athlete's Foot, Pains in the Back, Incomplete Elimination? Are you Insured against Sickness, Old Age, Unemployment, Battle, Murder and Sudden Death? Is your Lavatory Clean? Does Dry-Rot Lurk in your Roof? Do you Feel Too Old at Forty? Swat that Fly, it Carries Disease! Do not Neglect that Cold – it may turn into Goodness Knows What! Take Vitamins under Pain of Losing your job! Wave your Hair, under Pain of Losing your Husband's Love! Use Blank's Pure Dusting-Powder, under Pain of Poisoning your Baby! Beware of Substitutes! Beware of Germs! Beware Of Everything!

By Sloth-gate go in the armies of Leisure; the Ready-Cooked Foods, the Chromium that Needs no Cleaning, the Clothes that Wash Themselves, all the Gadgets and Machines that Take the Irk out of Work. And behind them come the devices for taking all effort out of the employment even of Leisure – the Cinema-posters, the Radio sets with easy tuning, the Gramophones that change their own records, the Gearless Cars, the Book-Societies that spare you the trouble of choosing your own reading. And since (by the ineluctable irony of things) the human machine revs fiercer and faster the more it is raced in neutral, these battalions are accompanied by an Ambulance Corps dispensing Soothing Syrups to nerves, worn out by too much Leisure.

Greed-gate is the entrance for all the schemes that promise Something for Nothing. The magistrates of the city work very hard to close Greed-gate; Lotteries can now scarcely find entrance in this country; Free-Gift Coupons have received a shrewd knock and Guessing-Competitions and Pools have sustained severe reverses. But surprise parties still bring off successful raids from time to time and carry off a good deal of loot before the authorities intervene. Common-sense, the sentinel, is frequently asleep at his post and forgets to utter the warning cry, "*Ex nihilo nihil fit.*"[4]

The troops that attack Snob-gate are the best turned-out regiments in the army. They are made up of Discriminating Men and Smart Women, of Typists who Marry the Boss, of Men who can Judge Whisky blindfold and Hostesses who kowtow to give their Patties that Air of Distinction. They offer Luxury Goods under the brand of the Life Beautiful; and perhaps the worst that can be said of them is that their notion of Beauty is trivial. The finest Snob-assault I ever saw with my eyes was the advertisement of a firm of American morticians in the pre-Slump era: "Why lay your loved ones in the cold ground? Let us electroplate them in gold or silver." But this example strikes a rare note of bravura.

There is something pathetic in this ruthless exploitation of human foibles. The advertising writer has to harden his heart, preserve his sense of humour and remind himself that, however loudly he shouts and however exaggerated his statements, he will be lucky if one-tenth of what he says is heard or the hundredth part of it attended to. He is obliged to be a hypocrite to

---

4   Out of nothing comes nothing.

some extent. He must seize on whatever virtue happens to be fashionable and turn it to commercial advantage. When physical fitness is the idol of the moment, he must select his "slogans" accordingly. He will not say that "wine maketh glad the heart of man,"[5] he must say that it is slimming or assists elimination, or that malt beverages contain vitamins, build up the constitution and increase resistance to infection. If patriotism is in vogue, he must say that his product is British, therefore best. If there is a wave of interest in psychotherapy he must assure us that Krazy Kinema Kartoons sublimate unconscious anxieties; and if, *per impossibile,* there were to be a sudden boom in asceticism, he would be obliged to assert that Asterisk's Sheets were so rough as to be practically a hair-shirt in themselves. His business is to sell the goods; and under whatever mask we disguise our appetites to ourselves, that is the mask he must assume to make his appeal effective. Anybody who wants to know what our national weaknesses are has only to study the advertisement columns of the daily Press. There he will find them all, reduced to their simplest elements, decked out in whatever motley is in the mode: the truth about ourselves and the name by which we are agreed to call it. . . .

The moral of all this (said the Duchess[6]) is that we have the kind of advertising we deserve; since advertisements only pander to our own proclaimed appetites, and with whatsoever measure we mete our desires they are (most lavishly and attractively) measured to us again.[7]

---

5 And wine that maketh glad the heart of man, and oil to make his face to shine, and bread which strengtheneth man's heart. Ps. 104:15 KJV.

6 "Tut, tut, child!" said the Duchess. "Everything's got a moral, if only you can find it.", Lewis Carroll, *Alice's Adventures in Wonderland* (London: Macmillan & Co., 1865).

7 "The Psychology of Advertising," *The Spectator,* November 19, 1937.

From a letter:

... the one point in your letter about which I should like to raise a query is the statement about the upper limit of production for the fruit of the earth. In a sense we do not know it – yet there are signs that there is a limit and that we are within measurable distance of reaching it. It may be true, for example, that the applications of coal to production have been touched upon: but there is a fixed quantity of coal in the earth and no more, and if we too brutally exploit the source of power we may find ourselves up against a limit of another kind. The same is true of oil – and, in a more alarming way, of the actual fruits of agriculture. If we make ourselves greedy and grasping tyrants of the earth – ravishing and not serving it – it takes its revenge in waste lands, barren soil, flood, drought and dearth. Every time we upset the balance of natural forces by over-cultivation, either of earth, animals or what-not, we seem to come up against some law which sends back to us in famine or disease the catastrophes we tried to avoid. And there seems to be also some compensatory law about the use of machines, by which, the more vigorously we endeavour to eliminate labour, the harder and more desperately we have to work to keep things going. . . . We have got it into our heads that, as a speaker remarked to me the other day at a [Workers' Educational Association] meeting, "the earth is for us to *use*," but I think we shall be making a great mistake if we interpret this as meaning that it is there for us to exploit without reverence and without caution. That is to make nature, our fellow-creature, into our slave – and not much better, perhaps, than making slaves of our fellow-men.[8]

---

8   Sayers to Flight-Lieutenant Bryan W. Monahan, R A A F Overseas Headquarters, January 15, 1943, *Letters*, 2:385.

10

The Nine Tailors

Creativity

In The Nine Tailors, *Lord Peter Wimsey's car breaks down in a small village in the fens of East Anglia, and he and his valet, Bunter, are forced to stay overnight with the village rector, Mr. Venables. It is New Year's Eve at Fenchurch St. Paul, and Wimsey has promised the rector to help with the bell ringing after the midnight service.*

He was roused by the pealing of bells.

For a moment, memory eluded him – then he flung the eiderdown aside and sat up, ruffled and reproachful, to encounter the calm gaze of Bunter.

"Good God! I've been asleep! Why didn't you call me? They've begun without me."

"Mrs. Venables gave orders, my lord, that you were not to be disturbed until half-past eleven, and the reverend gentleman instructed me to say, my lord, that they would content themselves with ringing six bells as a preliminary to the service."

"What time is it now?"

"Nearly five minutes to eleven, my lord."

As he spoke, the pealing ceased, and Jubilee began to ring the five-minute bell.

"Dash it all!" said Wimsey. "This will never do. Must go and hear the old boy's sermon. Give me a hair-brush. Is it still snowing?"

"Harder than ever, my lord."

Wimsey made a hasty toilet and ran downstairs, Bunter following him decorously. They let themselves out by the front door, and, guided by Bunter's electric torch, made their way through the shrubbery and across the road to the church, entering just as the organ boomed out its final notes. Choir and parson were in their places and Wimsey, blinking in the yellow lamplight, at length discovered his seven fellow-ringers seated on a row of chairs beneath the tower. He picked his way cautiously over the cocoa-nut matting towards them, while Bunter, who had apparently acquired all the necessary information beforehand, made his unperturbed way to a pew in the north aisle and sat down beside Emily from the Rectory. Old Hezekiah Lavender greeted Wimsey with a welcoming chuckle and thrust a prayer-book under his nose as he knelt down to pray.

"Dearly beloved brethren – "

Wimsey scrambled to his feet and looked round.

At the first glance he felt himself sobered and awe-stricken by the noble proportions of the church, in whose vast spaces the congregation – though a good one for so small a parish in the dead of a winter's night – seemed almost lost. The wide nave and shadowy aisles, the lofty span of the chancel arch – crossed, though not obscured, by the delicate fan-tracery and crenellated moulding of the screen – the intimate and cloistered loveliness of the chancel, with its pointed arcading, graceful ribbed vault and five narrow east lancets, led his attention on and focused it first upon the remote glow of the sanctuary. Then his gaze, returning to the nave, followed the strong yet slender shafting that sprang fountain-like from floor to foliated column-head, spraying into the light, wide arches that carried the clerestory. And there, mounting to the steep pitch of the roof, his eyes were held entranced with wonder and delight. Incredibly aloof, flinging back the light in a dusky shimmer of bright hair and gilded outspread wings, soared the ranked angels, cherubim and seraphim, choir over choir, from corbel and hammer-beam floating face to face uplifted.

"My God!" muttered Wimsey, not without reverence. And he softly repeated to himself: "He rode upon the cherubims and did fly; He came flying upon the wings of the wind" [Psalm 18:10].

Mr. Hezekiah Lavender poked his new colleague sharply in the ribs, and Wimsey became aware that the congregation had settled down to the General Confession, leaving him alone and agape upon his feet. Hurriedly he turned the leaves of his prayer-book and applied himself to making the proper responses. Mr. Lavender, who had obviously decided that he was either a half-wit or a heathen, assisted him by finding the Psalms for him and by bawling every verse very loudly in his ear.

". . . Praise Him in the cymbals and dances: praise Him upon the strings and pipe."

The shrill voices of the surpliced choir mounted to the roof, and seemed to find their echo in the golden mouths of the angels.

"Praise Him upon the well-tuned cymbals; praise Him upon the loud cymbals.

"Let everything that hath breath praise the Lord" [Psalm 150:5–6].[1]

---

[1] Dorothy L. Sayers, *The Nine Tailors* (London: Victor Gollancz, 1934), "The Bells in Their Courses."

Saluting skilled craftsmen in her poem "The Makers," Sayers points to God – the trinity that is at once the architect, craftsman, and cornerstone – as the source of all human creativity.

The Makers

The Architect stood forth and said:
"I am the master of the art:
I have a thought within my head,
I have a dream within my heart.

"Come now, good craftsman, ply your trade
With tool and stone obediently;
Behold the plan that I have made –
I am the master; serve you me."

The Craftsman answered: "Sir, I will,
Yet look to it that this your draft
Be of a sort to serve my skill –
You are not master of the craft.

"It is by me the towers grow tall,
I lay the course, I shape and hew;
You make a little inky scrawl,
And that is all that you can do.

"Account me, then, the master man,
Laying my rigid rule upon
The plan, and that which serves the plan –
The uncomplaining, helpless stone."

The Stone made answer: "Masters mine,
Know this: that I can bless or damn
The thing that both of you design
By being but the thing I am;

"For I am granite and not gold,
 For I am marble and not clay,
 You may not hammer me nor mould –
 I am the master of the way.

"Yet once that mastery bestowed
 Then I will suffer patiently
 The cleaving steel, the crushing load,
 That make a calvary of me;

"And you may carve me with your hand
 To arch and buttress, roof and wall,
 Until the dream rise up and stand –
 Serve but the stone, the stone serves all.

"Let each do well what each knows best,
 Nothing refuse and nothing shirk,
 Since none is master of the rest,
 But all are servants of the work –

"The work no master may subject
 Save He to whom the whole is known,
 Being Himself the Architect,
 The Craftsman and the Corner-stone.

"Then, when the greatest and the least
 Have finished all their laboring
 And sit together at the feast,
 You shall behold a wonder thing:

"The Maker of the men that make
 Will stoop between the cherubim,
 The towel and the basin take,
 And serve the servants who serve Him."

The Architect and Craftsman both
 Agreed, the Stone had spoken well;

Bound them to service by an oath
And each to his own labour fell.[2]

From a letter:

Public Enemy No. 1 – if you must use these expressions – is a flabby and sentimental theology which necessarily produces flabby and sentimental religious art. The first business for Church officials and churchmen is, I think, to look to their own mote and preach and teach better theology. But the point which they do not recognize is this; that for any work of art to be acceptable to God it must first be right with itself. That is to say, the artist must serve God in the technique of his craft; for example, a good religious play must first and foremost be a good play before it can begin to be good religion. Similarly, actors for religious films and plays should be chosen for their good acting and not chosen for their Christian sentiment or moral worth regardless of whether they are good actors or not. (A notorious case to the contrary is the religious film society which chose its photographers for their piety, with the result that a great number of the films were quite blasphemously incompetent.) The practice, very common among pious officials of asking writers to produce stories and plays to illustrate a certain doctrine or church activities, shows how curiously little these good people as a class understand the way in which the mind of the writer works. The result in practice is that instead of the doctrines springing naturally out of the action of the narrative, the action and characters are distorted for the sake of the doctrine with disastrous results.

This is what I mean when I ask that the Church should use a decent humility before the artist, whose calling is as direct as

2   Introduction to *The Man Born to Be King*, 1943.

that of the priest, and whose business it is to serve God in his own technique and not in somebody else's. Matters are only made worse when Sunday Observance Societies and other groups talk wildly about modern tendencies in art and so bring the Church into contempt, not only for bigotry but also for ignorance.

I quite agree that a great deal of ecclesiastical bric-à-brac needs purging. It is, as you say, so difficult to choose the really sound authorities to pronounce on the artistic merit of hymns and so forth. I believe that here again the soundest method is to purge at once the works which express a sickly brand of religious sentiment. They are pretty certain to be bad on all counts; it is very noticeable how well the great mediæval hymns stand up to the test of time and the test of translation, on account of the soundness of the theology which inspired them. But I think they should be purged definitely on theological grounds, if the work is being done by Ecclesiastics as such, since here they are on their own ground and are not going outside their terms of reference. The whole question is extraordinarily complicated because of the gulf that has grown up between art on the one hand and on the other hand both the Church and secular society, so that the artists tend to be out of touch with the common man, while the latter, whether Christian or not, has only a very fumbling critical judgment to rely on.[3]

From The Mind of the Maker:

I suppose that of all Christian dogmas, the doctrine of the Trinity enjoys the greatest reputation for obscurity and remoteness from common experience. Whether the theologian extols

---

3   Sayers to Brother George Every of the House of the Sacred Mission, Kelham, Nottinghamshire, May 21, 1941, *Letters,* 2:261–262.

it as the splendour of the light invisible or the sceptic derides it as a horror of great darkness, there is a general conspiracy to assume that its effect upon those who contemplate it is blindness, either by absence or excess of light. There is some truth in the assumption, but there is also a great deal of exaggeration. God is mysterious, and so (for that matter) is the universe and one's fellow-man and one's self and the snail on the garden-path; but none of these is so mysterious as to correspond to nothing within human knowledge. There are, of course, some minds that cultivate mystery for mystery's sake: with these, St. Augustine of Hippo, who was no obscurantist, deals firmly:

> Holy Scripture, which suits itself to babes, has not avoided words drawn from any class of things really existing, through which, as by nourishment, our understanding might rise gradually to things divine and transcendent. . . . But it has drawn no words whatever, whereby to frame either figures of speech or enigmatic sayings, from things which do not exist at all. And hence it is that those who [in disputing about God strive to transcend the whole creation] are more mischievously and emptily vain than their fellows; in that they surmise concerning God, what can neither be found in Himself nor in any creature.[4]

He proceeds, in his great treatise, to expound the doctrine analogically, using again and again the appeal to experience. He says in effect: "a Trinitarian structure of being is not a thing incomprehensible or unfamiliar to you; you know of many such within the created universe. There is a trinity of sight, for example: the form seen, the act of vision, and the mental attention which correlates the two. These three, though separable in theory, are inseparably present whenever you use your sight. Again, every

---

4   Augustine of Hippo, *The Works of Aurelius Augustine: On the Trinity,* trans. by A. W. Haddan (Edinburgh: T. & T. Clark, 1873), I, I, 26.

thought is an inseparable trinity of memory, understanding and will.[5] This is a fact of which you are quite aware; it is not the concept of a trinity-in-unity that in itself presents any insuperable difficulty to the human imagination."

We may perhaps go so far as to assert that the Trinitarian structure of activity is mysterious to us just because it is universal – rather as the four-dimensional structure of space-time is mysterious because we cannot get outside it to look at it. The mathematician can, however, to some extent perform the intellectual feat of observing space-time from without, and we may similarly call upon the creative artist to extricate himself from his own activity far enough to examine and describe its threefold structure. . . .

Since this chapter – and indeed this whole book – is an expansion of the concluding speech of St. Michael in my play *The Zeal of Thy House*, it will perhaps be convenient to quote that speech here:

> For every work [*or act*] of creation is threefold, an earthly trinity to match the heavenly.
>
> First, [*not in time, but merely in order of enumeration*] there is the Creative Idea, passionless, timeless, beholding the whole work complete at once, the end in the beginning: and this is the image of the Father.
>
> Second, there is the Creative Energy [*or Activity*] begotten of that idea, working in time from the beginning to the end, with sweat and passion, being incarnate in the bonds of matter: and this is the image of the Word.

---

5   "Still less is a single sensation strictly separable from the environment of emotion, memory and intellectual activity in which it occurs; nor is it strictly separable from the volition which directs attention to it and the thought which embodies sapient knowledge of it." Sir Arthur Eddington, *Philosophy of Physical Science* (Cambridge: Cambridge University Press, 1939).

Third, there is the Creative Power, the meaning of the work and its response in the lively soul: and this is the image of the indwelling Spirit.

And these three are one, each equally in itself the whole work, whereof none can exist without other: and this is the image of the Trinity.

Of these clauses, the one which gives the most trouble to the hearer is that dealing with the Creative Idea. (The word is here used, not in the philosopher's sense, in which the "Idea" tends to be equated with the "Word," but quite simply in the sense intended by the writer when he says: "I have an idea for a book."[6])

The ordinary man is apt to say: "I thought you began by collecting material and working out the plot." The confusion here is not merely over the words "first" and "begin." In fact the "Idea" – or rather the writer's realisation of his own idea – does precede any mental or physical work upon the materials or on the course of the story within a time-series. But apart from this, the very formulation of the Idea in the writer's mind is not the Idea itself, but its self-awareness in the Energy. Everything that is conscious, everything that has to do with form and time, and everything that has to do with process, belongs to the working of the Energy or Activity or "Word." The Idea, that is, cannot be said to precede the Energy in time, because (so far as that act of creation is concerned) it is the Energy that creates the time-process. This is the analogy of the theological expressions that "the Word was in the beginning with God" and was "eternally begotten of the Father." If, that is, the act has a beginning in time at all, it is because of the presence of the Energy or Activity.

6 Similarly, of course, "Energy" is not to be understood in the physicist's technical sense (e.g. Mass X Acceleration X Distance), or "Power" in the engineer's sense (e.g. applied force); both these words are used in the sense intended by the poet and the common man.

The writer cannot even be conscious of his Idea except by the working of the Energy which formulates it to himself.

That being so, how can we know that the Idea itself has any real existence apart from the Energy? Very strangely; by the fact that the Energy itself is conscious of referring all its acts to an existing and complete whole. In theological terms, the Son does the will of the Father. Quite simply, every choice of an episode, or a phrase, or a word is made to conform to a pattern of the entire book, which is revealed by that choice as already existing. This truth, which is difficult to convey in explanation, is quite clear and obvious in experience. It manifests itself plainly enough when the writer says or thinks: "That is, or is not, the right phrase" – meaning that it is a phrase which does or does not correspond to the reality of the Idea.

Further, although the book – that is, the activity of writing the book – is a process in space and time, it is known to the writer as *also* a complete and timeless whole, "the end in the beginning," and this knowledge of it is with him always, while writing it and after it is finished, just as it was at the beginning. It is not changed or affected by the toils and troubles of composition, nor is the writer aware of his book as merely a succession of words and situations. The Idea of the book is a thing-in-itself quite apart from its awareness or its manifestation in Energy, though it still remains true that it cannot be known as a thing-in-itself except as the Energy reveals it. The Idea is thus timeless and without parts or passions, though it is never seen, either by writer or reader, except in terms of time, parts and passion.

The Energy itself is an easier concept to grasp, because it is the thing of which the writer is conscious and which the reader can see when it is manifest in material form. It is dynamic – the sum and process of all the activity which brings the book into temporal and spatial existence. "All things are made by it, and without it nothing is made that has been made." To it belongs everything that can be included under the word "passion" – feeling, thought, toil, trouble, difficulty, choice, triumph – all the accidents which attend a manifestation in time. It is the Energy that is the creator in the sense in which the common man understands the word, because it brings about an expression in temporal form of the eternal and immutable Idea. It is, for the writer, what he means by "the writing of the book," and it includes, though it is not confined to, the manifestation of the book in material form. . . .

The Creative Power is the third "Person" of the writer's trinity. It is not the same thing as the Energy (which for greater clearness I ought perhaps to have called "the Activity"), though it proceeds from the Idea and the Energy together. It is the thing which flows back to the writer from his own activity and makes him, as it were, the reader of his own book. It is also, of course, the means by which the Activity is communicated to other readers and which produces a corresponding response in them. In fact, from the readers' point of view, it *is* the book. By it, they perceive the book, both as a process in time and as an eternal whole, and react to it dynamically. It is at this point we begin to understand what St. Hilary means in saying of the Trinity: "Eternity is in the Father, form in the Image, and use in the Gift."

Lastly: "these three are one, each equally in itself the whole work, whereof none can exist without other." If you were to ask a writer which is "the real book" – his Idea of it, his Activity in writing it, or its return to himself in Power, he would be at a loss to tell you, because these things are essentially inseparable. Each of them is the complete book separately; yet in the complete book all of them exist together. He can, by an act of the intellect, "distinguish the persons" but he cannot by any means "divide the substance." How could he? He cannot know the Idea, except by the Power interpreting his own Activity to him; he knows the Activity only as it reveals the Idea in Power; he knows the Power only as the revelation of the Idea in the Activity. All he can say is that these three are equally and eternally present in his own act of creation, and at every moment of it, whether or not the act ever becomes manifest in the form of a written and printed book. These things are not confined to the material manifestation: they exist in – they *are* – the creative mind itself.

I ought perhaps to emphasise this point a little. The whole complex relation that I have been trying to describe may remain entirely within the sphere of the imagination, and is there complete. The Trinity abides and works and is responsive to itself "in Heaven." A writer may be heard to say: "My book is finished – I have only to write it"; or even, "My book is written – I have only to put it on paper." The creative act, that is, does not depend for its fulfilment upon its manifestation in a material creation. The glib assertion that "God needs His creation as much as His creation needs Him" is not a true analogy from the mind of the human creator. Nevertheless, it is true that the urgent desire of the creative mind is towards expression in material form. The writer, in writing his book on paper, is expressing the freedom of his own nature in accordance with the law of his being; and we argue from this that material creation expresses the nature of the Divine Imagination. We may perhaps say that creation in some form or another is necessary to the nature of God; what we cannot say is that this or any particular form of creation is necessary to Him. It is in His mind, complete, whether He writes it down or not. To say that God depends on His creation as a poet depends on his written poem is an abuse of metaphor: the poet does nothing of the sort. To write the poem (or, of course, to give it material form in speech or song), is an act of love towards the poet's own imaginative act and towards his fellow-beings. It is a social act; but the poet is, first and foremost, his own society, and would be none the less a poet if the means of material expression were refused by him or denied him. . . .

In the metaphors used by the Christian creeds about the mind of the maker, the creative artist can recognise a true relation to his own experience; and it is his business to record the fact of that recognition in any further metaphor that the reader may understand and apply.[7]

---

7   *The Mind of the Maker,* 1941, ch. 3.

The Greatest Drama

Resurrection

In The Nine Tailors, *after a mysterious second body is found in a recently filled-in grave, the parishioners of Fenchurch St. Paul agree to bury it in the churchyard, even though they don't know who the stranger was or if he was baptized. After church on Sunday morning, Harry Gotobed, the sexton, asks Wimsey if he'd like to see the newly dug grave, along with Mr. Russell, the village undertaker.*

"We're giving him a nice bit of elm," said Mr. Russell, with some satisfaction, when the handsome proportions of the grave had been duly admired. "He did ought by rights to have come on the parish, and that means deal, as you know, but Rector says to me, 'Poor fellow,' he says, 'let's put him away nice and seemly, and I'll pay for it,' he says. And I've trued up the boards good and tight, so there won't be no unpleasantness. Of course, lead would be the right thing for him, but it ain't a thing as I'm often asked for, and I didn't think as I could get it in time, and the fact is, the sooner he's underground again, the better. Besides, lead is cruel 'ard work on the bearers. Six of them we're giving him – I wouldn't want to be thought lacking in respect for the dead, however come by, so I says to Rector, 'No, sir,' I says, 'not that old handcart,' I says, 'but six bearers just the same as if he was one of ourselves.' And Rector, he quite agreed with me. Ah! I daresay there'd be a sight of folk come in from round about, and I wouldn't like them to see the thing done mean or careless like."

"That's right," said Mr. Gotobed. "I've heerd as there's a reglar party comin' from St. Stephen in Jack Brownlow's sharrer. It'll be a rare frolic for 'em."

"Rector's giving a wreath, too," pursued Mr. Russell, "and Miss Thorpe's sending another. And there'll be a nice bunch o' flowers from the school-children and a wreath from the Women's Institute. My missus was round collecting the pennies just as soon as we knowed we'd have the buryin' of him."

"Ah! she's a quick worker and no mistake," said the sexton, admiringly.

"Ah! and Mrs. Venables, she made the money up to a guinea, so it'll be a real good one. I like to see a nice lot of flowers at a funeral. Gives it tone, like."

"Is it to be choral?"

"Well, not what you might call fully choral, but just a 'ymn at the graveside. Rector says, 'Not too much about parted friends,' he says, ''Twouldn't be suitable, seeing we don't know who his friends was.' So I says, '*What about God moves in a myster'ous way?*' I says. 'That's a good solemn-like, mournful 'ymn, as we all knows the tune on, and if anything can be said to be myster'ous, it's this here death,' I says. So that's what was settled."

"Ah!" said the voice of Mr. Lavender, "you're right there, Bob Russell. When I was a lad, there wasn't none o' this myster'ousness about. Everything was straightforward an' proper. But ever since eddication come in, it's been nothing but puzzlement, and fillin' up forms and 'ospital papers and sustificates and such, before you can even get as much as your Lord George pension."

"That may be, Hezekiah," replied the sexton, "but to my mind it all started with that business of Jeff Deacon at the Red House, bringin' strangers into the place. First thing as 'appened arter that was the War, and since then we been all topsy-turvy, like."

"As to the War," said Mr. Russell, "I daresay we'd a-had that anyhow, Jeff Deacon or no Jeff Deacon. But in a general way you're quite right. He was a bad 'un, was Jeff, though even now, poor Mary won't hear a word again' him."

"That's the way with women," said Mr. Lavender, sourly. "The wusser a man is, the more they dotes on him. Too soft-spoken he were, to my liking, were that Deacon. I don't trust these London folk, if you'll excuse me, sir."

"Don't mention it," said Wimsey.

"Why, Hezekiah," remonstrated Mr. Russell, "you thought a sight o' Jeff Deacon yourself at one time. Said he was the quickest chap at learning Kent Treble Bob [bell ringing] as you ever had to do with."

"That's a different thing," retorted the old gentleman. "Quick he was, there ain't no denyin', and he pulled a very good rope. But quickness in the 'ed don't mean a good 'eart. There's many evil men is as quick as monkeys. Didn't the good Lord say as much? The children o' this world is wiser in their generation than the children o' light. He commended the unjust steward, no doubt, but he give the fellow the sack just the same, none the more for that."

"Ah, well," said the sexton, "Jeff Deacon 'ull be put in his proper place where he've gone, and the same with this poor chap, whoever he be. We ain't got nothing to meddle wi' that, only to do our dooties in the station whereto we are called. That's

Scripture, that is, and so I says, Give him a proper funeral, for we don't know when it may be our turn next."

"That's very true, Harry; very true, that is. It may be you or me to be 'it on the 'ed one o' these days – though who can be going about to do such things beats me."[1]

Wimsey muses on death and resurrection as he listens to the internment service. Since he does not believe in life after death, the words of the Bible seem inexplicable and somewhat sinister to him. For the people of the congregation, however, a Christian burial is the right response, even to a stranger's death. The bells in the church tower toll for the deceased; one of the bells is named "Tailor Paul."

Lord Peter watched the coffin borne up the road.

"Here comes my problem," said he to himself, "going to earth on the shoulders of six stout fellows. Finally, this time, I suppose, and I don't seem to have got very much out of it. What a gathering of the local worthies – and how we are all enjoying it! Except dear old Venables – he's honestly distressed. . . . This everlasting tolling makes your bones move in your body. . . . Tailor Paul . . . Tailor Paul . . . two mortal tons of bawling bronze. . . . 'I am the Resurrection and the Life . . .' that's all rather sobering. This chap's first resurrection was ghastly enough – let's hope there won't be another this side of Doomsday. . . Silence that dreadful bell! . . . Tailor Paul . . . though even that might happen, if Lubbock finds anything funny. . . . 'Though after my skin worms destroy this body. . . .' How queer that fellow Thoday looks . . . something wrong there, I shouldn't wonder. . . . Tailor Paul . . . 'We brought nothing into this world and it is certain we can carry nothing

---

1   *The Nine Tailors*, 1934, "Lord Peter Called Into Hunt."

out . . .' except our secrets, old Patriarch; we take those with us all right." The deep shadows of the porch swallowed up priest, corpse and bearers, and Wimsey, following with Mrs. Venables, felt how strange it was that he and she should follow that strange corpse as sole and unexpected mourners.

"And people may say what they like," thought Wimsey again, "about the services of the Church of England, but there was genius in the choosing of these psalms. 'That I may be certi-fied how long I have to live' – what a terrifying prayer! Lord, let me never be certified of anything of the kind. 'A stranger with Thee and a sojourner' – that's a fact, God knows. . . . 'Thou hast set our misdeeds before Thee' . . . very likely, and why should I, Peter Wimsey, busy myself with digging them up? I haven't got so very much to boast about myself, if it comes to that. . . . Oh, well! . . . 'world without end, Amen.' Now the lesson. I suppose we sit down for this – I'm not very well up in the book of the words. . . . Yes. . . . This is the place where the friends and rela-tions usually begin to cry – but there's nobody here to do it – not a friend, nor a – How do I know that? I don't know it. . . . 'I have fought with beasts at Ephesus' . . . what on earth has that got to do with it? . . . 'raised a spiritual body' – what does old Donne say? 'God knows in what part of the world every grain of every man's dust lies. . . . He whispers, he hisses, he beckons for the bodies of his saints'[2] . . . do all these people believe that? Do I? Does anybody? We all take it pretty placidly, don't we? 'In a flash, at a trumpet crash, this Jack, joke, poor potsherd, patch, match-wood, immortal diamond is – immortal diamond.'[3] Did the

---

2 John Donne, "Sermon LXXXI," *The Works of John Donne, D. D. Vol. IV* (London: John W. Parker, 1839), 5.

3 Gerard Manley Hopkins, "That Nature is a Heraclitean Fire and of the comfort of the Resurrection," *Poems of Gerard Manley Hopkins* (London: Humphrey Milford, 1918).

old boys who made that amazing roof believe? Or did they just make those wide wings and adoring hands for fun, because they liked the pattern? At any rate, they made them *look* as though they believed something, and that's where they have us beat. What next? Oh, yes, out again to the grave, of course. Hymn 373 ... there must be some touch of imagination in the good Mr. Russell to have suggested this, though he looks as if he thought of nothing but having tinned salmon to his tea. . . . 'Man that is born of a woman . . .' not very much further to go now; we're coming into the straight. . . . 'Thou knowest, Lord, the secrets of our hearts. . . .' I knew it, I knew it! Will Thoday's going to faint. . . . No, he's got hold of himself again. I shall have to have a word with that gentleman before long ... 'for any pains of death, to fall from Thee.' Damn it! that goes home. Why? Mere splendour of rhythm, I expect – there are plenty of worse pains. . . . 'Our dear brother here departed' ... *brother* ... [4]

This newspaper article by Dorothy L. Sayers, "The Greatest Drama Ever Staged is the Official Creed of Christendom," appeared in the Sunday Times *two weeks before Easter 1938:*

Official Christianity, of late years, has been having what is known as "a bad press." We are constantly assured that the churches are empty because preachers insist too much upon doctrine – "dull dogma," as people call it. The fact is the precise opposite. It is the neglect of dogma that makes for dullness. The Christian faith is the most exciting drama that ever staggered the imagination of man – and the dogma is the drama.

That drama is summarised quite clearly in the creeds of the Church, and if we think it dull it is because we either have never

---

4   *The Nine Tailors*, 1934, "Lord Peter Taken from Lead."

really read those amazing documents, or have recited them so often and so mechanically as to have lost all sense of their meaning. The plot pivots upon a single character, and the whole action is the answer to a single central problem: *What think ye of Christ?* Before we adopt any of the unofficial solutions (some of which are indeed excessively dull) – before we dismiss Christ as a myth, an idealist, a demagogue, a liar or a lunatic – it will do no harm to find out what the creeds really say about Him. What does the Church think of Christ?

The Church's answer is categorical and uncompromising, and it is this: That Jesus Bar-Joseph, the carpenter of Nazareth, was in fact and in truth, and in the most exact and literal sense of the words, the God "by Whom all things were made." His body and brain were those of a common man; His personality was the personality of God, so far as that personality could be expressed in human terms. He was not a kind of dæmon or fairy pretending to be human; He was in every respect a genuine living man. He was not merely a man so good as to be "like God" – He *was* God.

Now, this is not just a pious commonplace; it is not commonplace at all. For what it means is this, among other things: that for whatever reason God chose to make man as he is – limited and suffering and subject to sorrows and death – He had the honesty and the courage to take His own medicine. Whatever game He is playing with His creation, He has kept His own rules and played fair. He can exact nothing from man that He has not exacted from Himself. He has Himself gone through the whole of human experience, from the trivial irritations of family life and the cramping restrictions of hard work and lack of money to the worst horrors of pain and humiliation, defeat, despair and death. When He was a man, He played the man. He was born in poverty and died in disgrace and thought it well worth while.

Christianity is, of course, not the only religion that has found the best explanation of human life in the idea of an incarnate and suffering god. The Egyptian Osiris died and rose again; Æschylus in his play, *The Eumenides,* reconciled man to God by the theory of a suffering Zeus. But in most theologies, the god is supposed to have suffered and died in some remote and mythical period of pre-history. The Christian story, on the other hand, starts off briskly in St. Matthew's account with a place and a date: "When Jesus was born in Bethlehem of Judæa in the days of Herod the King." St. Luke, still more practically and prosaically, pins the thing down by a reference to a piece of government finance. God, he says, was made man in the year when Cæsar Augustus was taking a census in connection with a scheme of taxation. Similarly, we might date an event by saying that it took place in the year that Great Britain went off the gold standard. About thirty-three years later (we are informed) God was executed, for being a political nuisance, "under Pontius Pilate" – much as we might say, "when Mr. Joynson-Hicks[5] was Home Secretary." It is as definite and concrete as all that.

Possibly we might prefer not to take this tale too seriously – there are disquieting points about it. Here we had a man of Divine character walking and talking among us – and what did we find to do with Him? The common people, indeed, "heard Him gladly"; but our leading authorities in Church and State considered that He talked too much and uttered too many disconcerting truths. So we bribed one of His friends to hand Him over quietly to the police, and we tried Him on a rather vague charge of creating a disturbance, and had Him publicly flogged and hanged on the common gallows, "thanking God we were

5   William Joynson Hicks, 1st Viscount Brentford (1865–1932), British Home Secretary from 1924 to 1929.

rid of a knave."[6] All this was not very creditable to us, even if He was (as many people thought and think) only a harmless crazy preacher. But if the Church is right about Him, it was more discreditable still; for the man we hanged was God Almighty.

So that is the outline of the official story – the tale of the time when God was the under-dog and got beaten, when He submitted to the conditions He had laid down and became a man like the men He had made, and the men He had made broke Him and killed Him. This is the dogma we find so dull – this terrifying drama of which God is the victim and hero.

If this is dull, then what, in Heaven's name, is worthy to be called exciting? The people who hanged Christ never, to do them justice, accused Him of being a bore – on the contrary; they thought Him too dynamic to be safe. It has been left for later generations to muffle up that shattering personality and surround Him with an atmosphere of tedium. We have very efficiently pared the claws of the Lion of Judah, certified Him "meek and mild," and recommended Him as a fitting household pet for pale curates and pious old ladies. To those who knew Him, however, He in no way suggested a milk-and-water person; *they* objected to Him as a dangerous firebrand. True, He was tender to the unfortunate, patient with honest inquirers, and humble before Heaven; but He insulted respectable clergymen by calling them hypocrites; He referred to King Herod as "that fox"; He went to parties in disreputable company and was looked upon as a "gluttonous man and a wine-bibber, a friend of publicans and sinners"; He assaulted indignant tradesmen and threw them and their belongings out of the Temple; He drove a coach-and-horses

---

6   Shakespeare, *Much Ado About Nothing,* Act 3, Scene 3, Dogberry: "Why, then, take no note of him, but let him go; and / presently call the rest of the watch together / and thank God you are rid of a knave."

through a number of sacrosanct and hoary regulations; He cured diseases by any means that came handy, with a shocking casualness in the matter of other people's pigs and property; He showed no proper deference for wealth or social position; when confronted with neat dialectical traps, He displayed a paradoxical humour that affronted serious-minded people, and He retorted by asking disagreeably searching questions that could not be answered by rule of thumb. He was emphatically not a dull man in His human lifetime, and if He was God, there can be nothing dull about God either. But He had "a daily beauty in His life that made us ugly,"[7] and officialdom felt that the established order of things would be more secure without Him. So they did away with God in the name of peace and quietness.

"And the third day He rose again"; what are we to make of that? One thing is certain: if He was God and nothing else, His immortality means nothing to us; if He was man and no more, His death is no more important than yours or mine. But if He really was both God and man, then when the man Jesus died, God died too, and when the God Jesus rose from the dead, man rose too, because they were one and the same person. The Church binds us to no theory about the exact composition of Christ's Resurrection Body. A body of some kind there had to be, since man cannot perceive the Infinite otherwise than in terms of space and time. It may have been made from the same elements as the body that disappeared so strangely from the guarded tomb, but it was not that old, limited, mortal body, though it was recognisably like it. In any case, those who saw the risen Christ remained persuaded that life was worth living

---

7   Shakespeare, *Othello,* Act 5, Scene 1, Iago: "It must not be: if Cassio do remain, / He hath a daily beauty in his life / That makes me ugly; and, besides, the Moor / May unfold me to him; there stand I in much peril: / No, he must die."

and death a triviality – an attitude curiously unlike that of the modern defeatist, who is firmly persuaded that life is a disaster and death (rather inconsistently) a major catastrophe.

Now, nobody is compelled to believe a single word of this remarkable story. God (says the Church) has created us perfectly free to disbelieve in Him as much as we choose. If we do disbelieve, then He and we must take the consequences in a world ruled by cause and effect. The Church says further, that man did, in fact, disbelieve, and that God did, in fact, take the consequences. All the same, if we are going to disbelieve a thing, it seems on the whole to be desirable that we should first find out what, exactly, we are disbelieving. Very well, then: "The right Faith is, that we believe that Jesus Christ is God and Man. Perfect God and perfect Man, of a reasonable soul and human flesh subsisting. Who although He be God and Man, yet is He not two, but one Christ."[8] There is the essential doctrine, of which the whole elaborate structure of Christian faith and morals is only the logical consequence.

Now, we may call that doctrine exhilarating or we may call it devastating; we may call it revelation or we may call it rubbish; but if we call it dull, then words have no meaning at all. That God should play the tyrant over man is a dismal story of unrelieved oppression; that man should play the tyrant over man is the usual dreary record of human futility; but that man should play the tyrant over God and find Him a better man than himself is an astonishing drama indeed. Any journalist, hearing of it for the first time, would recognise it as News; those who did hear it for the first time actually called it News, and good news at that;

---

8 "Perfect God and perfect man, of a reasonable soul and human flesh subsisting. Equal to the Father as touching His Godhead, and inferior to the Father as touching His manhood. Who, although He is God and man, yet He is not two, but one Christ." *Athanasian Creed.*

though we are apt to forget that the word Gospel ever meant anything so sensational.

Perhaps the drama is played out now, and Jesus is safely dead and buried. Perhaps. It is ironical and entertaining to consider that once at least in the world's history those words might have been spoken with complete conviction, and that was upon the eve of the Resurrection.[9]

---

9   Dorothy L. Sayers, "The Greatest Drama Ever Staged is the Official Creed of Christendom." *The Sunday Times*, April 3, 1938, published in *Creed or Chaos?* 1949.

12

The Mind of the Maker

Sacrificial Love

Toward the end of The Nine Tailors, *after the identity of the dead stranger at Fenchurch St. Paul is unraveled, Wimsey and Bunter return to spend Christmas with the villagers. On the way home to London they encounter a group of workmen zealously sandbagging the sluice gates. One of them, Will Thoday, hails them.*

"My lord!" he cried, "my lord! Thank God you are here! Go and warn them at St. Paul's that the sluice gates are going. We've done what we can with sandbags and beams, but we can't do no more and there's a message come down from the old Bank Sluice that the water is over the Great Leam at Lympsey, and they'll have to send it down here or be drowned themselves. She's held this tide, but she'll go the next with this wind and the tide at springs. It'll lay the whole country under water, my lord, and there's no time to lose."

"All right," said Wimsey. "Can I send you more men?"

"A regiment of men couldn't do nothing now, my lord. They old gates is going, and there won't be a foot of dry land in the three Fenchurches six hours from now."

Wimsey glanced at his watch. "I'll tell 'em," he said, and the car leapt forward.

The Rector was in his study when Wimsey burst in upon him with the news.

"Great Heavens!" cried Mr. Venables. "I've been afraid of this. I've warned the drainage authorities over and over again about those gates but they wouldn't listen. But it's no good crying over spilt milk. We must act quickly. If they open the Old Bank Sluice and Van Leyden's Sluice blows up, you see what will happen. All the Upper Water will be turned back up the Wale and drown us ten feet deep or more. My poor parishioners – all those outlying farms and cottages! But we mustn't lose our heads. We have taken our precautions. Two Sundays ago I warned the congregation what might happen and I put a note in the December Parish Magazine. And the Nonconformist minister has co-operated in the most friendly manner with us. Yes, yes. The first thing to do is to ring the alarm. They know what that means, thank God! They learnt it during the War. I never thought I should thank God for the War, but He moves in a mysterious way. Ring the bell for Emily, please. The church will be safe, whatever happens, unless we get a rise of over twelve feet, which is hardly likely. Out of the deep, O Lord, out of the deep. Oh, Emily, run and tell Hinkins that Van Leyden's Sluice is giving way. Tell him to fetch one of the other men and ring the alarm on Gaude and Tailor Paul at once. Here are the keys of the church and belfry. Warn your mistress and get all the valuables taken over to the church. Carry them up the tower. Now keep cool, there's a good girl. I don't think the house will be touched, but one cannot be too careful. Find somebody to help you with this chest – I've secured all the parish registers in it – and see that the church plate is taken up the tower as well. Now, where is my hat? We must get on the telephone to St. Peter and St. Stephen and make sure that they are prepared. And we will see what we can do with the people at the Old Bank Sluice. We haven't a moment to lose. Is your car here?"

They ran the car up to the village, the Rector leaning out perilously and shouting warnings to everyone they met. At the post-office they called up the other Fenchurches and then communicated with the keeper of the Old Bank Sluice. His report was not encouraging.

"Very sorry, sir, but we can't help ourselves. If we don't let the water through there'll be the best part of four mile o' the bank washed away. We've got six gangs a-working on it now, but they can't do a lot with all these thousands o' tons o' water coming down. And there's more to come, so they say."

The Rector made a gesture of despair, and turned to the post-mistress.

"You'd best get down to the church, Mrs. West. You know what to do. Documents and valuables in the tower, personal belongings in the nave. Animals in the churchyard. Cats, rabbits and guinea-pigs in *baskets, please* – we can't have then running round loose. Ah! there go the alarm-bells. Good! I am more alarmed for the remote farms than for the village. Now, Lord Peter, we must go and keep order as best we can at the church."

The village was already a scene of confusion. Furniture was being stacked on handcarts, pigs were being driven down the street, squealing; hens, squawking and terrified, were being huddled into crates. At the door of the school-house Miss Snoot was peering agitatedly out.

"When ought we to go, Mr. Venables?"

"Not yet, not yet – let the people move their heavy things first. I will send you a message when the time comes, and then you will get the children together and march them down in an orderly way. You can rely on me. But keep them cheerful – reassure them and don't on any account let them go home. They are far safer here. Oh, Miss Thorpe! Miss Thorpe! I see you have heard the news."

"Yes, Mr. Venables. Can we do anything?"

"My dear, you are the very person! Could you and Mrs. Gates see that the school-children are kept amused and happy, and give them tea later on if necessary? The urns are in the parish-room. Just a moment, I must speak to Mr. Hensman. How are we off for stores, Mr. Hensman?"

"Pretty well stocked, sir," replied the grocer. "We're getting ready to move as you suggested, sir."

"That's fine," said the Rector. "You know where to go. The refreshment room will be in the Lady chapel. Have you the key of the parish-room for the boards and trestles?"

"Yes, sir."

"Good, good. Get a tackle rigged over the church well for your drinking-water, and be sure and remember to boil it first. Or use the Rectory pump, if it is spared to us. Now, Lord Peter, back to the church."

Mrs. Venables had already taken charge in the church. Assisted by Emily and some of the women of the parish, she was busily roping off areas – so many pews for the schoolchildren, so many other pews near the stoves for the sick and aged, the area beneath the tower for furniture, a large placard on the parclose screen REFRESHMENTS. Mr. Gotobed and his son, staggering under buckets of coke, were lighting the stoves. In the churchyard, Jack Godfrey and a couple of other farmers were marking out cattle-pens and erecting shelters among the tombs. Just over the wall which separated the consecrated ground from the bell-field, a squad of voluntary diggers were digging out a handsome set of sanitary trenches.

"Good lord, sir," said Wimsey, impressed, "anybody would think you'd done this all your life."

"I have devoted much prayer and thought to the situation in the last few weeks," said Mr. Venables. "But my wife is the real manager. She has a marvellous head for organisation. Hinkins! right up to the bell-chamber with that plate – it'll be out of the way there. Alf! Alf Donnington! How about that beer?"

"Coming along, sir."

"Splendid – into the Lady chapel, please. You're bringing some of it bottled, I hope. It'll take two days for the casks to settle."

"That's all right, sir. Tebbutt and me are seeing to that."

The Rector nodded, and dodging past some of Mr. Hensman's contingent, who were staggering in with cases of groceries, he went out to the gates, where he encountered P.C. Priest, stolidly directing the traffic.

"We're having all the cars parked along the wall, sir."

"That's right. And we shall want volunteers with cars to run out to outlying places and bring in the women and sick people. Will you see to that?"

"Very good, sir."

"Lord Peter, will you act as our Mercury between here and Van Leyden's Sluice? Keep us posted as to what is happening."

"Right you are," said Wimsey. "I hope, by the way, that Bunter – where is Bunter?"

"Here, my lord. I was about to suggest that I might lend some assistance with the commissariat, if not required elsewhere."

"Do, Bunter, do," said the Rector.

"I understand, my lord, that no immediate trouble is expected at the Rectory, and I was about to suggest that, with the kind help of the butcher, sir, a sufficiency of hot soup might be prepared in the wash-house copper, and brought over in the wheeled watering tub – after the utensil has been adequately scalded, of course. And if there were such a thing as a paraffin-oil stove anywhere – ”

"By all means – but be careful with the paraffin. We do not want to escape the water to fall into the fire."

"Certainly not, sir."

"You can get paraffin from Wilderspin. Better send some more ringers up to the tower. Let them pull the bells as they like and fire them at intervals. Oh, here are the Chief Constable and Superintendent Blundell – how good of them to come over. We are expecting a little trouble here, Colonel."

"Just so, just so. I see you are handling the situation admirably. I fear a lot of valuable property will be destroyed. Would you like any police sent over?"

"Better patrol the roads between the Fenchurches," suggested Blundell. "St. Peter is greatly alarmed – they're afraid for the bridges. We are arranging a service of ferryboats. They lie even lower than you do and are, I fear, not so well prepared as you, sir."

"We can offer them shelter here," said the Rector. "The church will hold nearly a thousand at a pinch, but they must bring what food they can. And their bedding, of course. Mrs. Venables is arranging it all. Men's sleeping-quarters on the cantoris side, women and children on the decani side. And we can put the sick and aged people in the Rectory in greater comfort, if all goes well. St. Stephen will be safe enough, I imagine, but if not, we must do our best for them too. And, dear me! We shall rely on you, Superintendent, to send us victuals by boat as soon as it can be arranged. The roads will be clear between Leamholt and the Thirty-Foot, and the supplies can be brought from there by water."

126 + ✦ THE GOSPEL IN DOROTHY L. SAYERS

"I'll organise a service," said Mr. Blundell.

"If the railway embankment goes, you will have to see to St. Stephen as well. Good-day, Mrs. Giddings, good-day to you! We are having quite an adventure, are we not? So glad to see you here in good time. Well, Mrs. Leach! So here you are! How's Baby? Enjoying himself, I expect. You'll find Mrs. Venables in the church. Jack! Jackie Holliday! You must put that kitten in a basket. Run and ask Joe Hinkins to find you one. Ah, Mary! I hear your husband is doing fine work down at the Sluice. We must see that he doesn't come to any harm. Yes, my dear, what is it? I am just coming."

For three hours Wimsey worked among the fugitives – fetching and carrying, cheering and exhorting, helping to stall cattle and making himself as useful as he could. At length he remembered his duty as a messenger and extricating his car from the crowd made his way east along the Thirty-Foot. It was growing dark, and the road was thronged with carts and cattle, hurrying to the safety of Church Hill. Pigs and cattle impeded his progress.

"The animals went in two by two," sang Wimsey, as he sped through the twilight, "the elephant and the kangaroo. Hurrah!"

Down at the Sluice, the situation looked dangerous. Barges had been drawn against both sides of the gates and an attempt had been made to buttress the sluice with beams and sandbags, but the piers were bulging dangerously and as fast as material was lowered into the water, it was swept down by the force of the current. The river was foaming over the top of the weir, and from the east, wind and tide were coming up in violent opposition.

"Can't hold her much longer, now, my lord," gasped a man, plunging up the bank and shaking the water from him like a wet dog. "She's going, God help us!"

The sluice-keeper was wringing his hands.

"I told 'em, I told 'em! What will become on us?"

"How long now?" asked Wimsey.

"An hour, my lord, if that."

"You'd better all get away. Have you cars enough?"

"Yes, my lord, thank you."

Will Thoday came up to him, his face white and working.

"My wife and children – are they safe?"

"Safe as houses, Will. The Rector's doing wonders. You'd better come back with me."

"I'll hang on here till the rest go, my lord, thank you. But tell them to lose no time."

Wimsey turned the car back again. In the short time that he had been away the organisation had almost completed itself. Men, women, children and household goods had been packed into the church. It was nearly seven o'clock and the dusk had fallen. The lamps were lit. Soup and tea were being served in the Lady chapel, babies were crying, the churchyard resounded with the forlorn lowing of cattle and the terrified bleating of sheep. Sides of bacon were being carried in, and thirty waggon-loads of hay and corn were ranged under the church wall. In the only clear space amid the confusion the Rector stood behind the rails of the Sanctuary. And over all, the bells tumbled and wrangled, shouting their alarm across the country. Gaude, Sabaoth, John, Jericho, Jubilee, Dimity, Batty Thomas and Tailor Paul – awake! make haste! save yourselves! The deep waters have gone over us! They call with the noise of the cataracts!

Wimsey made his way up to the altar-rails and gave his message. The Rector nodded. "Get the men away quickly," he said, "tell them they must come at once. Brave lads! I know they hate to give in, but they mustn't sacrifice themselves uselessly.

As you go through the village, tell Miss Snoot to bring the school-children down." And as Wimsey turned to go, he called anxiously after him – "and don't let them forget the other two tea-urns!"

The men were already piling into their waiting cars when Lord Peter again arrived at the Sluice. The tide was coming up like a race, and in the froth and flurry of water he could see the barges flung like battering rams against the piers. Somebody shouted: "Get out of it, lads, for your lives!" and was answered by a rending crash. The transverse beams that carried the footway over the weir, rocking and swaying upon the bulging piers, cracked and parted. The river poured over in a tumult to meet the battering force of the tide. There was a cry. A dark figure, stepping hurriedly across the reeling barges, plunged and was gone. Another form dived after it, and a rush was made to the bank. Wimsey, flinging off his coat, hurled himself down to the water's edge. Somebody caught and held him.

"No good, my lord, they're gone! My God! did you see that?"

Somebody threw the flare of a headlight across the river. "Caught between the barge and the pier – smashed like eggshells. Who is it? Johnnie Cross? Who went in after him? Will Thoday? That's bad, and him a married man. Stand back, my lord. We'll have no more lives lost. Save yourselves, lads, you can do them no good. Christ! the sluice gates are going. Drive like hell, men, it's all up!"

Wimsey found himself dragged and hurtled by strong hands to his car. Somebody scrambled in beside him. It was the sluice-keeper, still moaning, "I told 'em, I told 'em!" Another thunderous crash brought down the weir across the Thirty-Foot, in a deluge of tossing timbers. Beams and barges were whirled together like straws, and a great spout of water raged over the bank and flung itself across the road. Then the Sluice, that held the water back from the Old Wale River, yielded, and the roar of the engines as the cars sped away was lost in the thunder of the meeting and over-riding waters.

The banks of the Thirty-Foot held, but the swollen Wale, receiving the full force of the Upper Waters and the spring tide, gave at every point. Before the cars reached St. Paul, the flood was rising and pursuing them. Wimsey's car – the last to start – was submerged to the axles. They fled through the dusk, and behind and on their left, the great silver sheet of water spread and spread.[1]

From The Mind of the Maker:

"Sacrifice" is another word liable to misunderstanding. It is generally held to be noble and loving in proportion as its sacrificial nature is consciously felt by the person who is sacrificing himself. The direct contrary is the truth. To feel sacrifice consciously as self-sacrifice argues a failure in love. When a job is undertaken from necessity, or from a grim sense of disagreeable duty, the worker is self-consciously aware of the toils and pains he undergoes, and will say: "I have made such and such sacrifices for this." But when the job is a labour of love, the sacrifices will present themselves to the worker – strange as it may

---

1   *The Nine Tailors,* 1934, "The Waters Are Called Home."

seem – in the guise of enjoyment.[2] Moralists, looking on at this, will always judge that the former kind of sacrifice is more admirable than the latter, because the moralist, whatever he may pretend, has far more respect for pride than for love. The Puritan assumption that all action disagreeable to the doer is *ipso facto* more meritorious than enjoyable action, is firmly rooted in this exaggerated valuation set on pride. I do not mean that there is no nobility in doing unpleasant things from a sense of duty, but only that there is more nobility in doing them gladly out of sheer love of the job. The Puritan thinks otherwise; he is inclined to say, "Of course, So-and-so works very hard and has given up a good deal for such-and-such a cause, but there's no merit in that – he enjoys it." The merit, of course, lies precisely in the enjoyment, and the nobility of So-and-so consists in the very fact that he is the kind of person to whom the doing of that piece of work is delightful.

It is because, behind the restrictions of the moral code, we instinctively recognise the greater validity of the law of nature, that we do always in our heart of hearts prefer the children of grace to the children of legality. We recognise a false ring in the demanding voice which proclaims: "I have sacrificed the best years of my life to my profession (my family, my country, or whatever it may be), and have a right to expect some return."

---

2   Edmund Spenser, *The Faery Queene:* VI. 11, 2:
    For some so goodly gratious are by kind,
    That every action doth them much commend,
    And in the eyes of men great liking find,
    Which others that have greater skill in mind,
    Though they enforce themselves, cannot attaine;
    For everything to which one is enclin'd
    Doth best become and greatest grace doth gaine:
    Yet praise likewise deserve good thewes enforst with paine.

The code compels us to admit the claim, but there is something in the expression of it that repels us. Conversely, however, the children of legality are shocked by the resolute refusal of the children of light to insist on this kind of claim and – still more disconcertingly – by their angry assertion of love's right to self-sacrifice. Those, for example, who obligingly inform creative artists of methods by which (with a little corrupting of their creative purpose) they could make more money, are often very excusably shocked by the fury with which they are sent about their business. Indeed, creative love has its darker aspects, and will sacrifice, not only itself, but others to its overmastering ends. Somerset Maugham, in *The Moon and Sixpence,* has given convincing expression to these dark fires of the artist's devouring passion; and the meaning of the story is lost unless we recognise that Strickland's terrible sacrifices, suffered and exacted, are the assertion of a love so tremendous that it has passed beyond even the desire of happiness. A passion of this temper does not resign itself to sacrifice, but embraces it, and sweeps the world up in the same embrace. It is not without reason that we feel a certain uneasy suspicion of that inert phrase, "Christian resignation"; an inner voice reminds us that the Christian God is Love, and that love and resignation can find no common ground to stand on. So much the human creator can tell us, if we like to listen to him. Our confusion on the subject is caused by a dissipation and eclecticism in our associations with the word "love." We connect it too exclusively with the sexual and material passions, whose anti-passion is possessiveness, and with indulgent affection, whose anti-passion is sentimentality. Concentrated, and freed from its anti-passions, love is the Energy of creation:

> In the juvescence of the year
> Came Christ the tiger – [3]

a disturbing thought.

> Tyger, Tyger, burning bright
> In the forests of the night,
> What immortal hand or eye
> Could frame thy fearful symmetry? . . .
>
> And what shoulder and what art,
> Could twist the sinews of thy heart?
> And when thy heart began to beat,
> What dread hand? and what dread feet? . . .
>
> When the stars threw down their spears,
> And water'd heaven with their tears,
> Did he smile his work to see?
> Did he who made the Lamb make thee? [4]

To that question, the creative artist returns an unqualified Yes, exciting thereby consternation, and the hasty passing of resolutions by the guardians of the moral code that artists are dangerous people and a subversive element in the state.

> And the kings of the earth, and the great men and the rich men, and the chief captains, and the mighty men, and every bondman, and every free man, hid themselves in the dens and in the rocks of the mountains, and said to the mountains and rocks, Fall on us, and hide us from the face of him that sitteth on the throne, and from the wrath of the Lamb; for the great day of his wrath is come; and who shall be able to stand? (Rev. 6:16, 17.)

---

3 T. S. Eliot, "Gerontion," *Poems* (New York: A. A. Knopf, 1920).

4 William Blake, "The Tyger," *Songs of Experience* (1794).

Who indeed? Neither resistance nor resignation will do anything here. To Love-in-Energy, the only effective response is Love-in-Power, eagerly embracing its own sacrifice.[5]

The Emperor Constantine is a four-hour play written for the Colchester Festival in 1951. In it, Sayers delved into two themes: the relationship between church and state, and the nature of Jesus Christ. Constantine, the first Roman Emperor to convert to Christianity and proclaim religious tolerance, was not baptized until a few days before his death. Sayers's play posits that his faith was merely politically expedient until he had a true experience of repentance in the last years of his life. In this scene, Constantine is confessing to his mother, Helena, all the sins that crowd upon him.

CONSTANTINE: What were you praying for?

HELENA: For mercy upon all sinners.

CONSTANTINE: You told me once that until I understood sin I should never understand God. Now I know sin – I *am* sin; and understand nothing at all.

HELENA: The sin was not all yours. You were cruelly deceived.

CONSTANTINE: That's not what I mean. Sin is more terrible than you think. It is not lying and cruelty and murder – it is a corruption of life at the source. I and mine are so knit together in evil that no one can tell where the guilt begins or ends. And I who called myself God's emperor – I find now that all my justice is sin and all my mercy bloodshed.

HELENA: You have discovered that? *(She sits down.)*

---

5   *The Mind of the Maker*, 1941, ch. 9.

CONSTANTINE: . . . I have founded Christ's empire in the grave, and purchased the blood of the martyrs with the slaughter of armies. The clemency of Constantine is more deadly than his vengeance; and if I were to pardon now, more and more deaths would follow. Yet how shall I sit in judgment who am a partner in the crime?

HELENA: You must, my child; that is the bitter portion of princes. It is sin to judge and sin to refrain from judgment, because evil can never be undone, but only purged and redeemed.

CONSTANTINE: Crispus . . . when I saw him lie there dead, I understood how she came to do it. I believe that was the first time I had ever really thought about her. I could almost have forgiven her – but the Empire must not forgive.

HELENA: To forgive and to spare are not always the same. You spared Maximian and Licinius once – did you forgive them?

CONSTANTINE (surprised by a new idea): Why, no – I suppose not. I didn't care for them enough. I wanted to be magnanimous. . . . I see. One can spare and not forgive – and one can also forgive, and not spare. . . . God forgives us – but does he spare us?

HELENA (sighing): Not very often. He did not spare Himself. The price is always paid, but not always by the guilty.

CONSTANTINE: By whom, then?

HELENA: By the blood of the innocent.

CONSTANTINE: Oh no!

HELENA: By nothing else, my child. Every man's innocence belongs to Christ, and Christ's to him. And innocence alone can pardon without injustice, because it has paid the price.

CONSTANTINE: That is intolerable.

HELENA: It is the hardest thing in the world – to receive salvation at the hand of those we have injured. But if they do not plead for us there is nobody else who can. That is why there is no redemption except in the cross of Christ. For He alone is true God and true Man, wholly innocent and wholly wronged, and we shed His blood every day.

CONSTANTINE: True God out of true God. . . . *(He falls on his knees before Helena.)* Mother, tell me, whose blood is on my hands? . . .

HELENA: The blood of God *(Constantine buries his face in her lap)* which makes intercession for us. . . .[6]

6   Dorothy L. Sayers, *The Emperor Constantine: A Chronicle* (London: Victor Gollancz, 1951).

13

Gaudy Night

Work

Harriet visits her old college for a "Gaudy" (reunion) in Gaudy Night, *and finds that the staff is upset by a vandal who is playing destructive pranks and sending nasty anonymous letters. She is asked to investigate, but after several fruitless months reluctantly turns to Lord Peter to help her find the culprit. All of the staff have gathered to meet him. He puts several leading questions to the group of women, looking for clues to their personalities.*

"How about the artist of genius who has to choose between letting his family starve and painting pot-boilers to keep them?"

"He's no business to have a wife and family," said Miss Hillyard.

"Poor devil! Then he has the further interesting choice between repressions and immorality. Mrs. Goodwin, I gather, would object to the repressions and some people might object to the immorality."

"That doesn't matter," said Miss Pyke. "You have hypothesized a wife and family. Well – he could stop painting. That, if he really is a genius, would be a loss to the world. But he mustn't paint bad pictures – that would be really immoral."

"Why?" asked Miss Edwards. "What do a few bad pictures matter, more or less?"

"Of course they matter," said Miss Shaw. She knew a good deal about painting. "A bad picture by a good painter is a betrayal of truth – his own truth."

"That's only a relative kind of truth," objected Miss Edwards. . . .

"If you can't agree about painters," [said Harriet] "make it someone else. Make it a scientist."

"I've no objection to scientific pot-boilers," said Miss Edwards. "I mean, a popular book isn't necessarily unscientific."

"So long," said Wimsey, "as it doesn't falsify the facts. But it might be a different kind of thing. To take a concrete instance – somebody wrote a novel called *The Search* – "

"C.P. Snow," said Miss Burrows. "It's funny you should mention that. It was the book that the – "

"I know," said Peter. "That's possibly why it was in my mind."

"I never read the book," said the Warden.

"Oh, I did," said the Dean. "It's about a man who starts out to be a scientist and gets on very well till, just as he's going to be appointed to an important executive post, he finds he's made a careless error in a scientific paper. He didn't check his assistant's results, or something. Somebody finds out, and he doesn't get the job. So he decides he doesn't really care about science after all."

"Obviously not," said Miss Edwards. "He only cared about the post."

"But," said Miss Chilperic, "if it was only a mistake – "

"The point about it," said Wimsey, "is what an elderly scientist says to him. He tells him: 'The only ethical principle which has made science possible is that the truth shall be told all the time. If we do not penalize false statements made in error, we open up the way for false statements by intention. And a false statement of fact, made deliberately, is the most serious crime a scientist can commit.' Words to that effect. I may not be quoting quite correctly."

"Well, that's true, of course. Nothing could possibly excuse deliberate falsification. . . ."

"In the same novel," said the Dean, "somebody deliberately falsifies a result – later on, I mean – in order to get a job. And the man who made the original mistake finds it out. But he says nothing, because the other man is very badly off and has a wife and family to keep."

"These wives and families!" said Peter.

"Does the author approve?" inquired the Warden.

"Well," said the Dean, "the book ends there, so I suppose he does."

"But does anybody here approve? A false statement is published and the man who could correct it lets it go, out of charitable considerations. Would anybody here do that? There's your test case, Miss Barton, with no personalities attached."

"Of course one couldn't do that," said Miss Barton. "Not for ten wives and fifty children."

"Not for Solomon and all his wives and concubines? I congratulate you, Miss Barton, on striking such a fine, unfeminine note. Will nobody say a word for the women and children?"

("I knew he was going to be mischievous," thought Harriet.)

"You'd like to hear it, wouldn't you?" said Miss Hillyard.

"You've got us in a cleft stick," said the Dean. "If we say it, you can point out that womanliness unfits us for learning; and if we don't, you can point out that learning makes us unwomanly."

"Since I can make myself offensive either way," said Wimsey, "you have nothing to gain by not telling the truth."

"The truth is," said Mrs. Goodwin, "that nobody could possibly defend the indefensible."

"It sounds, anyway, like a manufactured case," said Miss Allison, briskly. "It could very seldom happen; and if it did – "

"Oh, it happens," said Miss De Vine. "It has happened. It happened to me. I don't mind telling you – without names, of course. When I was at Flamborough College, examining for the professorial theses in York University, there was a man who sent in a very interesting paper on a historical subject. It was a most persuasive piece of argument; only I happened to know that the whole contention was quite untrue, because a letter that absolutely contradicted it was actually in existence in a certain very obscure library in a foreign town. I'd come across it when I was reading up something else. That wouldn't have mattered, of course. But the internal evidence showed that the man must have had access to that library. So I had to make an inquiry, and I found that he really had been there and must have seen the letter and deliberately suppressed it."

"But how could you be so sure he had seen the letter?" asked Miss Lydgate anxiously. "He might carelessly have overlooked it. That would be a very different matter."

"He not only had seen it," replied Miss de Vine; "he stole it. We made him admit as much. He had come upon that letter when his thesis was nearly complete, and he had no time to re-write it. And it was a great blow to him apart from that, because he had grown enamoured of his own theory and couldn't bear to give it up."

"That's the mark of an unsound scholar, I'm afraid," said Miss Lydgate in a mournful tone, as one speaks of an incurable cancer.

"But here is the curious thing," went on Miss de Vine. "He was unscrupulous enough to let the false conclusion stand; but he was too good a historian to destroy the letter. He kept it."

"You'd think," said Miss Pyke, "it would be as painful as biting on a sore tooth."

"Perhaps he had some idea of rediscovering it some day," said Miss de Vine, "and setting himself right with his conscience. I don't know, and I don't think he knew very well himself."

"What happened to him?" asked Harriet.

"Well, that was the end of him, of course. He lost the professorship, naturally, and they took away his M.A. degree as well. A pity, because he was brilliant in his own way – and very good-looking, if that has anything to do with it."

"Poor man!" said Miss Lydgate. "He must have needed the post very badly."

"It meant a good deal to him financially. He was married and not well off. I don't know what became of him. That was about six years ago. He dropped out completely. One was sorry about it, but there it was."

"You couldn't possibly have done anything else," said Miss Edwards.

"Of course not. A man as undependable as that is not only useless, but dangerous. He might do anything."

"You'd think it would be a lesson to him," said Miss Hillyard. "It didn't pay, did it? Say he sacrificed his professional honour for the women and children we hear so much about – but in the end it left him worse off."

"But that," said Peter, "was only because he committed the extra sin of being found out."

"It seems to me," began Miss Chilperic, timidly – and then stopped.

"Yes?" said Peter.

"Well," said Miss Chilperic, "oughtn't the women and children to have a point of view? I mean – suppose the wife knew that her husband had done a thing like that for her, what would she feel about it?"

"That's a very important point," said Harriet. "You'd think she'd feel too ghastly for words."

"It depends," said the Dean. "I don't believe nine women out of ten would care a dash."

"That's a monstrous thing to say," cried Miss Hillyard.

"You think a wife might feel sensitive about her husband's honour – even if it was sacrificed on her account?" said Miss Stevens. "Well – I don't know."

"I should think," said Miss Chilperic, stammering a little in her earnestness, "she would feel like a man who – I mean, wouldn't it be like living on somebody's immoral earnings?"

"There," said Peter, "if I may say so, I think you are exaggerating. The man who does that – if he isn't too far gone to have any feelings at all – is hit by other considerations, some of which have nothing whatever to do with ethics. But it is extremely interesting that you should make the comparison." He looked at Miss Chilperic so intently that she blushed.

"Perhaps that was rather a stupid thing to say."

"No. But if it ever occurs to people to value the honour of the mind equally with the honour of the body, we shall get a social revolution of a quite unparalleled sort – and very different from the kind that is being made at the moment."[1]

---

1 Dorothy L. Sayers, *Gaudy Night* (London: Victor Gollancz, 1935), ch. 17.

From Sayers's talk "Creed or Chaos?":

The unsacramental attitude of modern society to man and matter is probably closely connected with its unsacramental attitude to work. The Church is a good deal to blame for having connived at this. From the eighteenth Century onwards, she has tended to acquiesce in what I may call the "industrious apprentice" view of the matter: "Work hard and be thrifty, and God will bless you with a contented mind and a competence." This is nothing but enlightened self-interest in its vulgarest form, and plays directly into the hands of the monopolist and the financier. Nothing has so deeply discredited the Christian Church as her squalid submission to the economic theory of society. The burning question of the Christian attitude to money is being so eagerly debated nowadays that it is scarcely necessary to do more than remind ourselves that the present unrest, both in Russia and in Central Europe, is an immediate judgment upon a financial system that has subordinated man to economics, and that no mere readjustment of economic machinery will have any lasting effect if it keeps man a prisoner inside the machine.

This is the burning question; but I believe there is a still more important and fundamental question waiting to be dealt with, and that is, what men in a Christian society ought to think and feel about work. Curiously enough, apart from the passage in Genesis which suggests that work is a hardship and a judgment on sin, Christian doctrine is not very explicit about work. I believe, however, that there is a Christian doctrine of work, very closely related to the doctrines of the creative energy of God and the divine image in man. The modern tendency seems to be to identify work with gainful employment; and this is, I maintain, the essential heresy at the back of the great economic fallacy which allows wheat and coffee to be burnt and fish to be used for manure while whole populations stand in need of food. The fallacy being that work is not the expression of man's creative energy in the service of Society, but only something he does in order to obtain money and leisure.

A very able surgeon put it to me like this: "What is happening," he said, "is that nobody works for the sake of getting the thing done. The result of the work is a byproduct; the aim of the work is to make money to do something else. Doctors practice medicine, not primarily to relieve suffering, but to make a living – the cure of the patient is something that happens on the way. Lawyers accept briefs, not because they have a passion for justice, but because the law is the profession which enables them to live. The reason," he added, "why men often find themselves happy and satisfied in the army is that for the first time in their lives they find themselves doing something, not for the sake of the pay, which is miserable, but for the sake of getting the thing done."

I will only add to this one thing which seems to me very symptomatic. I was shown a "scheme for a Christian Society" drawn up by a number of young and earnest Roman Catholics. It contained a number of clauses dealing with work and employment – minimum wages, hours of labour, treatment of employees, housing and so on – all very proper and Christian. But it offered no machinery whatever for ensuring that the work itself should be properly done. In its lack of a sacramental attitude to work, that is, it was as empty as a set of trade union regulations. We may remember that a mediæval guild did insist, not only on the employer's duty to his workmen, but also on the labourer's duty to his work.

If man's fulfilment of his nature is to be found in the full expression of his divine creativeness, then we urgently need a

Christian doctrine of work, which shall provide, not only for proper conditions of employment, but also that the work shall be such as a man may do with his whole heart, and that he shall do it for the very work's sake. But we cannot expect a sacramental attitude to work, while many people are forced, by our evil standard of values, to do work which is a spiritual degradation – a long series of financial trickeries, for example, or the manufacture of vulgar and useless trivialities.[2]

In this scene from Sayers's play, The Zeal of Thy House, *the arrogance of the architect William of Sens is contrasted with the attitude of the angels Cassiel, Michael, and Gabriel, who express the author's belief in the spiritual value of work. As Sayers once wrote in a letter, "Basically I see perfectly that an Incarnate Creator is the fundamental sanction for looking on all man's work in a sacramental light – the manifestation of his divine creativeness in matter."*[3]

WILLIAM: Listen to me, young man. At my age one learns that sometimes one has to damn one's soul for the sake of the work. Trust me, God shall have a choir fit for His service. Does anything else really matter?

(He and Gervase follow the others out. During the singing of the following Interlude, the scene-shifters set the stage to represent the site of the choir. The other three angels go up and stand above with Gabriel.)

INTERLUDE: Every carpenter and workmaster that laboureth night and day, and they that give themselves to counterfeit imagery, and watch to finish a work;

---

2   "Creed or Chaos?," *Creed or Chaos?,* 1949.

3   Sayers to the Rev. V. A. Demant, April 10, 1941, *Letters,* 2:248.

The smith also sitting by the anvil, and considering the iron
work, he setteth his mind to finish his work, and watcheth to
polish it perfectly.

So doth the potter sitting at his work, and turning the wheel
about with his feet, who is always carefully set at his work, and
maketh all his work by number.

All these trust to their hands, and every one is wise in his work.

Without these cannot a city be inhabited, and they shall not
dwell where they will nor go up and down;

They shall not be sought for in public council, nor sit high in
the congregation;

But they will maintain the state of the world, and all their
desire is in the work of their craft. . . .[4]

CASSIEL: Two years of toil are passed; what shall I write About
this architect?

MICHAEL: A schedule here,
Long as my sword, crammed full of deadly sins;
Jugglings with truth, and gross lusts of the body,
Drink, drabbing, swearing; slothfulness in prayer;
With a devouring, insolent ambition
That challenges disaster.

CASSIEL: These are debts;
What shall I set upon the credit side?

GABRIEL: Six columns, and their aisles, with covering vaults
From wall to arcading, and from thence again
To the centre, with the keystones locking them,
All well and truly laid without a fault.

---

4   Extracts from Sirach 38.

CASSIEL: No sum of prayer to balance the account?

GABRIEL: Ask Raphael, for prayers are in his charge.

CASSIEL: Come, Raphael, speak; or is thy censer cold?
Canst thou indeed find any grace in William
The builder-up of Canterbury?

RAPHAEL: Yes.

(He swings his censer, which gives out a cloud of incense.)

Behold, he prayeth; not with the lips alone,
But with the hand and with the cunning brain
Men worship the Eternal Architect.
So, when the mouth is dumb, the work shall speak
And save the workman. True as a mason's rule
And line can make them, the shafted columns rise
Singing like music; and by day and night
The unsleeping arches with perpetual voice
Proclaim in Heaven, to labour is to pray.

MICHAEL: Glory to God, that made the Firmament![5]

From "Why Work?," a lecture Sayers gave in April 1942:

What is the Christian understanding of work? . . . I should like
to put before you two or three propositions. . . . You will find that
any of them, if given in effect everyday practice, is so revolutionary (as compared with the habits of thinking into which we have
fallen), as to make all political revolutions look like conformity.

The first, stated quite briefly, is that work is not, primarily,
a thing one does to live, but the thing one lives to do. It is, or it

---

5   Act II, *The Zeal of Thy House*, 1937, published in *Four Sacred Plays*, 1948.

should be, the full expression of the worker's faculties, the thing in which he finds spiritual, mental and bodily satisfaction, and the medium in which he offers himself to God.

Now the consequences of this are not merely that the work should be performed under decent living and working conditions. That is a point we have begun to grasp, and it a perfectly sound point. But we have tended to concentrate on it to the exclusion of other considerations far more revolutionary.

(a) There is, for instance, the question of profits and remuneration. We have all got it fixed in our heads that the proper end of work is to be paid for – to produce a return in profits or payment to the worker which fully or more than compensates the effort he puts into it. But if our proposition is true, this does not follow at all. So long as Society provides the worker with a sufficient return in real wealth to enable him to carry on the work properly, then he has his reward. For his work is the measure of his life, and his satisfaction is found in the fulfilment of his own nature, and in contemplation of the perfection of his work. . . .

(b) Here is the second consequence. At present we have no clear grasp of the principle that every man should do the work for which he is fitted by nature. The employer is obsessed by the notion that he must find cheap labour, and the worker by the notion that the best-paid job is the job for him. Only feebly, inadequately, and spasmodically do we ever attempt to tackle the problem from the other end, and inquire: What type of worker is suited to this type of work? People engaged in education see clearly that this is the right end to start from: but they are frustrated by economic pressure, and by the failure of parents on the one hand and employers on the other to grasp the fundamental importance of this approach. . . .

(c) A third consequence is that, if we really believed this proposition and arranged our work and our standard of values accordingly, we should no longer think of work as something that we hastened to get through in order to enjoy our leisure; we should look on our leisure as the period of changed rhythm that refreshed us for the delightful purpose of getting on with our work. . . .

(d) A fourth consequence is that we should fight tooth and nail, not for mere employment, but for the quality of the work that we had to do. We should clamor to be engaged in work that was worth doing, and in which we could take pride. The worker would demand that the stuff he helped to turn out should be good stuff – he would no longer be content to take the cash and let the credit go. . . .

This first proposition chiefly concerns the worker as such. My second proposition directly concerns Christians as such, and it is this: it is the business of the Church to recognize that the secular vocation, as such, is sacred. Christian people, and particularly perhaps the Christian clergy, must get it firmly into their heads that when a man or woman is called to a particular job of secular work, that is as true a vocation as though he or she were called to specifically religious work. The Church must concern Herself not only with such questions as the just price and proper working conditions: She must concern Herself with seeing that work itself is such as a human being can perform without degradation – that no one is required by economic or any other considerations to devote himself to work that is contemptible, soul destroying, or harmful. It is not right for Her to acquiesce in the notion that a man's life is divided into the time he spends on his work and the time he spends in serving God. He must be able to serve God in his work, and the work itself must be accepted and respected as the medium of divine creation.

In nothing has the Church so lost Her hold on reality as in Her failure to understand and respect the secular vocation. She has allowed work and religion to become separate departments, and is astonished to find that, as result, the secular work of the world is turned to purely selfish and destructive ends, and that the greater part of the world's intelligent workers have become irreligious, or at least, uninterested in religion.

But is it astonishing? How can any one remain interested in a religion which seems to have no concern with nine-tenths of his life? The Church's approach to an intelligent carpenter is usually confined to exhorting him not to be drunk and disorderly in his leisure hours, and to come to church on Sundays. What the Church should be telling him is this: that the very first demand that his religion makes upon him is that he should make good tables.

Church by all means, and decent forms of amusement, certainly – but what use is all that if in the very center of his life and occupation he is insulting God with bad carpentry? No crooked table legs or ill-fitting drawers ever, I dare swear, came out of the carpenter's shop at Nazareth. Nor, if they did, could anyone believe that they were made by the same hand that made Heaven and earth. No piety in the worker will compensate for work that is not true to itself; for any work that is untrue to its own technique is a living lie.

Yet in Her own buildings, in Her own ecclesiastical art and music, in Her hymns and prayers, in Her sermons and in Her little books of devotion, the Church will tolerate or permit a pious intention to excuse so ugly, so pretentious, so tawdry and twaddling, so insincere and insipid, so *bad* as to shock and horrify any decent draftsman.

And why? Simply because She has lost all sense of the fact that the living and eternal truth is expressed in work only so far as that work is true in itself, to itself, to the standards of its own technique. She has forgotten that the secular vocation is sacred. Forgotten that a building must be good architecture before it can be a good church; that a painting must be well painted before it can be a good sacred picture; that work must be good work before it can call itself God's work. . . .

And conversely: when you find a man who is a Christian praising God by the excellence of his work – do not distract him and take him away from his proper vocation to address religious meetings and open church bazaars. Let him serve God in the way to which God has called him. If you take him away from that, he will exhaust himself in an alien technique and lose his capacity to do his dedicated work.

It is your business, you churchmen, to get what good you can from observing his work – not to take him away from it, so that he may do ecclesiastical work for you. But, if you have any power, see that he is set free to do this own work as well as it may be done. He is not there to serve you; he is there to serve God by serving his work.

This brings me to my third proposition; and this may sound to you the most revolutionary of all. It is this: the worker's first duty is to serve the work. The popular catchphrase of today is that it is everybody's duty to serve the community, but there *is* a catch in it. It is the old catch about the two great commandments. "Love God – and your neighbor: on those two commandments hang all the Law and the Prophets."[6]

---

6   Matthew 22:36–40: "Teacher, which commandment in the law is the greatest?" He said to him, "'You shall love the Lord your God with all your heart, and with all your soul, and with all your mind.' This is the greatest and first commandment. And a second is like it: 'You shall love your neighbor as yourself.' On these two commandments hang all the law and the prophets."

The catch in it, which nowadays the world has largely forgotten, is that the second commandment depends upon the first, and that without the first, it is a delusion and a snare. Much of our present trouble and disillusionment have come from putting the second commandment before the first.

If we put our neighbor first, we are putting man above God, and that is what we have been doing ever since we began to worship humanity and make man the measure of all things. Whenever man is made the center of things, he becomes the storm center of trouble – and that is precisely the catch about serving the community. It ought perhaps to make us suspicious of that phrase when we consider that it is the slogan of every commercial scoundrel and swindler who wants to make sharp business practice pass muster as social improvement.

"Service" is the motto of the advertiser, of big business, and of fraudulent finance. And of others, too. Listen to this: "I expect the judiciary to understand that the nation does not exist for their convenience, but that justice exists to serve the nation." That was Hitler yesterday – and that is what becomes of "service," when the community, and not the work, becomes its idol. There is, in fact, a paradox about working to serve the community, and it is this: that to aim directly at serving the community is to falsify the work; the only way to serve the community is to forget the community and serve the work. . . .

The only true way of serving the community is to be truly in sympathy with the community, to be oneself part of the community and then to serve the work without giving the community another thought. Then the work will endure, because it will be true to itself. It is the work that serves the community; the business of the worker is to serve the work.

Where we have become confused is in mixing up the *ends* to which our work is put with the way in which the work is done. The end of the work will be decided by our religious outlook: as we *are* so we *make*. It is the business of religion to make us Christian people, and then our work will naturally be turned to Christian ends, because our work is the expression of ourselves. But the way in which the work is done is governed by no sanction except the good of the work itself; and religion has no direct connection with that, except to insist that the workman should be free to do his work well according to its own integrity. . . . If work is to find its right place in the world, it is the duty of the Church to see to it that the work serves God, and that the worker serves the work.[7]

---

7 "Why Work?" an address delivered at Eastbourne, England, April 23, 1942, published in *Creed or Chaos?*, 1949.

14

Are Women Human?

Equality

In Gaudy Night, *Harriet Vane is investigating a mystery at one of the new women's colleges at Oxford. There she meets Miss Cattermole, a rebellious student about to be disciplined by the head of the college.*

Miss Cattermole was understood to say, rather incoherently, that she hated College and loathed Oxford, and felt no responsibility towards those institutions.

"Then why," said Harriet, "are you here?"

"I don't want to be here; I never did. Only my parents were so keen. My mother's one of those people who work to get things open to women – you know – professions and things. And father's a lecturer in a small provincial University. And they've made a lot of sacrifices and things."

Harriet thought Miss Cattermole was probably the sacrificial victim.

"I didn't mind coming up, so much," went on Miss Cattermole; "because I was engaged to somebody, and he was up, too, and I thought it would be fun and the silly old Schools wouldn't matter much. But I'm not engaged to him any more and how on earth can I be expected to bother about all this dead-and-gone History?"

"I wonder they bothered to send you to Oxford, if you didn't want to go, and were engaged."

"Oh! But they said that didn't make any difference. Every woman ought to have a University education, even if she married. And *now*, of course, they say what a good thing it is I still have my College career. And I can't make them understand that I *hate* it! They can't see that being brought up with everybody talking education all round one is enough to make one loathe the sound of it. I'm sick of education."

Harriet was not surprised.

"What should you have liked to do? I mean, supposing the complication about your engagement hadn't happened?"

"I think," said Miss Cattermole, blowing her nose in a final manner and taking another cigarette, "I think I should have liked to be a cook. Or possibly a hospital nurse, but I think I should have been better at cooking. Only, you see, those are two of the things Mother's always trying to get people out of the way of thinking women's sphere ought to be restricted to."

"There's a lot of money in good cooking," said Harriet.

"Yes – but it's not an educational advance. Besides, there's no school of Cookery at Oxford, and it had to be Oxford, you see, or Cambridge, because of the opportunity of making the right kind of friends. Only I haven't made any friends. They all hate me. . . ."

"I'll tell you what I'd do. I'd stop trying to do sensational things, because it's apt to get you into positions where you have to be grateful. And I'd stop chasing undergraduates, because it bores them to tears and interrupts their work. I'd tackle the

History and get through Schools. And then I'd turn around and say, 'Now I've done what you want me to, and I'm going to be a cook.' And stick to it."

"Would you?"

"I expect you want to be very truly run after, like Old Man Kangaroo. Well, good cooks are. Still, as you've started here on History, you'd better worry on at it. It won't hurt you, you know. If you learn how to tackle one subject – any subject – you've learnt how to tackle all subjects."

"Well," said Miss Cattermole, in rather an unconvinced tone, "I'll try."

Harriet went away in a rage and tackled the Dean.

"Why do they send these people here? Making themselves miserable and taking up the place of people who *would* enjoy Oxford? *We* haven't got room for women who aren't and never will be scholars. It's alright for the men's colleges to have hearty passmen who gambol round and learn to play games, so that they can gambol and game in Prep. Schools. But this dreary little devil isn't even hearty. She's a wet mess."[1]

From "Are Women Human?," an address given to a women's society in 1938:

When I was asked to come and speak to you, your Secretary made the suggestion that she thought I must be interested in the feminist movement. I replied – a little irritably, I am afraid – that I was not sure I wanted to "identify myself," as the phrase goes, with feminism, and that the time for "feminism," in the old-fashioned sense of the word, had gone past. In fact, I think I went so far as to say that, under present conditions, an aggressive

---

1   *Gaudy Night*, 1935, ch. 8.

feminism might do more harm than good. As a result I was, perhaps not unnaturally, invited to explain myself.

I do not know that it is very easy to explain, without offence or risk of misunderstanding, exactly what I do mean, but I will try.

The question of "sex-equality" is, like all questions affecting human relationships, delicate and complicated. It cannot be settled by loud slogans or hard-and-fast assertions like "a woman is as good as a man" – or "woman's place is the home" – or "women ought not to take men's jobs." The minute one makes such assertions, one finds one has to qualify them. "A woman is as good as a man" is as meaningless as to say, "a Kaffir is as good as a Frenchman" or "a poet is as good as an engineer" or "an elephant is as good as a racehorse" – it means nothing whatever until you add: "at doing what?" In a religious sense, no doubt, the Kaffir is as valuable in the eyes of God as a Frenchman – but the average Kaffir is probably less skilled in literary criticism than the average Frenchman, and the average Frenchman less skilled than the average Kaffir in tracing the spoor of big game. There might be exceptions on either side: it is largely a matter of heredity and education. When we balance the poet against the engineer, we are faced with a fundamental difference of temperament – so that here our question is complicated by the enormous social problem whether poetry or engineering is "better" for the State, or for humanity in general. There may be people who would like a world that was all engineers or all poets – but most of us would like to have a certain number of each; though here again, we should all differ about the desirable proportion of engineering to poetry. The only proviso we should make is that people with dreaming and poetical temperaments should not entangle themselves in engines, and that mechanically-minded persons should not issue booklets of bad verse. When we come to the elephant and the racehorse, we come down to bed-rock physical differences – the elephant would make a poor showing in the Derby, and the unbeaten Eclipse himself would be speedily eclipsed by an elephant when it came to hauling logs.

That is so obvious that it hardly seems worth saying. But it is the mark of all movements, however well-intentioned, that their pioneers tend, by much lashing of themselves into excitement, to lose sight of the obvious. In reaction against the age-old slogan, "woman is the weaker vessel," or the still more offensive, "woman is a divine creature," we have, I think, allowed ourselves to drift into asserting that "a woman is as good as a man," without always pausing to think what exactly we mean by that. What, I feel, we ought to mean is something so obvious that it is apt to escape attention altogether, viz: not that every woman is, in virtue of her sex, as strong, clever, artistic, level-headed, industrious and so forth as any man that can be mentioned; but, that a woman is just as much an ordinary human being as a man, with the same individual preferences, and with just as much right to the tastes and preferences of an individual. What is repugnant to every human being is to be reckoned always as a member of a class and not as an individual person. . . . What is unreasonable and irritating is to assume that *all* one's tastes and preferences have to be conditioned by the class to which one belongs. That has been the very common error into which men have frequently fallen about women – and it is the error into which feminist women are, perhaps, a little inclined to fall into about themselves.

Take, for example, the very usual reproach that women nowadays always want to "copy what men do." In that reproach there is a great deal of truth and a great deal of sheer, unmitigated and indeed quite wicked nonsense. There are a number of jobs and pleasures which men have in times past cornered for themselves. At one time, for instance, men had a monopoly of classical education. When the pioneers of university training for women demanded that women should be admitted to the universities, the cry went up at once: "Why should women want to know about Aristotle?" The answer is NOT that *all* women would be the better for knowing about Aristotle – still less, as Lord Tennyson seemed to think, that they would be more companionable wives for their husbands if they did know about Aristotle – but simply: "What women want as a class is irrelevant. *I* want to know about Aristotle. It is true that most women care nothing about him, and a great many male undergraduates turn pale and faint at the thought of him – but I, eccentric individual that I am, do want to know about Aristotle, and I submit that there is nothing in my shape or bodily functions which need prevent my knowing about him." . . .

Which brings us back to this question of what jobs, if any, are women's jobs. Few people would go so far as to say that all women are well fitted for all men's jobs. When people do say this, it is particularly exasperating. It is stupid to insist that there are as many female musicians and mathematicians as male – the facts are otherwise, and the most we can ask is that if a Dame Ethel Smyth or a Mary Somerville turns up, she shall be allowed to do her work without having aspersions cast either on her sex or her ability. What we ask is to be human individuals, however peculiar and unexpected. It is no good saying: "You are a little girl and therefore you ought to like dolls"; if the answer is, "But I don't," there is no more to be said. Few women happen to be natural born mechanics; but if there is one, it is useless to try and argue her into being something different. What we must *not* do is to argue that the occasional appearance of a female mechanical genius proves that all women would be mechanical geniuses if they were educated. They would not.

Where, I think, a great deal of confusion has arisen is in a failure to distinguish between special *knowledge* and special *ability*. There are certain questions on which what is called "the woman's point of view" is valuable, because they involve special *knowledge*. Women should be consulted about such things as housing and domestic architecture because, under present circumstances, they have still to wrestle a good deal with houses and kitchen sinks and can bring special knowledge to the problem. Similarly, some of them (though not all) know more about children than the majority of men, and their opinion, as *women*, is of value. In the same way, the opinion of colliers is of value about coal-mining, and the opinion of doctors is valuable about disease. But there are other questions – as for example, about literature or finance – on which the "woman's point of view" has no value at all. In fact, it does not exist. No special knowledge is involved, and a woman's opinion on literature or finance is valuable only as the judgment of an individual. I am occasionally desired by congenital imbeciles and the editors of magazines to say something about the writing of detective fiction "from the woman's point of view." To such demands, one can only say, "Go away and don't be silly. You might as well ask what is the female angle on an equilateral triangle." . . .

Indeed, it is my experience that both men and women are fundamentally human, and that there is very little mystery about either sex, except the exasperating mysteriousness of human beings in general. And though for certain purposes it may still be necessary, as it undoubtedly was in the immediate past, for women to band themselves together, as women, to secure recognition of their requirements as a sex, I am sure that the time has now come to insist more strongly on each woman's – and indeed each man's – requirements as an individual person. It used to be said that women had no *esprit de corps;* we have proved that we have – do not let us run into the opposite error of insisting that there is an aggressively feminist "point of view" about everything. To oppose one class perpetually to another – young against old, manual labour against brain-worker, rich against poor, woman against man – is to split the foundations of the State; and if the cleavage runs too deep, there remains no remedy but force and dictatorship. If you wish to preserve a free democracy, you must base it – not on classes and categories, for this will land you in the totalitarian State, where no one may act or think except as the member of a category. You must base it upon the individual Tom, Dick and Harry, on the individual Jack and Jill – in fact, upon you and me.[2]

Here is the ageless story of Mary and Martha as told in The Light and the Life, *the seventh play in* The Man Born to Be King.

MARTHA *(arriving in a flurry)*: That careless girl has broken the big yellow pitcher. And something has gone wrong with the scullery door. It won't shut properly. How much longer are Peter and James going to be? The meat will be dried to a cinder. Mary, I do wish you'd take a little interest in the housekeeping. There's too much work for one pair of hands, and that Abigail's no use at all. It's all very well for men to sit about talking all day, but a woman's place is in the kitchen. Rabbi, why do you encourage Mary to leave everything to me? Don't you think it's a little unfair? Do tell her to come and help me.

---

2   "Are Women Human?," an address given to a women's society in 1938, published in *Unpopular Opinions,* 1946.

JESUS: Martha dear, you are the kindest soul alive. You work so hard and you take so much trouble about everything – except, perhaps, the greatest thing of all, the thing that Mary cares about. She has chosen the better part, and you must not take it away from her.

MARTHA: Rabbi, I don't grudge Mary anything. But I still don't think it's quite fair. She was away from home long enough, goodness knows – and considering *everything,* I think the least she can do——

JESUS: Martha, can the cooking get on without you for just five minutes?

MARTHA *(grudgingly)*: Well, I daresay it *could*——

JESUS: Then stop worrying about it for one moment and think. Sit down. Do you remember a story I told you the first time I ever came to see you?

MARTHA: The day you brought Mary back to us? About the younger son who ran away abroad to see life, and he wasted all his money and had to keep pigs? And then he was sorry and came home and his father forgave him?

JESUS: Yes, that one. Did I tell you about his elder brother?

MARTHA: No, Rabbi. It ended with the father having a feast for the one who'd come home.

JESUS: Well, the elder brother was working in the fields all this time, and when he came back, he was surprised to hear music and dancing and a party going on. So he called one of the servants, and asked, "What's happening?" And the servant said: "Your brother's come home, sir, and your father has killed the fatted calf, because he's so glad to have him back safe and sound." But the elder brother was angry, and wouldn't go in, but sat sulking outside, till his father came out and begged him to join in the merry-making. "Look here, sir," said the young man, "I've worked for you all these years, and been a good son to you, and you've never let me have so much as a roast kid to entertain my friends. And here's this brother of mine, who's squandered your money in dissipation and bad company, and you go and kill the fatted calf for him. It isn't fair." And the father said: "Son, you are with me all the time and everything I have is yours. But it is right that we should rejoice and make merry to-day, for your brother is alive when we all thought he was dead: he was lost, and now we have found him."

MARTHA *(upset)*: Oh Rabbi! Have I really been behaving so unkindly?

MARY *(distressed)*: No, no, never! Rabbi, indeed she hasn't. She and Lazarus have been perfect angels to me.

MARTHA: I don't know. Perhaps I *have* resented things a little bit. Down underneath, not on top. Rather pleased with myself, you know, for acting more generously than I felt. Staying at home all day, one gets a bit narrow and exacting – a bit – Yes, Rabbi – I know what you're going to say: don't say it.

JESUS: Very well, then, I won't.

MARTHA: "Self-righteous" – I can see it in your face. . . . Mary, my lamb, don't take on so. He's quite right – and I'm sorry. There, there! Come along in now. We won't wait for the others. If their supper's spoilt it'll be their own fault for being late.[3]

---

3   Scene I, *The Light and the Life,* play seven of *The Man Born to Be King,* 1943.

From a magazine article:

God, of course, may have His own opinion, but the Church is reluctant to endorse it. I think I have never heard a sermon preached on the story of Martha and Mary that did not attempt, somehow, somewhere, to explain away its text. Mary's, of course, was the better part – the Lord said so, and we must not precisely contradict Him. But we will be careful not to despise Martha. No doubt, He approved of her too. We could not get on without her, and indeed (having paid lip-service to God's opinion) we must admit that we greatly prefer her. For Martha was doing a really feminine job, whereas Mary was just behaving like any other disciple, male or female; and that is a hard pill to swallow.

Perhaps it is no wonder that the women were first at the Cradle and last at the Cross. They had never known a man like this Man – there never has been such another. A prophet and teacher who never nagged at them, never flattered or coaxed or patronised; who never made arch jokes about them, never treated them either as "The women, God help us!" or "The ladies, God bless them!"; who rebuked without querulousness and praised without condescension; who took their questions and arguments seriously; who never mapped out their sphere for them, never urged them to be feminine or jeered at them for being female; who had no axe to grind and no uneasy male dignity to defend; who took them as he found them and was completely unself-conscious. There is no act, no sermon, no parable in the whole Gospel that borrows its pungency from female perversity; nobody could possibly guess from the words and deeds of Jesus that there was anything "funny" about woman's nature.

But we might easily deduce it from His contemporaries, and from His prophets before Him, and from His Church to this day. Women are not human; nobody shall persuade that they are human; let them say what they like, we will not believe it, though One rose from the dead.[4]

4   "The-Human-Not-Quite-Human," *Christendom: A Journal of Christian Sociology,* September 1941, republished in *Unpopular Opinions,* 1946.

15

Creed or Chaos?

Envy

In Gaudy Night, *Wimsey discovers that Annie, one of the maids at Somerville College, has a festering grudge against a scholar, Miss de Vine, who had previously exposed a deliberate falsification in an academic work by Annie's husband, thus causing the loss of his job. Alcoholism, and then suicide, followed. Annie blames the tragedy on the new role that women have in academia, women's colleges in general, and these educated women in particular.*

"Annie," said Dr. Baring, "are we to understand that you admit being responsible for all these abominable disturbances? I sent for you in order that you might clear yourself of certain suspicions which – "

"Clear myself! I wouldn't trouble to clear myself. You smug hypocrites – I'd like to see you bring me into court. I'd laugh in your faces. How would you look, sitting there while I told the judge how that woman there killed my husband?"

"I am exceedingly disturbed," said Miss de Vine, "to hear about all this. I knew nothing of it till just now. But indeed I had no choice in the matter. I could not foresee the consequences – and even if I had – "

"You wouldn't have cared. You killed him and you didn't care. I say you murdered him. What had he done to you? What harm had he done to anybody? He only wanted to live and be happy. You took the bread out of his mouth and flung his children and me out to starve. What did it matter to you? You had no children. You hadn't a man to care about. I know all about you. You had a man once and you threw him over because it was too much bother to look after him. But couldn't you leave my man alone? He told a lie about somebody else who was dead and dust hundreds of years ago. Nobody was the worse for that. Was a dirty bit of paper more important than all our lives and happiness? You broke him and killed him – all for nothing. Do you think that's a woman's job?"

"Most unhappily," said Miss de Vine, "it was my job."

"What business had you with a job like that? A woman's job is to look after a husband and children. I wish I had killed you. I wish I could kill you all. I wish I could burn down this place and all the places like it – where you teach women to take men's jobs and rob them first and kill them afterwards."

She turned to the Warden.

"Don't you know what you're doing? I've heard you sit round sniveling about unemployment – but it's you, it's women like you who take the work away from the men and break their hearts and lives. No wonder you can't get men for yourselves and hate the women who can. God keep the men out of your hands, that's what I say. You'd destroy your own husbands, if you had any, for an old book or bit of writing. . . . I loved my husband and you broke his heart. If he'd been a thief or a murderer, I'd have loved him and stuck to him. He didn't mean to steal that old bit of paper – he only put it away. It made no difference to anybody. It wouldn't have helped a single man or woman or child in the world – it wouldn't have kept a cat alive; but you killed him for it. . . .

"There's nothing in your books about life and marriage and children, is there? Nothing about desperate people – or love – or hate or anything human. You're ignorant and stupid and helpless. You're a lot of fools. You can't do anything for yourselves. Even you, you silly old hags – you had to get a man to do your work for you.

"You brought him here." She leaned over Harriet with her fierce eyes, as though she would have fallen on her and torn her to pieces. . . . "You don't know what love means. It means sticking to your man through thick and thin and putting up with everything. But you take men and use them and throw them away when you've finished with them. They come after you like wasps round a jam-jar, and then they fall in and die. What are you going to do with that one there? You send for him when you need him to do your dirty work, and when you've finished with him you'll get rid of him. You don't want to cook his meals and mend his clothes and bear his children like a decent woman. You'll use him, like any other tool, to break me. You'd like to see me in prison and my children in a home, because you haven't the guts to do your proper job in the world. The whole bunch of you together haven't flesh and blood enough to make you fit for a man. As for *you*—"

Peter had come back to his place and was sitting with his head in his hands. She went over and shook him furiously by the shoulder, and as he looked up, spat in his face. "You! You dirty traitor! You rotten little white-faced rat! It's men like you that make women like this. You don't know how to do anything but talk. What do you know about life, with your title and your money and your clothes and motor-cars? You've never done a hand's turn of honest work. You can buy all the women you want. Wives and mothers may rot and die for all you care, while you chatter about duty and honour. . . . What are you going to do now, all of you? Run away and squeal to the magistrate because I made fools of you all? You daren't. You're afraid to come out into the light. You're afraid for your precious college and your precious selves. *I'm* not afraid. I did nothing but stand up for my own flesh and blood. Damn you! I can laugh at you all! You daren't touch me. You're afraid of me. I had a husband and I loved him – and you were jealous of me and you killed him. Oh, God! You killed him among you, and we never had a happy moment again."[1]

From "The Other Six Deadly Sins":

Hand in hand with Covetousness goes its close companion – *Invidia* or Envy, which hates to see other men happy. The names by which it offers itself to the world's applause are *Right* and *Justice,* and it makes a great parade of these austere virtues. It begins by asking, plausibly: "Why should not I enjoy what others enjoy?" and it ends by demanding: "Why should others enjoy what I may not?" Envy is the great leveller: if it cannot level things up, it will level them down; and the words constantly in its mouth are: "My Rights" and "My Wrongs." At its best, Envy is a climber and a snob; at its worst, it is a destroyer – rather than have anybody happier than itself, it will see us all miserable together.

In love, Envy is cruel, jealous, and possessive. My friend and my married partner must be wholly wrapped up in me, and must find no interests outside me. That is my right. No person, no work, no hobby must rob me of any part of that right. If we

---

1   *Gaudy Night,* 1935, ch. 22.

cannot be happy together, we will be unhappy together – but there must be no escape into pleasures that I cannot share. If my husband's work means more to him than I do, I will see him ruined rather than preoccupied; if my wife is so abandoned as to enjoy Beethoven or dancing, or anything else which I do not appreciate, I will so nag and insult her that she will no longer be able to indulge these tastes with a mind at ease. If my neighbours are able to take pleasure in intellectual interests which are above my head, I will sneer at them and call them by derisive names, because they make me feel inferior, and that is a thing I cannot bear. All men have equal rights – and if these people were born with any sort of privilege, I will see to it that that privilege shall be made worthless – if I can, and by any means I can devise. Let justice be done to me, though the heavens fall and the earth be shot to pieces.

If Avarice is the sin of the Haves against the Have-nots, Envy is the sin of the Have-nots against the Haves. If we want to see what they look like on a big scale, we may say that Avarice has been the sin of the Anglo-Saxon democracies, and Envy the sin of Germany. Both are cruel – the one with a heavy, complacent, and bloodless cruelty; the other with a violent, calculated, and savage cruelty. But Germany only displays in accentuated form an evil of which we have plenty at home.

The difficulty about dealing with Envy is precisely that it *is* the sin of the Have-nots, and that, on that account, it can always find support among those who are just and generous-minded. Its demands for a place in the sun are highly plausible, and those who detect any egotism in the demand can readily be silenced by accusing them of oppression, inertia, and a readiness to grind the face of the poor. Let us look for a moment at some of the means by which Envy holds the world to ransom.

One of its achievements has been to change the former order by which society was based on status and substitute a new basis – that of contract. Status means, roughly speaking, that the relations of social units are ordered according to the intrinsic qualities which those units possess by nature. Men and institutions are valued for what they are. Contract means that they are valued, and their relations ordered, in virtue of what bargain they are able to strike. Knowledge, for example, and the man of knowledge, can be rated at a market value – prized, that is, not for the sake of knowledge, but for what is called their contribution to society. The family is esteemed, or not esteemed, according as it can show its value as an economic unit. Thus, all inequalities can, theoretically, be reduced to financial and utilitarian terms, and the very notion of intrinsic superiority can be denied and derided. In other words, all pretension to superiority can be debunked.

The years between the wars saw the most ruthless campaign of debunking ever undertaken by nominally civilized nations. Great artists were debunked by disclosures of their private weaknesses; great statesmen, by attributing to them mercenary and petty motives, or by alleging that all their work was meaningless, or done for them by other people. Religion was debunked, and shown to consist of a mixture of craven superstition and greed. Courage was debunked, patriotism was debunked, learning and art were debunked, love was debunked, and with it family affection and the virtues of obedience, veneration, and solidarity. Age was debunked by youth and youth by age. Psychologists stripped bare the pretensions of reason and self-control and conscience, saying that these were only the respectable disguises of unmentionable unconscious impulses. Honour was debunked with peculiar virulence, and good faith, and unselfishness. Everything that could possibly be held to constitute an essential superiority had the garments of honour torn from its back and was cast out into the darkness of derision. Civilization was finally debunked till it had not a rag left to cover its nakedness.

It is well that the hypocrisies which breed like mushrooms in the shadow of great virtues should be discovered and removed; but Envy is not the right instrument for that purpose; for it tears down the whole fabric to get at the parasitic growths. In fact, virtues themselves are the enemy of Envy. Envy cannot bear to admire or respect; it cannot bear to be grateful. But it is very plausible; it always announces that it works in the name of truth and equity.

Sometimes it may be a good thing to debunk Envy a little. For example: here is a phrase which we have heard a good deal of late: "These services (payments, compensations, or what not) ought not to be made a matter of charity. We have a right to demand that they should be borne by the State."

It sounds splendid; but what does it mean?

Now, you and I are the State; and where the bearing of financial burdens is concerned, the taxpayer is the State. The heaviest burden of taxation is, naturally, borne by those who can best afford to pay. When a new burden is imposed, the rich will have to pay most of it.

Of the money expended in charity, the greater part, for obvious reasons, is contributed by the rich. Consequently, if the burden hitherto borne by charity is transferred to the shoulders of the taxpayer, it will inevitably continue to be carried by exactly the same class of people. The only difference is this: that people will no longer pay because they want to eagerly and for love – but because they must, reluctantly and under pain of fine or imprisonment. The result, roughly speaking, is financially the same: the only difference is the elimination of the two detested virtues of love and gratitude.

I do not say for a moment that certain things should not be the responsibility of the State – that is, of everybody. No doubt those who formerly contributed out of love should be very willing to pay a tax instead. But what I see very clearly is the hatred of the gracious act, and the determination that nobody shall be allowed any kind of spontaneous pleasure in well-doing if Envy can prevent it. "This ointment might have been sold for much and given to the poor" [Matt. 26:9]. Then our nostrils would not be offended by any odour of sanctity – the house would not be "filled with the smell of the ointment." It is characteristic that it should have been Judas who debunked that act of charity.[2]

---

2   "The Other Six Deadly Sins," *Creed or Chaos?*, 1949.

16

Unpopular Opinions

Faith

Sayers addressed various aspects of war on the home front in a series of articles published weekly in the Spectator *between November 17, 1939, and January 26, 1940. Ostensibly the wartime letters and documents of the Wimsey family, they gave advice for navigating streets during blackouts and the proper attitudes to rationing, with Sayers posing as various characters in her books. In the following "extracts from the private diary of Lord Peter Wimsey, somewhere abroad" Lord Peter is writing just after the Soviet invasion of Finland on November 30, 1939.*

Friday

. . . Poor P——! he avoided me in the street today. At least I think so. Why else should he dive so hurriedly into the baby-linen shop by mistake for the café next door? It must have been an error of haste – even if some unfortunate indiscretion had brought baby-linen into his life, he would scarcely be making his purchases in person. He probably thought I was going to tackle him about

Russia. I wasn't. Does one button-hole a man in the street for a chat about his wife's elopement? *Le chef de gare il est cocu,*[1] poor devil, and that's all there is to be said about it. He's sincere, and the Helsinki business has been a severe shock to him. He isn't one of the whole-hoggers who are ready to accept an interregnum of fraud and violence as a necessary preliminary to the Kingdom of Man on earth. . . .

Still, oddly enough, my own immediate feeling is a queer sense of liberation. All these years, to express any doubts about the Russian experiment has laid one under the imputation of upholding capitalism, class-privilege, and so on, for the sake of one's own advantage. As though one had been shown God and had slammed the door in His face for fear of judgment. Difficult to explain that the fear was of another kind – or perhaps not fear, but an instinctive mistrust – something in the back of one's mind saying *"C'est louche."*[2] "A plague o' both your houses," one said, "Moscow and Berlin alike; the moment you get inside the door there's the same bad smell in the basement." Now the offence is rank, and stinks in P——'s nostrils. Lilies that fester smell far worse than weeds. But was Soviet doctrine ever anything but a weed at root, like the other?

The Catholic padre makes no bones about it. "Both started," he says, "by denying God, and no figs could grow from that thistle." But I have no such rational grounds for saying, "I told you so." For me to say, "I object as a Christian" would be rather like saying "I object as a native of Norfolk" – the one qualification bearing about as much relation to my conduct as the other, and being just about as geographical. I don't demand that my bootmaker should have Christian principles. I don't object to an

1   The stationmaster is cuckolded.

2   It's weird.

atheist barber – though, come to think of it, I suppose nothing *in theory* need prevent an atheist barber from cutting my throat if he feels like it. The law is framed on the assumption that my life is sacred; but upon my word I can see no sanction for that assumption at all, except on the hypothesis that I am an image of God – made, I should say, by a shockingly bad sculptor. And if I see no sanctity in myself, why should I see it in Finland? But I do. It seems altogether irrational. All the same, I still have the sense of liberation. "Fall into the hand of God, not into the hand of economic humanity."[3] One can say it now without feeling obliged to apologise for one's class prejudices. . . .

Saturday

. . . Like the gentleman in the carol, I have seen a wonder sight – the Catholic padre and the refugee Lutheran minister *having a drink together* and discussing, in very bad Latin, the persecution of the Orthodox Church in Russia. I have seldom heard so much religious toleration or so many false quantities. . . .

Tuesday

. . . My papers have arrived, so the balloon goes up tonight. When M—— handed them over, he said, "You have a wife and family, haven't you?" I said "Yes," and felt curiously self-conscious. The first time it has mattered a curse whether I went west or not. M—— looked at me as I used to look at my own married officers when they volunteered for a dirty bit of work, and it all seemed absurd and incongruous.

---

3   2 Samuel 24:14: "Then David said to Gad, 'I am in great distress; let us fall into the hand of the Lord, for his mercy is great; but let me not fall into human hands.'"

I shall not keep a diary *over there*. So, in case of accident, I will write my own epitaph now: HERE LIES AN ANACHRONISM IN THE VAGUE EXPECTATION OF ETERNITY.[4]

The following article, "What Do We Believe?," appeared in the Sunday Times *one week after Britain and France declared war on Germany.*

In ordinary times we get along surprisingly well, on the whole, without ever discovering what our faith really is. If, now and again, this remote and academic problem is so unmannerly as to thrust its way into our minds, there are plenty of things we can do to drive the intruder away. We can get the car out, or go to a party or the cinema, or read a detective story, or have a row with the district council, or write a letter to the papers about the habits of the night-jar or Shakespeare's use of nautical metaphor. Thus we build up a defence mechanism against self-questioning, because, to tell the truth, we are very much afraid of ourselves.

"When a strong man armed keepeth his palace his goods are in peace. But when a stronger than he shall come upon him . . . he taketh from him all his armour wherein he trusted" [Luke 11:21–22]. So to us in wartime, cut off from mental distractions by restrictions and blackouts, and cowering in a cellar with a gas-mask under threat of imminent death, comes in the stronger fear and sits down beside us.

"What," he demands, rather disagreeably, "do you make of all this? Is there indeed anything you value more than life, or are you making a virtue of necessity? What do you believe? Is your faith a comfort to you under the present circumstances?"

---

4   "The Wimsey Papers – IV," *The Spectator,* December 8, 1939.

At this point, before he has time to side-track the argument and entangle us in irrelevancies, we shall do well to reply boldly that a faith is not primarily a "comfort," but a truth about ourselves. What we in fact believe is not necessarily the theory we most desire or admire. It is the thing which, consciously or unconsciously, we take for granted and act on. Thus, it is useless to say that we "believe in" the friendly treatment of minorities if, in practice, we habitually bully the office-boy; our actions clearly show that we believe in nothing of the sort. Only when we know what we truly believe can we decide whether it is "comforting." If we are comforted by something we do not really believe, then we had better think again.

Now, there does exist an official statement of Christian belief, and if we examine it with a genuine determination to discover what the words mean, we shall find that it is a very strange one. And whether, as Christians declare, man was made in the image of God or, as the cynic said, man has made God in the image of man, the conclusion is the same – namely, that this strange creed purports to tell us the essential facts, not only about God, but about the true nature of man. And the first important thing it proclaims about that nature is one which we may not always admit in words, though I think we do act upon it more often than we suppose.

I believe in God the Father Almighty, Maker of all things. That is the thundering assertion with which we start: that the great fundamental quality that makes God, and us with Him, what we are is creative activity. After this, we can scarcely pretend that there is anything negative, static, or sedative about the Christian religion. "In the beginning God created"; from everlasting to everlasting, He is God the Father and Maker. And, by implication, man is most godlike and most himself when he is occupied in creation. And by this statement we assert further that the will and power to make is an absolute value, the ultimate good-in-itself, self-justified, and self-explanatory.

How far can we check this assertion as it concerns ourselves? The men who create with their minds and those who create (not merely labour) with their hands will, I think, agree that their periods of creative activity are those in which they feel right with themselves and the world. And those who bring life into the world will tell you the same thing. There is a psychological theory that artistic creation is merely a "compensation" for the frustration of sexual creativeness; but it is more probable that the making of life is only one manifestation of the universal urge to create. Our worst trouble to-day is our feeble hold on creation. To sit down and let ourselves be spoon-fed with the ready-made is to lose grip on our only true life and our only real selves.

And in the only-begotten Son of God, by whom all things were made. He was incarnate; crucified, dead and buried; and rose again. The second statement warns us what to expect when the creative energy is manifested in a world subject to the forces of destruction. It makes things and manifests Itself in time and matter, and can no other, because It is begotten of the creative will. So doing, It suffers through the opposition of other wills, as well as through the dead resistance of inertia. (There is no room here to discuss whether will is "really" free; if we did not, in fact, *believe* it to be free, we could neither act nor live.)

The creative will presses on to Its end, regardless of what It may suffer by the way. It does not choose suffering, but It will not avoid it, and must expect it. We say that It is Love, and "sacrifices" Itself for what It loves; and this is true, provided we understand what we mean by sacrifice. Sacrifice is what it looks like to other people, but to That-which-Loves I think it does not appear so. When one really cares, the self is forgotten, and the sacrifice becomes only a part of the activity. Ask yourself: If there is something you supremely want to do, do you count as "self-sacrifice" the difficulties encountered or the other possible activities cast aside? You do not. The time when you deliberately say, "I must sacrifice this, that, or the other" is when you do not *supremely* desire the end in view. At such times you are doing your duty, and that is admirable, but it is not love. But as soon as your duty becomes your love the "self-sacrifice" is taken for granted, and, whatever the world calls it, you call it so no longer.

Moreover, defeat cannot hold the creative will; it can pass through the grave and rise again. If It cannot go by the path of co-operation, It will go by the path of death and victory. But it does us no credit if we force It to go that way. It is our business to recognise It when It appears and lead It into the city with hosannas. If we betray It or do nothing to assist It, we may earn the unenviable distinction of going down to history with Judas and Pontius Pilate.

I believe in the Holy Ghost, the lord and life-giver. In this odd and difficult phrase the Christian affirms that the life in him proceeds from the eternal creativeness; and that therefore so far as he is moved by that creativeness, and so far only, he is truly alive. The word "ghost" is difficult to us; the alternative word "spirit" is in some ways more difficult still, for it carries with it still more complicated mental associations. The Greek word is *pneuma,* breath: "I believe in the breath of life."

And indeed, when we are asked, "What do you value more than life?" the answer can only be, "Life – the right kind of life, the creative and godlike life." And life, of any kind, can only be had if we are ready to lose life altogether – a plain observation of fact which we acknowledge every time a child is born, or, indeed, whenever we plunge into a stream of traffic in the hope of attaining a more desirable life on the other side.

And I believe in one Church and baptism, in the resurrection of the body and the life everlasting. The final clauses define what Christians believe about man and matter. First, that all those who believe in the creative life are members of one another and make up the present body in which that life is manifest. They accept for themselves everything that was affirmed of creative life incarnate, including the love and, if necessary, the crucifixion, death and victory. Looking at what happened to that Life, they will expect to be saved, not *from* danger and suffering, but *in* danger and suffering. And the resurrection of the body means more, I think, than we are accustomed to suppose. It means that, whatever happens, there can be no end to the manifestation of creative life. Whether the life makes its old body again, or an improved body, or a totally new body, it will and must create, since that is its true nature.

"This is the Christian faith, which except a man believe faithfully he cannot be saved."[5] The harsh and much-disputed statement begins to look like a blunt statement of fact; for how can anyone make anything of his life if he does not believe in life? If we truly desire a creative life for ourselves and other people, it is our task to rebuild the world along creative lines; but we must be sure that we desire it enough.[6]

---

5 This statement is from the Athanasian Creed, used by some Christian churches since the sixth century.

6 "What Do We Believe?," *The Sunday Times*, September 10, 1939, republished in *Unpopular Opinions*, 1946.

17

The Man Born to Be King

Incarnation

He That Should Come is a nativity play first broadcast by the BBC on Christmas Day 1938. In the introduction, Sayers outlines her overarching goal – articulating an underlying objective of many of her writings.

The whole effect and character of the play depend on its being played in an absolutely natural and realistic style. Any touch of the ecclesiastical intonation or of "religious unction" will destroy its intention. The whole idea in writing it was to show the miracle that was to change the whole course of human life enacted in a world casual, inattentive, contemptuous, absorbed in its own affairs and completely unaware of what was happening: to illustrate, in fact, the tremendous irony of history. It may be found advisable to make this point clear to the actors before they start, lest some preconceptions as to what is or is not "reverent" in a Nativity Play should hamper the freedom of their performance. I feel sure that it is in the interests of a true reverence towards the Incarnate Godhead to show that His Manhood was a real manhood, subject to the common realities of daily life; that the men and women surrounding Him were living human beings, not just characters in a story; that, in short, He was born, not into "the Bible," but into the world. That an audience will take the play in this spirit is proved to me by the various letters I received after the first broadcast. As one man in a country village put it, "It's nice to think that people in the Bible were folks like us." And another correspondent: "None of us realised before how much we had just *accepted* the story without properly visualising it. It . . . brought home to us as never before the *real* humanity of Jesus." There will always be a few voices raised to protest against the introduction of "reality" into religion; but I feel that the great obstacle in the path of Christianity today is that to so many it has become unreal, shadowy, "a tale that is told," so that it is of the utmost importance to remind people by every means in our power that the thing actually happened – that it is, and was from the beginning, closely in contact with real life.[1]

When Sayers wrote The Man Born To Be King, *she worked from early Greek and Hebrew manuscripts and eschewed the familiar language of the King James Version of the Bible. Speaking contemporary English, her characters truly are "closely in contact with real life." This caused an outcry from conservative Christian groups, giving the broadcasts an added boost of publicity. The plays were aired at four week intervals starting on December 21, 1941. An excerpt from the first of the series illustrates why they were met with both admiration and dismay:*

SHEPHERD'S WIFE: Zillah, Zillah! Have you laid the table?

ZILLAH: Yes, Mother.

---

1   Introduction to *He That Should Come*, 1938, published in *Four Sacred Plays*, 1948.

WIFE: Then run and tell Father Joseph supper's ready. You'll find him out at the back. And have a look up the road to see if your Dad's coming.

ZILLAH: Yes, Mother. *(She runs out, calling)* Father Joseph, Father Joseph!

WIFE: Now, Mother Mary, let me take the Baby and lay him in the cradle while you have your bit of supper. Come along, lovey, aren't you a beautiful boy, then? There! Now you go off to sleep like a good boy. But he's always wonderful good, ain't he? Never cries hardly at all. Happiest baby as ever I see.

MARY: He is happy in your kind home. But when he was born, he wept.

WIFE: Ah! they all do that, and can you blame them, poor little things, seeing what a cruel hard world it is they come into? Never mind. We all has our ups and downs. Here's your good man. Come along, Father Joseph. Here's a nice dish of broiled meat for you. I'm sure you need it, working so late, too. I wonder you could see what you were doing.

JOSEPH: It's a grand night. That great white star do shine well – nigh as bright as the moon – right over the house, seemingly. I've mended the fence.

WIFE: Isn't it a real bit of luck for us, you being such a fine carpenter? And so kind, doing all these jobs about the place.

JOSEPH: Well, that's the least I can do, when you've been so generous and shared your home with us.

WIFE: Well, that was the least *we* could do. We couldn't leave you in that old stable over in the inn. We'd never a-slept easy in our beds, knowing there was a mother and baby without no proper roof to their heads – especially after what Dad told us about seein' them there angels, and the little boy bein' the blessed Messiah and all. . . . There, Mother Mary, you take and eat that. It'll do you good. . . . D'you think it's really true? About him bein' the promised Saviour as is to bring back the Kingdom to Israel?

MARY: I know it is true.

WIFE: How proud you must feel. Don't it seem strange, now, when you look at him and think about it?

MARY: Sometimes – very strange. I feel as though I were holding the whole world in my arms – the sky and the sea and the green earth, and all the seraphim. And then, again, every-thing becomes quite simple and familiar, and I know that he is just my own dear son. If he grew up to be wiser than Moses, holier than Aaron, or more splendid than Solomon, that would still be true. He will always be my baby, my sweet Jesus, whom I love – nothing can ever change that.

WIFE: No more it can't; and the queen on her throne can't say no different. When all's said and done, children are a great blessing. What's gone with Zillah, I wonder? I hope she ain't run off too far. There might be wolves about. Hark!

ZILLAH (*running in from outside*): Oh, Mother! Mother!

WIFE: What's up now?

JOSEPH: Hallo, my lass! What's the matter?

ZILLAH: They're coming here! They're coming here! Dad's bringing them!

WIFE: Who're coming, for goodness' sake?

ZILLAH: Kings – three great kings! riding horseback! They're coming to see the Baby.

WIFE: Kings? Don't talk so soft! Kings, indeed!

ZILLAH: But they *are*. They've got crowns on their heads and rings on their fingers, and servants carrying torches. And they asked Dad, is this where the Baby is? And he said, Yes, and I was to run ahead and say they were coming.

JOSEPH: She's quite right. I can see them from the window. Just turning the corner by the palm-trees.

WIFE: Bless me! and supper not cleared away and everything upside down. Here, Mother, let me take your plate. That's better. Zillah, look in the dresser drawer and find a clean bib for Baby Jesus.

ZILLAH: Here you are, Mum. . . . One of the kings is a very old gentleman with a long beard and a beautiful scarlet cloak, and the second's all in glittering armour – ooh! and the third's a black man with big gold rings in his ears and the jewels in his turban twinkling like the stars – and his horse is as white as milk, with silver bells on the bridle.

WIFE: Fancy! and all to do honour to our Baby.

JOSEPH: Take heart, Mary. It's all coming true as the Prophet said: The nations shall come to thy light, and kings to the brightness of thy rising.

MARY: Give me my son into my arms.

WIFE: To be sure. He'll set on your knee so brave as a king on his golden throne. Look at him now, the precious lamb. . . . Mercy me, here they are.

CASPAR (at door): Is this the house?

SHEPHERD (at door): Ay, sirs, this is the house. Pray go in, and ye'll find the Child Jesus wi' his mother.

WIFE: Come in, my lords, come in. Please mind your heads. I fear 'tis but a poor, lowly place.

CASPAR: No place is too lowly to kneel in. There is more holiness here than in King Herod's Temple.

MELCHIOR: More beauty here than in King Herod's palace.

BALTHAZAR: More charity here than in King Herod's heart.

CASPAR: O lady clear as the sun, fair as the moon, the nations of the earth salute your son, the Man born to be King. Hail, Jesus, King of the Jews!

MELCHIOR: Hail, Jesus, King of the World!

BALTHAZAR: Hail, Jesus, King of Heaven!

CASPAR, MELCHIOR, BALTHAZAR: All hail!

MARY: God bless you, wise old man; and you, tall warrior; and you, dark traveller from desert lands. You come in a strange way, and with a strange message. But that God sent you I am sure, for you and His angels speak with one voice. "King of the Jews" – why, yes; they told me my son should be the Messiah of Israel. "King of the World" – that is a very great title; yet when he was born, they proclaimed tidings of joy to all nations. "King of Heaven" – I don't quite understand that; and yet indeed they said that he should be called the Son of God. You are great and learned men, and I am a very simple woman. What can I say to you, till the time comes when my son can answer for himself?

CASPAR: Alas! the more we know, the less we understand life. Doubts make us afraid to act, and much learning dries the heart. And the riddle that torments the world is this: Shall Wisdom and Love live together at last, when the promised Kingdom comes?

MELCHIOR: We are rulers, and we see that what men need most is good government, with freedom and order. But order puts fetters on freedom, and freedom rebels against order, so that love and power are always at war together. And the riddle that torments the world is this: Shall Power and Love dwell together at last, when the promised Kingdom comes?

BALTHAZAR: I speak for a sorrowful people – for the ignorant and the poor. We rise up to labour and lie down to sleep, and night is only a pause between one burden and another. Fear is our daily companion – the fear of want, the fear of war, the fear of cruel death, and of still more cruel life. But all this we could bear if we knew that we did not suffer in vain; that God was beside us in the struggle, sharing the miseries of His own world. For the riddle that torments the world is this: Shall Sorrow and Love be reconciled at last, when the promised Kingdom comes?

MARY: These are very difficult but with me, you see, it is like this. When the Angel's message came to me, the Lord put a song into my heart. I suddenly saw that wealth and cleverness were nothing to God – no one is too unimportant to be His friend. That was the thought that came to me, because of the thing that happened to *me*. I am quite humbly born, yet the Power of God came upon me; very foolish and unlearned, yet the Word of God was spoken to me; and I was in deep distress, when my Baby was born and filled my life with love. So I know very well that Wisdom and Power and Sorrow *can* live together with Love; and for me, the Child in my arms is the answer to all the riddles.

CASPAR: You have spoken a wise word, Mary. Blessed are you among women, and blessed is Jesus your son. Caspar, King of Chaldaea, salutes the King of the Jews with a gift of frankincense.

MELCHIOR: O Mary, you have spoken a word of power. Blessed are you among women, and blessed is Jesus your son. Melchior, King of Pamphylia, salutes the King of the World with a gift of gold.

BALTHAZAR: You have spoken a loving word, Mary, Mother of God. Blessed are you among women, and blessed is Jesus your son. Balthazar, King of Ethiopia, salutes the King of Heaven with a gift of myrrh and spices.

ZILLAH: Oh, look at the great gold crown! Look at the censer all shining with rubies and diamonds, and the blue smoke curling up. How sweet it smells – and the myrrh and aloes, the sweet cloves and the cinnamon. Isn't it lovely? And all for our little Jesus! Let's see which of his presents he likes best. Come, Baby, smile at the pretty crown.

WIFE: Oh, what a solemn, old-fashioned look he gives it.

ZILLAH: He's laughing at the censer –

WIFE: He likes the tinkling of the silver chains.

JOSEPH: He has stretched out his little hand and grasped the bundle of myrrh.

WIFE: Well, there now! You never can tell what they'll take a fancy to.

MARY: Do they not embalm the dead with myrrh? See, now, you sorrowful king, my son has taken your sorrows for his own.

JOSEPH: Myrrh is for love also; as Solomon writes in his Song: A bundle of myrrh is my beloved unto me.

MARY: My lords, we are very grateful to you for all your gifts. And as for the words you have said, be sure that I shall keep all these things and ponder them in my heart.[2]

From "Creed or Chaos?":

At the risk of appearing quite insolently obvious, I shall say that if the Church is to make any impression on the modern mind she will have to preach Christ and the cross.

Of late years, the Church has not succeeded very well in preaching Christ: she has preached Jesus, which is not quite the same thing. I find that the ordinary man simply does not grasp at all the idea that Jesus Christ and God the Creator are held to be literally the same Person. They believe Catholic doctrine to be that God the Father made the world and that Jesus Christ redeemed mankind, and that these two characters are quite separate personalities. The phrasing of the Nicene Creed is here a little unfortunate – it is easy to read it as: "being of one substance with the Father-by-whom-all-things-were made." The Church Catechism – again rather unfortunately – emphasises the distinction: "God the Father who hath made me and all the world, God the Son who hath redeemed me and all mankind." The distinction of the Persons within the unity of the Substance is philosophically quite proper, and familiar enough to any creative artist: but the majority of people are not creative artists, and they have it very firmly fixed in their heads that the Person who bore the sins of the world was not the eternal creative

2   Scene 2, "Kings in Judea," *The Man Born to Be King,* 1943.

life of the world, but an entirely different person, who was in fact the victim of God the Creator. It is dangerous to emphasise one aspect of a doctrine at the expense of the other, but at this present moment the danger that anybody will confound the Persons is so remote as to be negligible. What everybody does is to divide the substance – with the result that the whole Jesus history becomes an unmeaning anecdote of the brutality of God to man.

It is only with the confident assertion of the creative divinity of the Son that the doctrine of the Incarnation becomes a real revelation of the structure of the world. And here Christianity has its enormous advantage over every other religion in the world. It is the only religion which gives value to evil and suffering. It affirms – not, like Christian Science, that evil has no real existence, nor yet, like Buddhism, that good consists in a refusal to experience evil – but that perfection is attained through the active and positive effort to wrench a real good out of a real evil.

I will not now go into the very difficult question of the nature of evil and the reality of not-being, though the modern physicists seem to be giving us a very valuable lead about that particular philosophic dilemma. But it seems to me most important that, in face of present world conditions, the doctrines of the reality of evil and the value of suffering should be kept in the very front line of Christian affirmation. I mean, it is not enough to say that religion produces virtues and personal consolations side by side with the very obvious evils and pains that afflict mankind, but that God is alive and at work within the evil and the suffering, perpetually transforming them by the positive energy which He had with the Father before the world was made. . . .

At this point we shall find ourselves compelled to lay down the Christian doctrine concerning the material universe; and it is here, I think, that we shall have our best opportunity to explain the meaning of sacramentalism. The common man labours under a delusion that for the Christian, matter is evil and the body is evil. For this misapprehension, St. Paul must bear some blame, St. Augustine of Hippo a good deal more, and Calvin a very great deal. But so long as the Church continues to teach the manhood of God and to celebrate the sacraments of the Eucharist and of marriage, no living man should dare to say that matter and body are not sacred to her. She must insist strongly that the whole material universe is an expression and incarnation of the creative energy of God, as a book or a picture is the material expression of the creative soul of the artist. For that reason, all good and creative handling of the material universe is holy and beautiful, and all abuse of the material universe is a crucifixion of the body of Christ. The whole question of the right use to be made of art, of the intellect and of the material resources of the world is bound up in this. Because of this, the exploitation of man or of matter for commercial uses stands condemned, together with all debasement of the arts and perversions of the intellect. If matter and the physical nature of man are evil, or if they are of no importance except as they serve an economic system, then there is nothing to restrain us from abusing them as we choose – nothing, except the absolute certainty that any such abuse will eventually come up against the unalterable law, and issue in judgment and destruction. In these as in all other matters we cannot escape the law; we have only the choice of fulfilling it freely by the way of grace or willy-nilly by the way of judgment.[3]

---

3   "Creed or Chaos?," *Creed or Chaos?,* 1949.

18

King of Sorrows

The Cross

In the crucifixion scene from The Man Born to Be King, *Sayers brings the gospel into the real world with a brutality that might shock even those who know the story well.*

(CALVARY HILL)

THE EVANGELIST: And when they were come to the place which is called Calvary, there they crucified him, and the robbers, one on the right hand and the other on the left.

1ST SOLDIER: Whew! . . . well, that's two of 'em.

2ND SOLDIER: That Gestas is a sturdy rogue. We had to break his fingers to make him open his fists.

3RD SOLDIER: Yes – he put up a stiff fight. You'll have a black eye, Corvus.

(Laughter)

1ST SOLDIER *(vindictively)*: He'll ache for it. We strung him out tight as a bowstring.

2ND SOLDIER: Come on, come on, let's have the next ... got him stripped?

3RD SOLDIER: Yes. Here you are.

4TH SOLDIER: This one won't give trouble.

3RD SOLDIER: Dunno about that. He wouldn't drink the myrrh and vinegar.

1ST SOLDIER: Why not?

3RD SOLDIER: Said he wanted to keep his head clear.

1ST SOLDIER: If he thinks he can make a get-away –

4TH SOLDIER: Ah! He's only crazy. *(persuasively)* Here, my lad – don't be so obstinate. Drink it. It'll deaden you like. You won't feel so much. . . . No? . . . Well, if you won't you won't. . . . You're a queer one, ain't you? . . . Come on, then, get down to it.

1ST SOLDIER *(whose temper has been soured by the black eye)*: Kick his feet from under him.

2ND SOLDIER: No need. He's down. . . . Take the feet, Corvus.

1ST SOLDIER: Stretch your legs. I'll give you king of the Jews.

2ND SOLDIER: Hand me the mallet.

JESUS: Father, forgive them. They don't know what they are doing. *(His voice breaks off in a sharp gasp as the mallet falls. Fade out on the dull thud of the hammering.)* . . .

(AT THE FOOT OF THE CROSS)

VOICES: Who was going to destroy the Temple and build it in three days? . . . Looks as though the Temple 'ud see you out! . . . Come to that, why don't you destroy the cross? . . . Split the wood, melt the iron . . . that's nothing to a fellow who can over-throw the Temple. . . . Go to it, miracle-man! . . . Show us your power, Jesus of Nazareth. . . .

MARY MAGDALEN: Is it nothing to you, all you that pass by? What has he done to you that you should treat him like this?

VOICES: He said he was the Messiah. . . . King of Israel. . . . Son of David . . . greater than Solomon. . . . Does Israel get her kings from the carpenter's shop? . . . or out of the common gaol? . . . Will you reign from the gibbet, King of the Jews?

MARY MAGDALEN: He would have made you citizens of the Kingdom of God – and you have given him a crown of thorns.

VOICES: Where are all his mighty works now? . . . He saved others, but he can't save himself. . . . Come on, charlatan, heal your own wounds. . . . If you are the Son of God, come down from the cross.

MARY MAGDALEN: He gave power to your hands and strength to your feet – and you have nailed his hands and feet to the cross.

VOICES: Are you hungry, are you thirsty, Jesus of Nazareth? . . . Where's the water you talked about? . . . Where is the never-failing bread? . . . Nothing up your sleeve now, conjurer! *(Laughter)* Loaves and fishes! Loaves and fishes!

MARY MAGDALEN: He fed you with the bread of heaven and the water of life freely – and you have given him vinegar to drink.

VOICES: Charlatan! . . . Sorcerer! . . . Deceiver! . . . Boaster! . . .

MARY MAGDALEN: John – can't we get closer? It will be some comfort to him to have us near.

JOHN: I don't know if the soldiers will let us through. But we can ask them.

(Crowd background)

CENTURION: Pass along, there! Pass along, please! . . . Now then, my lad, stand back – you can't come any closer.

JOHN: Pray, good Centurion, let us pass. We are friends of Jesus of Nazareth.

CENTURION: Then you'd best steer clear of trouble. Take those women away. It's no place for them.

MARY VIRGIN: Sir, I am his mother. I implore you, let me go to him.

CENTURION: Sorry, ma'am. Can't be done. . . . . Corvus! Keep those people moving! . . . Now just you go home quietly.

MARY MAGDALEN: Marcellus – do you know me?

CENTURION: No, my girl. Never saw you in my life.

MARY MAGDALEN: Has grief so changed my face? . . . Quick, you Maries, pull off my veil, unpin my hair! . . . Look again, Marcellus! Is there another woman in Jerusalem with red hair like mine?

CENTURION: Mary of Magdala!

SOLDIERS: Mary! . . . Mary of Magdala! . . . Where have you been all this time, Magdalen?

MARY MAGDALEN: By the feet that danced for you, by the voice that sang for you, by the beauty that delighted you – Marcellus, let me pass!

MARCELLUS: Beauty? That's for living men. What is this dying gallows bird to you?

MARY MAGDALEN: He is my life, and you have killed him. . . . (*The soldiers laugh*)

Think what you like – laugh if you will – but for old sake's sake, let Mary of Magdala pass.

1ST SOLDIER: Oh, no, you don't, my lass!

2ND SOLDIER: Not without paying.

3RD SOLDIER: Sing us one of the old songs, Mary!

SOLDIERS: That's right! . . . Give us a tune. . . . Sing, girl, sing! . . . Make us laugh, make us cry, Mary Magdalen!

MARY MAGDALEN (*distracted*): My songs? . . . I have forgotten them all. . . . Wait. . . . Wait. . . . I will try. . . . What will you have, lads? "Roses of Sharon"? "Dinah Dear"? "Home Again"?

SOLDIERS (*applauding*): "Home Again"! "Home Again"! . . . S'sh!

(*As Mary sings, soldiers and crowd listen quietly.*)

MARY MAGDALEN (*sings*):

> Soldier, soldier, why will you roam?
> The flowers grow white in the hills at home,
> Where the little brown brook runs down to the sea –
> Come again, home again, love, to me.

(*Here the soldiers join in the chorus.*)

> Pick up your feet for the last long leagues,
> No more pack-drill, no more fatigues,
> No more roll-call, no more bugle-call,
> Company halt! And stand at ease.

Sunlight, starlight, twilight and dawn,
The door unbarred, and the latch undrawn
Waiting for the lad that I –

(She breaks down)

I can't go on.

CENTURION: All right, Mary. . . . Let her through, lads . . . and
the mother and the friend. . . . That'll do. . . . No more. . . . Keep
back, there. . . . Move along, now, move along. . . . Yes, Publius?

4TH SOLDIER: The prisoners' clothes, Centurion.

CENTURION: Oh, yes. They're your perquisite. Take 'em and
share 'em out evenly.[1]

From the introduction to the play:

For Jesus Christ is unique – unique among gods and men. There
have been incarnate gods a-plenty, and slain-and-resurrected
gods not a few; but He is the only God who has a date in history.
And plenty of founders of religions have had dates, and some
of them have been prophets or avatars of the Divine; but only
this one of them was personally God. There is no more astonishing collocation of phrases than that which, in the Nicene
Creed, sets these two statements flatly side by side: "Very God
of very God. . . . He suffered under Pontius Pilate." All over the
world, thousands of times a day, Christians recite the name of
a rather undistinguished Roman pro-consul – not in execration
(Judas and Caiaphas, more guilty, get off with fewer reminders
of their iniquities), but merely because that name fixes within a
few years the date of the death of God.

---

1   Scene II, "King of Sorrows," *The Man Born to Be King*, 1943.

In the light of that remarkable piece of chronology we can see an additional reason why the writer of realistic Gospel plays has to eschew the didactic approach to his subject. He has to display the words and actions of actual people engaged in living through a piece of recorded history. He cannot, like the writer of purely liturgical or symbolic religious drama, confine himself to the abstract and universal aspect of the life of Christ. He is brought up face to face with the "scandal of particularity." *Ecce homo* – not only Man-in-general and God-in-His-thusness, but also God-in-His-thisness, and *this* Man, *this* person, of a reasonable soul and human flesh subsisting, who walked and talked *then* and *there*, surrounded, not by human types, but by *those* individual people. This story of the life and murder and resurrection of God-in-Man is not only the symbol and epitome of the relations of God and man throughout time; it is also a series of events that took place at a particular point *in time. And the people of that time had not the faintest idea that it was happening.*

Of all examples of the classical tragic irony in fact or fiction, this is the greatest – the classic of classics. Beside it, the doom of Oedipus is trifling, and the nemesis of the Oresteian blood-bath a mere domestic incident. For the Christian affirmation is that a number of quite commonplace human beings, in an obscure province of the Roman Empire, killed and murdered God Almighty – quite casually, almost as a matter of religious and political routine, and certainly with no notion that they were doing anything out of the way. Their motives, on the whole, were defensible, and in some respects praiseworthy. There was some malice, some weakness, and no doubt some wresting of the law – but no more than we are accustomed to find in the conduct of human affairs. By no jugglings of fate, by no unforeseeable coincidence, by no supernatural machinations, but by that destiny which is character, and by the unimaginative following of their ordinary standards of behaviour, they were led, with a ghastly inevitability, to the commission of the crime of crimes. We, the audience, know what they were doing; the whole point and poignancy of the tragedy is lost unless we realise that they did not. It is in this knowledge by the audience of the appalling truth which is hidden from all the agonists in the drama that the tragic irony consists.

Consequently, it is necessary for the playwright to work with a divided mind. He must be able at will to strip off his knowledge of what is actually taking place, and present, through his characters, the events and people as they appeared to themselves at the time. This would seem obvious and elementary; but its results are in fact the very thing that gives offence to unimaginative piety. We are so much accustomed to viewing the whole story from a post-Resurrection, and indeed from a post-Nicene, point of view, that we are apt, without realising it, to attribute to all the New Testament characters the same kind of detailed theological awareness which we have ourselves. We judge their behaviour as though all of them – disciples, Pharisees, Romans, and men-in-the-street – had known with Whom they were dealing and what the meaning of all the events actually was. But they did not know it. The disciples had only the foggiest inkling of it, and nobody else came anywhere near grasping what it was all about. If the Chief Priests and the Roman Governor had been aware that they were engaged in crucifying God – if Herod the Great had ordered his famous massacre with the express intention of doing away with God – then they would have been quite exceptionally and diabolically wicked people. And indeed, we like to think that they were: it gives us a reassuring sensation that "it can't happen here." And to this comfortable persuasion we are assisted by the stately and ancient language of the Authorised Version, and by the general air of stained-glass-window decorum with which the tale is usually presented to us. The characters are not men and women: they are all "sacred personages," standing about in symbolic attitudes, and self-consciously awaiting the fulfilment of prophecies. That is how they were seen, for example, by a certain gentleman from Stoke Newington, who complained that the Centurion who was commended for building a Jewish synagogue had been made by me to "refer to the sacred building in a conversation, in a levitous (*sic*) and jocular manner." For him, the Centurion was not a Roman N.C.O., stationed in a foreign province, and looking on the local worship with such amiable indulgence as a British sergeant-major in India might extend to a Hindu cult. He was a sacred Centurion, whose lightest word was sacred, and the little Jewish edifice was sacred *to him,* as though he had no gods of his own. Still odder is the attitude of another correspondent, who objected to Herod's telling his court, "keep your mouths shut," on the grounds that such coarse expressions were jarring on the lips of any one "so closely connected with our Lord."

Sacred personages, living in a far-off land and time, using dignified rhythms of speech, making from time to time restrained gestures symbolic of brutality. They mocked and railed on Him and smote Him, they scourged and crucified Him. Well, they were people very remote from ourselves, and no doubt it was all done in the noblest and most beautiful manner. We should not like to think otherwise.

Unhappily, if we think about it at all, we must think otherwise. God was executed by people painfully like us, in a society very similar to our own – in the over-ripeness of the most splendid and sophisticated Empire the world has ever seen. In a nation famous for its religious genius and under a government renowned for its efficiency, He was executed by a corrupt church, a timid politician, and a fickle proletariat led by professional agitators. His executioners made vulgar jokes about Him, called Him filthy names, taunted Him, smacked Him in the face, flogged Him with the cat, and hanged Him on the common gibbet – a bloody, dusty, sweaty, and sordid business.

If you show people that, they are shocked. So they should be. If that does not shock them, nothing can. If the mere representation of it has an air of irreverence, what is to be said about the deed? It is curious that people who are filled with horrified indignation whenever a cat kills a sparrow can hear that story of the killing of God told Sunday after Sunday and not experience any shock at all.[2]

The Central Religious Advisory Committee vetted each play for the BBC. One of the members, the Bishop of Winchester, objected to the informality of Sayers's dialog. She entreated the director of religious broadcasting to negotiate with him:

I am frankly appalled at the idea of getting through the Trial and Crucifixion scenes with all the "bad people" having to be bottled down to expressions which could not possibly offend anybody. I will not allow the Roman soldiers to use barrack-room oaths, but they must behave like common soldiers hanging a common criminal, or where is the point of the story? The impenitent thief cannot curse and yell as you and I would if we were skewered up with nails to a post in the broiling sun, but he must not talk like a Sunday-school child. Nobody cares a dump nowadays that Christ was "scourged, railed upon, buffeted, mocked

2   Introduction to *The Man Born to be King*, 1943.

and crucified," because all those words have grown hypnotic with ecclesiastical use. But it does give people a slight shock to be shown that God was flogged, spat upon, called dirty names, slugged in the jaw, insulted with vulgar jokes, and spiked up on the gallows like an owl on a barn-door. That's the thing the priests and people did – has the Bishop forgotten it? It is an ugly, tear-stained, sweat-stained, blood-stained story, and the thing was done by callous, conceited and cruel people. Shocked? We damn well ought to be shocked. If nobody is going to be shocked we might as well not tell them about it.

It's very bad luck on you, and I *don't* want to make trouble. But I do want the Bishop to know what I feel about it – not from the "artistic" point of view, but from the point of view of *what we are trying to tell people*. The scandal of the Cross was a scandal – not a solemn bit of ritual symbolic of scandal. "The drunkards make songs upon me" – I daresay they did, and I don't suppose they were very pretty songs either, or in very good taste. I've made all the alterations required so far, but I'm now entering a formal protest, which I have tried to make a mild one, without threatenings and slaughters. But if the contemporary world is not much moved by the execution of God it is partly because pious phrases and reverent language have made it appear a more dignified crime than it was. It was a dirty piece of work, tell the Bishop.

Sympathetically yours,

Dorothy L. Sayers [3]

---

3   Sayers to Dr. James Welch, Director of Religious Broadcasting, BBC, February 19, 1942, *Letters*, 2:351–352.

19

The Just Vengeance
Images and Symbols

The Just Vengeance *was commissioned for Lichfield Cathedral's 750th anniversary festival. Sayers wrote it in the form of a miracle-play, meant to be performed in the church building. The entire play takes place in the moment of the death of an airman shot down during World War II, which had ended only the year before the play's presentation. As Sayers wrote in the introduction, the play is about "Man's insufficiency and God's redemptive act, set against the background of contemporary crisis." Here, the airman is listening as the Christ figure proclaims the glory of the incarnation, which will lead to the cross and atonement:*

PERSONA DEI: I the image of the Unimaginable
In the place where the Image and the Unimaged are one,
The Act of the Will, the Word of the Thought, the Son
In whom the Father's selfhood is known to Himself,
I being God and with God from the beginning
Speak to Man in the place of the Images.
You that We made for Ourself in Our own image,
Free like Us to experience good by choice,
Not of necessity, laying your will in Ours

For love's sake creaturely, to enjoy your peace,
What did you do? What did you do for Us
By what you did for yourselves in the moment of choice?
O Eve My daughter, and O My dear son Adam,
Whose flesh was fashioned to be My tabernacle,
Try to understand that when you chose your will
Rather than Mine, and when you chose to know evil
In your way and not in Mine, you chose for Me.
It is My will you should know Me as I am –
But how? For you chose to know your good as evil,
Therefore the face of God is evil to you,
And you know My love as terror, My mercy as judgment,
My innocence as a sword; My naked life
Would slay you. How can you ever know Me then?
Yet know you must, since you were made for that;
Thus either way you perish. Nay, but the hands
That made you, hold you still; and since you would not
Submit to God, God shall submit to you,
Not of necessity, but free to choose
For your love's sake what you refused to Mine.
God shall be man; that which man chose for man
God shall endure, and what man chose to know
God shall know too – the experience of evil
In the flesh of man; and certainly He shall feel
Terror and judgment and the point of the sword;
And God shall see God's face set like a flint
Against Him; and man shall see the Image of God
In the image of man; and man shall show no mercy.
Truly I will bear your sin and carry your sorrow,
And, if you will, bring you to the tree of life,
Where you may eat, and know your evil as good,
Redeeming that first knowledge. But all this

Still at your choice, and only as you choose,
Save as you choose to let Me choose in you.
Who then will choose to be the chosen of God,
And will to bear Me that I may bear you?

EVE: O my dear Lord, in me the promise stood –
Worst, weakest, yet in me. What must I do?

PERSONA: Woman, that bore the blame from the beginning,
Now in the end bring forth the remedy;
Go, call your daughter Mary, whose unsinning
Heart I have chosen that it may bear Me.

EVE: Mary!

CHORUS: O Mary maiden! Mary of pity!
Speak for us, Mary! Speak for a world in fear!
Mary, mother and maid, send help to the city!
Speak for us, choose for us, Mary!

(Enter Mary, above.)

MARY: You called? I am here.

CHORUS: All that is true in us, all we were meant to be,
The lost opportunity and the broken unity,
The dead innocence, the rejected obedience,
The forfeited chastity and the frozen charity,
The caged generosity, and the forbidden pity,
Speak in the mouth of Mary, in the name of the city!

PERSONA: In the speed of the Holy Ghost run, Gabriel;
Bear Our message to Mary, daughter of Eve,
That she may lay her will under Our will
Freely, and as she freely gives, receive.

(Gabriel comes down.)

CHORUS: Alpha and Omega, beginning and end,
Laid on a single head in the moment of choice!
Pray God now, pray that a woman lend
Her ear to God's, as once to the serpent's voice.
Paradise all to gain and all to lose
In the second race re-run from the old start;
What will the city do now, if a girl refuse
The weight of the glory, the seven swords in the heart?

GABRIEL: Hail, thou that art highly favoured!
The Lord is with thee;
Blessed art thou among women.

MARY: What may this be?

GABRIEL: Thou shalt conceive in the power of the Holy Ghost
The most high Child, the Prince of the heavenly host;
This is the word that I am charged to say:
Wilt thou receive that Guest without dismay?

MARY: Behold in me the handmaid of the Lord;
Be it unto me according to thy word.

PERSONA: Now I put off My crown and majesty
To take the vesture of humility.

(The Persona Dei takes off His imperial vesture and remains in His alb.)

GABRIEL: Rejoice, O daughter of Jerusalem,
Thy King shall come to thee in Bethlehem.

MARY: My heart is exalting the Lord
    and my spirit is glad of my Saviour,
Who stoops from the height of His heaven
    to look on me, maiden-in-meekness,
And all generations shall bless me
    in the sound of the great salutation,

For He that is highly exalted
    exalts me, and holy is He.

CHOIR: Who being the Father's Image,
    the expression and form of the Selfhood,
Thought the equal and infinite glory
    was nowise a thing to be clung to,
But came to the selfhood of Man,
    in the image and form of a servant,
Made lower and less than His angels,
    the Lord of them; holy is He. . . .

PERSONA: Mother and daughter, bear Me forth to the world;
Show to them who were made in the image of God
The image of the Image of the Unimaginable
From the place where the Image and the Unimaged are one.[1]

From a lecture, "Towards a Christian Æsthetic":

The true work of art, then, is something *new* – it is not primarily the copy or representation of anything. It may involve
representation, but that is not what makes it a work of art. It
is not manufactured to specification, as an engineer works to
a plan – though it may involve compliance with the accepted
rules for dramatic presentation, and may also contain verbal
"effects" which can be mechanically accounted for. We know
very well, when we compare it with so-called works of art which
are "turned out to pattern" that in this connection "neither cir-
cumcision availeth anything nor uncircumcision, but a new
creature" [Gal. 6:15]. Something has been created.

This word – this idea of Art as *creation* is, I believe, the one
important contribution that Christianity has made to æsthet-
ics. Unfortunately, we are apt to use the words "creation" and

---

1   *The Just Vengeance,* 1946, published in *Four Sacred Plays,* 1948.

208 ♦ THE GOSPEL IN DOROTHY L. SAYERS

"creativeness" very vaguely and loosely, because we do not relate them properly to our theology. But it is significant that the Greeks had not this word in their æsthetic at all. They looked on a work of art as a kind of *techné,* a manufacture. Neither, for that matter, was the word in their theology – they did not look on history as the continual act of God fulfilling itself in creation.

How do we say that God creates, and how does this compare with the act of creation by an artist? To begin with, of course, we say that God created the universe "out of nothing" – He was bound by no conditions of any kind. Here there can be no comparison: the human artist is *in* the universe and bound by its conditions. He can create only within that framework and out of that material which the universe supplies. Admitting that, let us ask in what way God creates. Christian theology replies that God, who is a Trinity, creates by, or through, His second Person, His Word or Son, who is continually begotten from the First Person, the Father, in an eternal creative activity. And certain theologians have added this very significant comment: the Father, they say, is only known to Himself by beholding His image in His Son.

Does that sound very mysterious? We will come back to the human artist, and see what it means in terms of *his* activity. But first, let us take note of a new word that has crept into the argument by way of Christian theology – the word *Image.* Suppose, having rejected the words "copy," "imitation" and "representation" as inadequate, we substitute the word "image" and say that what the artist is doing is *to image forth* something or the other, and connect that with St. Paul's phrase: "God . . . hath spoken to us by His Son, the brightness of this glory and *express image* of His person." – Something which, by being an image, expresses that which it images. Is that getting us a little nearer to something? There is something which is, in the deepest sense of the words, *unimaginable,* known to Itself (and still more, to us) only by the image in which it expresses Itself through creation; and, says Christian theology very emphatically, the Son, who is the express image, is not the copy, or imitation, or representation of the Father, nor yet inferior or subsequent to the Father in any way – in the last resort, in the depths of their mysterious being, the Unimaginable and the Image are *one and the same. . . .*

There is a school of criticism that is always trying to explain, or explain away, a man's works of art by trying to dig out the events of his life and his emotions *outside* the works themselves, and saying "these are the real Æschylus, the real Shakespeare, of which the poems are only faint imitations." But any poet will tell you that this is the wrong way to go to work. It is the old, pagan æsthetic which explains nothing – or which explains all sorts of things about the work *except* what makes it a work of art. The poet will say: "My poem is the expression of my experience." But if you then say, "What experience?" he will say, "I can't tell you anything about it, except what I have said in the poem – the poem is the experience." The Son and the Father are *one:* the poet himself did not know what his experience was until he created the poem which revealed his own experience to himself.

To save confusion, let us distinguish between an *event* and an *experience.* An event is something that happens to one – but one does not necessarily experience it. To take an extreme instance: suppose you are hit on the head and get concussion and, as often happens, when you come to, you cannot remember the blow. The blow on the head certainly happened to you, but you did not *experience* it all you experience is the after-effects. You only experience a thing when you can express it – however halt-ingly – to your own mind. You may remember the young man in T. S. Eliot's play, *The Family Reunion,* who says to his relations:

> You are all people
> To whom nothing has happened, at most a continual impact
> Of external events . . .

He means that they have got through life without ever really *experiencing* anything, because they have never tried to express to themselves the real nature of what has happened to them.

A poet is a man who not only suffers "the impact of exter-nal events," but experiences them. He puts the experience into words in his own mind, and in so doing recognises the experi-ence for what it is. To the extent that we can do that, we are all poets. A "poet" so-called is simply a man like ourselves with an exceptional power of revealing his experience by expressing it, so that not only he, but we ourselves, recognise that experience as our own.

I want to stress the word *recognise.* A poet does not see some-thing – say the full moon – and say: "This is a very beautiful sight – let me set about finding words for the appropriate expres-sion of what people ought to feel about it." That is what the literary artisan does, and it means nothing. What happens is that then, or at some time after, he finds himself saying words in his head and says to himself: "Yes – that is right. *That* is the experi-ence the full moon was to me. I recognise it in expressing it, and now I know what it was." And so, when it is a case of mental or spiritual experience – sin, grief, joy, sorrow, worship – the thing reveals itself to him in words, and so becomes fully experienced for the first time. By thus recognising it in its expression, he makes it his own – integrates it into himself. He no longer feels himself battered passively by the impact of external events – it is no longer something happening *to* him, but something happening *in* him, the reality of the event is communicated to him in activity and power. So that the act of the poet in creation is seen to be threefold – a trinity – experience, expression and recognition; the unknowable reality in the experience; the image of that reality known in its expression; and power in the recognition; the whole making up the single and indivisible act of creative mind.

Now, what the poet does for himself, he can also do for us. When he has imaged forth his experience he can incarnate it, so to speak, in a material body – words, music, painting – the thing we know as a work of art. And since he is a man like the rest of us, we shall expect that our experience will have something in common with his. In the image of *his* experience, we can *recognise* the image of some experience of our own – something that had happened to us, but which we had never understood, never formulated or expressed to ourselves, and therefore never known as a real experience. When we read the poem, or see the play or picture or hear the music, it is as though a light were turned on inside us. We say: "Ah! I recognise that! That is something which I obscurely felt to be going on in and about me, but I didn't know what it was and couldn't express it. But now that the artist has made its image – imaged it forth – for me, I can possess and take hold of it and make it my own, and turn it into a source of knowledge and strength." This is the *communication of the image in power*, by which the third person of the poet's trinity brings us, through the incarnate image, into direct knowledge of the in itself unknowable and unimaginable reality. "No man cometh to the Father save by Me," said the incarnate Image; and He added, "but the Spirit of Power will lead you into all truth."

This recognition of the truth that we get in the artist's work comes to us as a revelation of new truth. I want to be clear about that. I am not referring to the sort of patronising recognition we give to a writer by nodding our heads and observing: "Yes, yes, very good, very true – that's just what I'm always saying." I mean the recognition of a truth which tells us something about ourselves that we had *not* been "always saying" – something which puts a new knowledge of ourselves within our grasp. It is new, startling, and perhaps shattering – and yet it comes to us with a sense of familiarity. We did not know it before, but the moment the poet has shown it to us, we know that, somehow or other, we had always really known it.

Very well. But, frankly, is that the sort of thing the average British citizen gets, or expects to get, when he goes to the theatre or reads a book? No, it is not. In the majority of cases, it is not in the least what he expects, or what he wants. What he looks for is not this creative and Christian kind of Art at all. He does not expect or desire to be upset by sudden revelations about himself and the universe. Like the people of Plato's decadent Athens, he has forgotten or repudiated the religious origins of all Art. He wants entertainment, or, if he is a little more serious-minded, he wants something with a moral, or to have some spell or incantation put on him to instigate him to virtuous action.

Now, entertainment and moral spellbinding have their uses, but they are not Art in the proper sense. They may be the incidental effects of good art; but they may also be the very aim and essence of false art. And if we continue to demand of the Arts only these two things, we shall starve and silence the true artist and encourage in his place the false artist, who may become a very sinister force indeed.

Let us take the amusement-art: what does that give us? Generally speaking, what we demand and get from it is the enjoyment of the emotions which usually accompany experience without having had the experience. It does not reveal us to ourselves: it merely projects on to a mental screen a picture of ourselves as we already fancy ourselves to be – only bigger and brighter. The manufacturer of this kind of entertainment is not by any means interpreting and revealing his own experience to himself and us – he is either indulging his own day-dreams, or – still more falsely and venially – he is saying: "What is it the audience think they would like to have experienced? Let us show them that, so that they can wallow in emotion by pretending to have experienced it." This kind of pseudo-art is "wish-fulfilment" or "escape" literature in the worst sense – it is an escape, not from the "impact of external events" into the citadel of experienced reality, but an escape from reality and experience into a world of merely external events – the progressive externalisation of consciousness. For occasional relaxation this is all right; but it can be carried to the point where, not merely art, but the whole universe of phenomena becomes a screen on which we see the magnified projection of our unreal selves, as the object of equally unreal emotions. This brings about the complete corruption of the consciousness, which can no longer recognise reality in experience. When things come to this pass, we have a civilisation which "lives for amusement" – a civilisation without guts, without experience, and out of touch with reality.

Or take the spellbinding kind of art. This at first sight seems better because it spurs us to action; and it also has its uses. But it too is dangerous in excess, because once again it does not reveal reality in experience, but only projects a lying picture of the self. As the amusement-art seeks to produce the *emotions* without the experience, so *this* pseudo-art seeks to produce the *behaviour* without the experience. In the end it is directed to putting the behaviour of the audience beneath the will of the spellbinder, and its true name is not "art," but "art-magic." In its vulgarest form it becomes pure propaganda. It can (as we have reason to know) actually succeed in making its audience into the thing it desires to have them – it can really in the end corrupt the consciousness and destroy experience until the inner selves of its victims are wholly externalised and made the puppets and instruments of their own spurious passions. This is why it is dangerous for anybody – even for the Church – to urge artists to produce works of art for the express purpose of "doing good to people." Let her by all means encourage artists to express their own Christian experience and communicate it to others. That is the true artist saying: "Look! recognise your experience in my own." But "edifying art" may only too often be the pseudo-artist corruptly saying: "This is what you are supposed to believe and feel and do – and I propose to work you into a state of mind in which you will believe and feel and do as you are told." This pseudo-art does not really communicate power to us; it merely exerts power over us.

What is it, then, that these two pseudo-arts – the entertaining and the spellbinding – have in common? And how are they related to true Art? What they have in common is the falsification of the consciousness; and they are to Art as the *idol* is to the Image. The Jews were forbidden to make any image for worship, because before the revelation of the threefold unity in which Image and Unimaginable are one, it was only too fatally easy to substitute the idol for the Image. The Christian revelation set free all the images, by showing that the true Image subsisted within the Godhead Itself – it was neither copy, nor imitation, nor representation, nor inferior, nor subsequent, but the brightness of the glory, and the express image of the Person – the very mirror in which reality knows itself and communicates itself in power.

But the danger still exists; and it always will recur whenever the Christian doctrine of the Image is forgotten. In our æsthetic, that doctrine has never been fully used or understood, and in consequence our whole attitude to the artistic expression of reality has become confused, idolatrous and pagan. We see the Arts degenerating into mere entertainment which corrupts and relaxes our civilisation, and we try in alarm to correct this by demanding a more moralising and bracing kind of Art. But this is only setting up one idol in place of the other. Or we see that Art is becoming idolatrous, and suppose that we can put matters right by getting rid of the representational element in it. But what is wrong is not the representation itself, but the fact that what we are looking at, and what we are looking *for*, is not the Image but an idol. Little children, keep yourselves from idols.

It has become a commonplace to say that the Arts are in a bad way. We are in fact largely given over to the entertainers and the spellbinders; and because we do not understand that these two functions do not represent the true nature of Art, the true artists are, as it were, excommunicate, and have no audience. But there is here not, I think, so much a relapse from a Christian æsthetic as a failure ever to find and examine a real Christian æsthetic, based on dogma and not on ethics. This may not be a bad thing. We have at least a new line of country to explore, that has not been trampled on and built over and fought over by countless generations of quarrelsome critics. What we have to start from is the Trinitarian doctrine of creative mind, and the light which that doctrine throws on the true nature of images.

The great thing, I am sure, is not to be nervous about God – not to try and shut out the Lord Immanuel from *any* sphere of truth. Art is not He – we must not substitute Art for God; yet this also is He, for it is one of His Images and therefore reveals His nature.

Here we see in a mirror darkly – we behold only the images; else-where we shall see face to face, in the place where Image and Reality are one.[2]

2   "Towards a Christian Æsthetic," Edward Alleyn Lecture (1944), published in *Unpopular Opinions*, 1946.

20

Busman's Honeymoon

Time and Eternity

The last of the twelve Lord Peter Wimsey books is Busman's
Honeymoon. *Peter and Harriet are on their honeymoon when
they discover a body in the basement of the house that they have
just bought. In the course of the book they are able to discover the
murderer as well as begin discerning their new relationship. The
crisis comes on the night before the condemned man, Crutchley, is
to be executed at dawn. Lord Peter has tried to mitigate his responsibility toward the murderer by paying for the best legal defense in
the country, and arranging for the future of the man's girlfriend,
who is pregnant. But as in the first book,* Whose Body?, *Wimsey
is unable to avoid the flashbacks that return him to World War I,
when he was an officer making decisions that cost men their lives.
He retreats into himself, brooding on the past.*

It was past two o'clock when she heard the car return. There were
steps on the gravel, the opening and shutting of the door, a brief
murmur of voices – then silence. Then, unheralded by so much
as a shuffle on the stair, came Bunter's soft tap at the little door.

"Well, Bunter?"

"Everything has been done that could be done, my lady." They spoke in hushed tones, as though the doomed man lay already dead. "It was some considerable time before he would consent to see his lordship. At length the governor persuaded him, and his lordship was able to deliver the message and acquaint him with the arrangements made for the young woman's future. I understand that he seemed to take very little interest in the matter; they told me there that he continued to be a sullen and intractable prisoner. His lordship came away very much distressed. It is his custom under such circumstances to ask the condemned man's forgiveness. From his demeanour, I do not think he had it."

"Did you come straight back?"

"No, my lady. On leaving the prison at midnight, his lordship drove away in a westerly direction, very fast, for about fifty miles. That is not unusual; I have frequently known him drive all night. Then he stopped the car suddenly at a crossroads, waited for a few minutes as though he were endeavouring to make up his mind, turned round and came straight back here, driving even faster. He was shivering very much when we came in, but refused to eat or drink anything. He said he could not sleep, so I made up a good fire in the sitting-room. I left him seated on the settle. I came up by the back way, my lady, because I think he might not wish to feel that you were in any anxiety about him."

"Quite right, Bunter – I'm glad you did that. Where are you going to be?"

"I shall remain in the kitchen, my lady, within call. His lordship is not likely to require me, but if he should do so, he will find me at hand, making myself a little supper."

"That's an excellent plan. I expect his lordship will prefer to be left to himself, but if he should ask for me – not on any account unless or until he does – will you tell him – "

"Yes, my lady?"

"Tell him there is still a light in my room, and that you think I am very much concerned about Crutchley."

"Very good, my lady. Would your ladyship like me to bring you a cup of tea?"

"Oh, Bunter, thank you. Yes, I should."

When the tea came, she drank it thirstily, and then sat listening. Everything was silent, except the church clock chiming out the quarters; but when she went into the next room she could hear faintly the beat of restless feet on the floor below.

She went back and waited. She could think only one thing, and that over and over again. I must not go to him; he must come to me. If he does not want me, I have failed altogether, and that failure will be with us all our lives. But the decision must be his and not mine. I have got to accept it. I have got to be patient. Whatever happens, I must not go to him.

It was four by the church clock when she heard the sound she had been waiting for: the door at the bottom of the stair creaked. For a few moments nothing followed, and she thought he had changed his mind. She held her breath till she heard his footsteps mount slowly and reluctantly and enter the next room. She feared they might stop there, but this time he came straight on and pushed open the door which she had left ajar.

"Harriet. . . ."

"Come in, dear."

He came over and stood close beside her, mute and shivering. She put her hand out to him and he took it eagerly, laying his other hand in a fumbling gesture on her shoulder.

"You're cold, Peter. Come nearer the fire."

"It's not cold," he said, half-angrily, "it's my rotten nerves. I can't help it. I suppose I've never been really right since the War. I hate behaving like this. I tried to stick it out by myself."

"But why should you?"

"It's this damned waiting about till they've finished. . . ."

"I know. I couldn't sleep either."

He stood holding out his hands mechanically to the fire till he could control the chattering of his teeth.

"It's damnable for you too. I'm sorry. I'd forgotten. That sounds idiotic. But I've always been alone."

"Yes, of course. I'm like that, too. I like to crawl away and hide in a corner."

"Well," he said, with a transitory gleam of himself, "you're my corner and I've come to hide."

"Yes, my dearest."

(And the trumpets sounded for her on the other side.)

"It's not as bad as it might be. The worst times are when they haven't admitted it, and one goes over the evidence and wonders if one wasn't wrong, after all. . . . And sometimes they're so damned decent. . . ."

"What was Crutchley like?"

"He doesn't seem to care for anybody or regret anything except that he didn't pull it off. He hates old Noakes just as much as the day he killed him. He wasn't interested in Polly – only said she was a fool and a bitch, and I was a bigger fool to waste time and money on her. And Aggie Twitterton could go and rot with the whole pack of us, and the sooner the better."

"Peter, how horrible!"

"If there *is* a God or a judgment – what next? What have we done?"

"I don't know. But I don't suppose anything we could do would prejudice the defence."

"I suppose not. I wish we knew more about it." . . .

"They hate executions, you know. It upsets the other prisoners. They bang on the doors and make nuisances of themselves. Everybody's nervous. . . . Caged like beasts, separately. . . . That's the hell of it . . . we're all in separate cells. . . . I can't get out, said the starling. . . . If one could only get out for one moment, or go to sleep, or stop thinking. . . . Oh, damn that cursed clock! . . . Harriet, for God's sake, hold on to me . . . get me out of this . . . break down the door. . . ."

"Hush, dearest. I'm here. We'll see it out together."

Through the eastern side of the casement, the sky grew pale with the forerunners of the dawn.

"Don't let me go."

The light grew stronger as they waited.

Quite suddenly, he said, "Oh, damn!" and began to cry – in an awkward, unpractised way at first, and then more easily. So she held him, crouched at her knees, against her breast, huddling his head in her arms that he might not hear eight o'clock strike.[1]

From a newspaper article:

It is over twenty years since I first read the words, in some forgotten book. I remember neither the name of the author, nor that of the Saint from whose meditations he was quoting. Only the statement itself has survived the accidents of transmission: "*Cibus sum grandium; cresce, et manducabis Me*" – "I am the food of the full-grown; become a man, and thou shalt feed on Me." [2]

---

1 *Busman's Honeymoon*, 1936, "Epithalamion."

2 Augustine of Hippo, *Confessions*, trans. by Henry Chadwick, VII, X, 16: "I heard as it were your voice from on high. 'I am the food of the fully grown; grow and you will feed on me. And you will not change me into you like the food your flesh eats, but you will be changed into Me.'"

... Paradoxical as it may seem, to believe in youth is to look backward; to look forward, we must believe in age. "Except," said Christ, "ye become as little children" [Matt. 18:3] – and the words are sometimes quoted to justify the flight into infantilism. Now, children differ in many ways, but they have one thing in common. Peter Pan – if indeed he exists otherwise than in the nostalgic imagination of an adult – is a case for the pathologist. All normal children (however much we discourage them) look forward to growing up. "Except ye become as little children," except you can wake on your fiftieth birthday with the same forward-looking excitement and interest in life that you enjoyed when you were five, "ye cannot see the Kingdom of God." One must not only die daily, but every day one must be born again.

"How can a man be born when he is old?" asked Nicodemus [John 3:4]. His question has been ridiculed; but it is very reasonable and even profound. "Can he enter a second time into his mother's womb and be born?" Can he escape from Time, creep back into the comfortable pre-natal darkness, renounce the values of experience? The answer makes short work of all such fantasies. "That which is born of the flesh is flesh, and that which is born of the Spirit is spirit." The spirit alone is eternal youth; the mind and the body must learn to make terms with Time.

Time is a difficult subject for thought, because in a sense we know too much about it. It is perhaps the only phenomenon of which we have direct apprehension; if all our senses were destroyed, we should still remain aware of duration. Moreover, all conscious thought is a process in time; so that to think consciously about Time is like trying to use a foot-rule to measure its own length. The awareness of timelessness, which some people have, does not belong to the order of conscious thought and cannot be directly expressed in the language of conscious thought, which is temporal. For every conscious human purpose (including thought) we are compelled to reckon (in every sense of the word) with Time.

Now, the Christian Church has always taken a thoroughly realistic view of Time, and has been very particular to distinguish between Time and Eternity. In her view of the matter, Time is not an aspect or a fragment of Eternity, nor is Eternity an endless extension of Time; the two concepts belong to different categories. Both have a divine reality: God is the Ancient of Days and also the I AM; the Everlasting and also the Eternal Present; the Logos and also the Father. The Creeds, with their usual practicality, issue a sharp warning that we shall get into a nasty mess if we confuse the two or deny the reality of either. Moreover, the mystics – those rare spirits who are simultaneously aware of Time and Eternity – support the doctrine by their knowledge and example. They are never vague, woolly-minded people to whom Time means nothing; on the contrary, they insist more than anybody upon the validity of Time and the actuality of human experience. . . .

In contending with the problem of evil it is useless to try to escape either *from* the bad past or *into* the good past. The only way to deal with the past is to accept the whole past, and by accepting it, to change its meaning. The hero of T. S. Eliot's *The Family Reunion,* haunted by the guilt of a hereditary evil, seeks at first "to creep back through the little door" into the shelter of the unaltered past, and finds no refuge there from the pursuing hounds of heaven. "Now I know / That the last apparent refuge, the safe shelter, / That is where one meets them; that is the way of spectres. . . ." So long as he flees from Time and Evil he is thrall to them, not till he welcomes them does he find strength to transmute them. "And now I know / That my business is not to run away, but to pursue, / Not to avoid being found, but to seek. / . . . It is at once the hardest thing, and the only thing possible. / Now they will lead me; I shall be safe with them. / I am not safe here. / . . . I must follow the bright angels." Then, and only then, is he enabled to apprehend the good in the evil and to see the terrible hunters of the soul in their true angelic shape. "I feel quite happy, as if happiness / Did not consist in getting what one wanted / Or in getting rid of what can't be got rid of / But in a different vision." It is the release, not from, but into, Reality.

This is the great way of Christian acceptance – a very different thing from so-called "Christian" resignation, which merely submits without ecstasy. "Repentance," says a Christian writer, "is no more than a passionate intention to know all things after the mode of Heaven, and it is impossible to know evil as good if you insist on knowing it as evil." For man's evil knowledge, "there could be but one perfect remedy – to know the evil of the past itself as good, and to be free from the necessity of evil in the future – to find right knowledge and perfect freedom together; to know all things as occasions of love."[3]

The story of Passion-Tide and Easter is the story of the winning of that freedom and of that victory over the evils of Time. The burden of the guilt is accepted ("He was made Sin"[4]) the last agony of alienation from God is passed through (*Eloi, lama sabachthani*[5]); the temporal Body is broken and remade;

---

3 Charles Williams, "The Incarnation of the Kingdom," *He Came Down from Heaven* (1938).

4 2 Corinthians 5:21 (NRSV): "He made Him who knew no sin to be sin on our behalf, so that we might become the righteousness of God in Him."

5 Mark 15:34 (NRSV): "At three o'clock Jesus cried out with a loud voice, '*Eloi, Eloi, lama sabachthani?*' which means, 'My God, my God, why have you forsaken me?'"

and Time and Eternity are reconciled in a Single Person. There is no retreat here to the Paradise of primal ignorance; the new Kingdom of God is built upon the foundations of spiritual experience. Time is not denied; it is fulfilled. "I am the food of the full-grown."[6]

---

6 "The Food of the Full-Grown," *The Sunday Times,* April 9, 1939, republished as "Strong Meat" in *Creed or Chaos?,* 1949.

A Panegyric
for Dorothy L. Sayers

C. S. Lewis

The variety of Dorothy Sayers's work makes it almost impossible to find anyone who can deal properly with it all. Charles Williams might have done so; I certainly can't. It is embarrassing to admit that I am no great reader of detective stories: embarrassing because, in our present state of festering intellectual class consciousness, the admission might be taken as a boast. It is nothing of the sort: I respect, though I do not much enjoy, that severe and civilized form, which demands much fundamental brain work of those who write in it and assumes as its background uncorrupted and unbrutalised methods of criminal investigation.

Prigs have put it about that Dorothy in later life was ashamed of her "tekkies" and hated to hear them mentioned. A couple of years ago my wife asked her if this was true and was relieved to hear her deny it. She had stopped working in that genre because she felt she had done all she could with it. And indeed, I gather, a full process of development had taken place. I have heard it said that Lord Peter is the only imaginary detective who ever grew up – grew from the Duke's son, the fabulous amorist, the scholar swashbuckler, and connoisseur of wine, into the increasingly human character, not without quirks and flaws, who loves and marries, and is nursed by, Harriet Vane. Reviewers complained that Miss Sayers was falling in love with her hero. On which a better critic remarked to me, "It would be truer to say she was falling out of love with him; and ceased fondling a girl's dream – if she had ever done so – and began inventing a man."

There is in reality no cleavage between the detective stories and her other works. In them, as in it, she is first and foremost the craftsman, the professional. She always saw herself as one who has learned a trade, and respects it, and demands respect for it from others. We who loved her may (among ourselves) lovingly admit that this attitude was sometimes almost comically emphatic. One soon learned that "We authors, Ma'am"[1] was the most acceptable key. Gas about "inspiration," whimperings about critics or public, all the paraphernalia of *dandyisme* and "outsidership" were, I think, simply disgusting to her. She aspired to be, and was, at once a popular entertainer and a conscientious craftsman: like (in her degree) Chaucer, Cervantes, Shakespeare, or Molière. I have an idea that, with a very few exceptions, it is only such writers who matter much in the long run. "One shows one's greatness," says Pascal, "not by being at an extremity but by being simultaneously at two extremities." Much of her most valuable thought about writing was embodied in *The Mind of the Maker*: a book which is still too little read. It has faults. But books about writing by those who have

---

1 This expression, attributed to Benjamin Disraeli, was found to have a soothing effect upon Queen Victoria, who in 1868 published her *Leaves from a Journal of Our Life in the Highlands.*

themselves written viable books are too rare and too useful to be neglected.

For a Christian, of course, this pride in one's craft, which so easily withers into pride in oneself, raises a fiercely practical problem. It is delightfully characteristic of her extremely robust and forthright nature that she soon lifted this problem to the fully conscious level and made it the theme of one of her major works. The architect in *The Zeal of Thy House* is at the outset the incarnation of–and therefore doubtless the *Catharsis* from–a possible Dorothy who the actual Dorothy Sayers was offering for mortification. His disinterested zeal for the work itself has her full sympathy. But she knows that, without grace, it is a dangerous virtue: little better than the "artistic conscience" which every Bohemian bungler pleads as a justification for neglecting his parents, deserting his wife, and cheating his creditors. From the beginning, personal pride is entering into the architect's character: the play records his costly salvation.

As the detective stories do not stand quite apart, so neither do the explicitly religious works. She never sank the artist and entertainer in the evangelist. The very astringent (and admirable) preface to *The Man Born to Be King*, written when she had lately been assailed with a great deal of ignorant and spiteful obloquy, makes the point of view defiantly clear. "It was assumed," she writes, "that my object in writing was 'to do good.' But that was in fact not my object at all, though it was quite properly the object of those who commissioned the plays in the first place. My object was *to tell that story* to the best of my ability, within the medium at my disposal – in short, to make as good a work of art as I could. For a work of art that is not good and true *in art* is not true and good in any other respect." Of course, while art and evangelism were distinct, they turned out to demand one another. Bad art on this theme went hand in hand with bad theology. "Let me tell you, good Christian people, an honest writer would be ashamed to treat a nursery tale as you have treated the greatest drama in history: and this in virtue, not of his faith, but of his calling." And equally, of course, her disclaimer of an intention to "do good" was ironically rewarded by the immense amount of good she evidently did.

The architectonic qualities of this dramatic sequence will hardly be questioned. Some tell me they find it vulgar. Perhaps they do not quite know what they mean; perhaps they have not fully digested the answers to this charge given in the preface. Or perhaps it is simply not "addressed to their condition." Different souls take their nourishment in different vessels. For my own part, I have re-read it in every Holy Week since it first appeared, and never re-read it without being deeply moved.

Her later years were devoted to translation. The last letter I ever wrote to her was in acknowledgement of her *Song of Roland,* and I was lucky enough to say that the end-stopped lines and utterly unadorned style of the original must have made it a far harder job than Dante. Her delight at this (surely not very profound) remark suggested that she was rather starved for rational criticism. I do not think this one of her most successful works. It is too violently colloquial for my palate; but then, she knew far more Old French than I. In her Dante the problem is not quite the same. It should always be read in conjunction with the paper on Dante which she contributed to the *Essays Presented to Charles Williams.*[2] There you get the first impact of Dante on a mature, a scholarly, and an extremely independent mind. That impact determined the whole character of her translation.

---

2   "'. . . And Telling You a Story': A Note on The Divine Comedy," *Essays Presented to Charles Williams* (1947).

She had been startled and delighted by something in Dante for which no critic, and no earlier translator, had prepared her: his sheer narrative impetus, his frequent homeliness, his high comedy, his grotesque buffoonery. These qualities she was determined to preserve at all costs. If, in order to do so, she had to sacrifice sweetness or sublimity, then sacrificed they should be. Hence her audacities in both language and rhythm.

We must distinguish this from something rather discreditable that has been going on of recent years – I mean the attempt of some translators from Greek and Latin to make their readers believe that the *Aeneid* is written in service slang and that Attic Tragedy uses the language of the streets. What such versions implicitly assert is simply false; but what Dorothy was trying to represent by her audacities is quite certainly there in Dante. The question is how far you can do it justice without damage to other qualities which are also there and thus misrepresenting the *Comedy* as much in one direction as fussy, Miltonic old Cary[3] had done in the other. In the end, I suppose, one comes to a choice of evils. No version can give the whole of Dante. So at least I said when I read her *Inferno*. But, then, when I came to the *Purgatorio,* a little miracle seemed to be happening. She had risen, just as Dante himself rose in his second part: growing richer, more liquid, more elevated. Then first I began to have great hopes of her *Paradiso*. Would she go on rising? Was it possible? Dared we hope?

Well. She died instead; went, as one may in all humility hope, to learn more of Heaven than even the *Paradiso* could tell her. For all she did and was, for delight and instruction, for her militant loyalty as a friend, for courage and honesty, for the richly

---

3   *The Vision; or, Hell, Purgatory, and Paradise, of Dante Alighieri,* translated by Rev. Henry Francis Cary (London: William Smith, 1844).

feminine qualities which showed through a port and manner superficially masculine and even gleefully ogreish – let us thank the Author who invented her.[4]

---

4   C. S. Lewis, "A Panegyric for Dorothy L. Sayers," *On Stories and Other Essays on Literature,* ed. Walter Hooper (London: Harcourt Brace Jovanovich, 1966), 91–95.

Chronology

1893 Dorothy Leigh Sayers is born June 13 at Oxford, to Henry and Helen Mary Sayers, their only child.

1894 They move to Bluntisham-cum-Earith in Huntingdon-shire, where Henry is rector.

1909 Dorothy Sayers enters the Godolphin School, Salisbury.

1912 Wins a scholarship to Somerville College, Oxford

1915 Sayers graduates from Somerville College with first class honors in modern languages and medieval literature.

1916 *Op. I* (poetry) published by Blackwell Publishing

1918 *Catholic Tales and Christian Songs* (poetry) published by Blackwell

1919 Works for Blackwell as an intern, then as a secretary at L'Ecole des Roches in Normandy

1920 Women are finally awarded degrees from Oxford. Sayers receives her MA.

1921 Unhappy relationship with Russian poet John Cournos

1922 Advertising copywriter at Bensons in London

1923   *Whose Body?* (mystery)

1924   Sayers's son John Anthony is born out of wedlock. Bill White, the father, is already married. Sayers pays her cousin, Ivy Shrimpton, to foster the boy.

1926   Marries Captain Oswald Atherton "Mac" Fleming, a Scottish journalist and World War I veteran. They reside at 24 Great James Street in Bloomsbury.

1927   *Unnatural Death* (mystery)

1928   Sayers's father dies. *The Unpleasantness at the Bellona Club* (mystery), *Lord Peter Views the Body* (short stories)

1929   Mother dies. Sayers moves to her mother's house at 22 Newland Street, Witham. *Tristan in Brittany* by Thomas of Britain (translation)

1930   Sayers is one of the founding members of the Detection Club. *The Documents in the Case* (mystery), *Strong Poison* (mystery)

1931   Sayers quits her copywriting job at Benson's. She can live on the proceeds from her novels. *The Five Red Herrings* (mystery)

1932   *Have His Carcase* (mystery)

1933   *Murder Must Advertise* (mystery), *Hangman's Holiday* (short stories)

1934   Sayers "adopts" John Anthony, who now uses the surname Fleming. He still resides with Ivy Shrimpton. *The Nine Tailors* (mystery)

1935   *Gaudy Night* (mystery)

1936   *Busman's Honeymoon* (stage play and mystery)

1937 *The Zeal of Thy House* (stage play for the Canterbury Festival)

1938 *He That Should Come* (radio play) broadcast Christmas Day

1939 *The Devil to Pay* (stage play for the Canterbury Festival), *In the Teeth of the Evidence* (Short Stories), *Strong Meat* (book of essays)

1940 *Begin Here* (book of essays), *Love All* (stage play), *Creed or Chaos?* (book of essays), *The Christ of the Creeds* (radio broadcasts)

1941 *The Mind of the Maker* (book-length essay), *The Golden Cockerel* (radio play) adapted from Alexander Pushkin

1943 Declines a Lambeth Doctorate in Divinity. *The Man Born to Be King* (a series of twelve radio plays that aired December 1941–October 1942)

1944 *Even the Parrot* (satire)

1946 *The Just Vengeance* (stage play for the Lichfield Festival), *The Heart of Stone,* by Dante (translation), *Unpopular Opinions* (book of essays)

1949 *The "Comedy" of Dante Alighieri the Florentine. Cantica I: Hell* (translation)

1950 Mac Fleming dies. Sayers accepts an honorary doctorate of letters from the University of Durham.

1951 *The Emperor Constantine* (stage play for the Colchester Festival)

1952 Sayers becomes churchwarden of her London parish, St. Thomas-cum-St. Annes.

1955   *The "Comedy" of Dante Alighieri the Florentine. Cantica II: Purgatory* (translation), *Introductory Papers on Dante* (criticism)

1957   *Further Papers on Dante* (criticism), *The Song of Roland* (translation); Sayers dies of a heart attack on December 17, age 64. John Anthony Fleming is the sole beneficiary of her will and acknowledges that he is her son.

1962   Barbara Reynolds finishes Sayers's translation of *The "Comedy" of Dante Alighieri the Florentine, Cantica III: Paradise.*

Selected Bibliography

Brown, Janice. *The Seven Deadly Sins in the Work of Dorothy L. Sayers*. Kent, OH: Kent State University Press, 1979.

Dale, Alzina Stone. *Maker and Craftsman: The Story of Dorothy L. Sayers*. Lincoln, NE: iUniverse, 2003.

Dante, Alighieri. *The Divine Comedy I: Hell*. Translated by Dorothy L. Sayers. London: Penguin Books, 1949.

_____ . *The Divine Comedy II: Purgatory*. Translated by Dorothy L. Sayers. London: Penguin Books, 1955.

_____ . *The Divine Comedy III: Paradise*. Translated by Dorothy L. Sayers and Barbara Reynolds. London: Penguin Books, 1962.

Hone, Ralph E. *Poetry of Dorothy L. Sayers*. Cambridge: Dorothy L. Sayers Society, 1996.

Lewis, C. S. "A Panegyric for Dorothy L. Sayers," *On Stories and Other Essays on Literature*. Walter Hooper, ed. London: Harcourt Brace Jovanovich, 1966, 91–95.

Reynolds, Barbara, ed. *Dorothy L. Sayers: Her Life and Soul*. New York: St. Martin's Press, 1993.

_____ . *The Letters of Dorothy L. Sayers: Volume One: 1899–1936: The Making of a Detective Novelist*. Cambridge: Dorothy L. Sayers Society, 1995.

_____ . *The Letters of Dorothy L. Sayers: Volume Two: 1937–1943 From novelist to playwright*. Cambridge: Dorothy L. Sayers Society, 1997.

_____ . *The Letters of Dorothy L. Sayers: Volume Three: 1944–1950: A Noble Daring*. Cambridge: Dorothy L. Sayers Society, 1998.

———— . *The Letters of Dorothy L. Sayers: Volume Four: 1951–1957: In the Midst of Life.* Cambridge: Dorothy L. Sayers Society, 1998.

Sayers, Dorothy L. *Begin Here: A Statement of Faith.* London: Victor Gollancz, 1940.

———— . *Busman's Honeymoon: A Love Story with Detective Interruptions.* London: Victor Gollancz, 1937.

———— . *Catholic Tales and Christian Songs.* Oxford: B. H. Blackwell, 1918.

———— . *Clouds of Witness.* London: Victor Gollancz, 1958.

———— . *Creed or Chaos?* London: Methuen, 1947.

———— . *The Christ of the Creeds & Other Broadcast Messages to the British People during World War II.* West Sussex: Dorothy L. Sayers Society, 2008.

———— . *The Emperor Constantine: A Chronicle.* London: Victor Gollancz, 1951.

———— . *The Five Red Herrings.* London: Victor Gollancz, 1931.

———— . *Four Sacred Plays.* London: Victor Gollancz, 1948.

———— . *Gaudy Night.* London: Victor Gollancz, 1935.

———— . *Have His Carcase.* New York: Harper & Row, 1932.

———— . "Letter Addressed to 'Average People.'" *The City Temple Tidings,* July 1946, 166.

———— . *The Lost Tools of Learning.* London: Methuen, 1948.

———— . *The Man Born to Be King.* London: Victor Gollancz, 1943.

———— . *The Mind of the Maker.* New York: Harper & Row, 1941.

———— . "More Pantheon Papers." *Punch,* January 13, 1954, 84.

_____. *Murder Must Advertise: A Detective Story*. London: Victor Gollancz, 1933.

_____. *The Nine Tailors: Changes Rung on an Old Theme in Two Short Touches and Two Full Peals*. London: Victor Gollancz, 1934.

_____. *Op. I*. Oxford: Blackwell Publishers, 1916.

_____. "The Psychology of Advertising." *The Spectator*, November 19, 1937, 24–26.

_____. *Strong Poison*. London: Victor Gollancz, 1930.

_____. *A Treasury of Sayers Stories*. London: Victor Gollancz, 1958.

_____. *Unnatural Death*. London: Collins, 1927.

_____. *Unpopular Opinions*. London: Victor Gollancz, 1946.

_____. *The Unpleasantness at the Bellona Club*. London: Ernest Benn, 1928.

_____. *Whose Body?* London: T. Fisher Unwin, 1923.

_____. "The Wimsey Papers – IV." *The Spectator*, December 8, 1939, 809–10.

_____. *The Zeal of Thy House*. London: Victor Gollancz, 1937.

Sayers, Dorothy L., ed. *Great Short Stories of Detection, Mystery, and Horror, Third Series*. London: Victor Gollancz, 1934.

Sayers, Dorothy L. and Robert Eustace. *The Documents in the Case*. London: Ernest Benn, 1930.

Simmons, Laura K. *Creed without Chaos: Exploring Theology in the Writings of Dorothy L. Sayers*. Grand Rapids: Baker Academic, 2005.

The Song of Roland. Translated by Dorothy L. Sayers. Baltimore: Penguin Books, 1957.

Acknowledgments

The following selections are reprinted by permission of HarperCollins Publishers:

Pages 120–23, 127–31, 182–86, 195–97 [3234 words] from *Whose Body?* by Dorothy L. Sayers. Copyright © 1923 by Dorothy Leigh Sayers Fleming.

Pages 221–24 [996 words] from *Unnatural Death* by Dorothy L. Sayers. Copyright © 1927 by Dorothy Leigh Sayers Fleming. Copyright renewed © 1955 by Dorothy Leigh Sayers Fleming.

Pages 252–56 [1,209 words] from *The Unpleasantness at the Bellona Club* by Dorothy L. Sayers. Copyright © 1928 by Dorothy Leigh Sayers Fleming. Copyright renewed © 1956 by Dorothy Leigh Sayers Fleming.

Pages 63–66 [1,139 words] from *Strong Poison* by Dorothy L. Sayers. Copyright © 1930 by Dorothy L. Sayers Fleming. Copyright renewed © 1958 by Lloyds Bank, Ltd., Executor of the Estate of Dorothy L. Sayers.

Pages 131–35, 238–40 [1,741 words] from *The Documents in the Case* by Dorothy L. Sayers. Copyright © 1930 by Dorothy L. Sayers Fleming and Robert Eustace. Copyright renewed © 1958 by Lloyds Bank, Ltd.

Pages 59, 62, 195–96, 213–14 [645 words] from *The Five Red Herrings* by Dorothy L. Sayers. Copyright © 1931 by Dorothy Leigh Sayers Fleming. Copyright renewed © 1959 by Lloyds Bank, Ltd.

Pages 196–97 [433 words] from *Have His Carcase* by Dorothy L. Sayers. Copyright © 1932 by Dorothy Leigh Sayers Fleming. Copyright renewed © 1960 by Lloyds Bank, Ltd.

Pages 71, 54–5, 175–77, 237–39 [1,531 words] from *Murder Must Advertise* by Dorothy L. Sayers. Copyright © 1933 by Dorothy Leigh Sayers Fleming. Copyright renewed © 1961 by Lloyds Bank Ltd., Executor of the Estate of Dorothy L. Sayers.

Pages 178–80, 390–95, 510–14 [3,168 words] from *Gaudy Night* by Dorothy L. Sayers. Copyright © 1936 by Dorothy Leigh Sayers Fleming. Copyright renewed © 1964 by Anthony Fleming.

Pages 427–32 [1,158 words] from *Busman's Honeymoon* by Dorothy L. Sayers. Copyright © 1937 by Dorothy Leigh Sayers Fleming. Copyright renewed © 1965 by Anthony Fleming.

Excerpt from *The Nine Tailors* by Dorothy L. Sayers. Copyright © 1934 by Dorothy Sayers. Copyright renewed © 1962 by Lloyds Bank Limited. Reprinted by permission of Houghton Mifflin Harcourt Publishing Company. All rights reserved.

Selections from *Creed or Chaos?* taken from *Letters to a Diminished Church,* by Dorothy L. Sayers. Copyright © 2004 by W Publishing. Used by permission of Thomas Nelson. www.thomasnelson.com

Extracts from the following works reprinted by permission of the estate of Dorothy Sayers and the Watkins/Loomis Agency (for both print and ebook editions except where noted):

The Divine Comedy II: Purgatory by Dante, Alighieri, translated by Dorothy L. Sayers. [201 words] Copyright © 1955 by Dorothy L. Sayers.

Begin Here: A Statement of Faith. [189 words] Copyright © 1940 by The Lost Tools of Learning

The Emperor Constantine: A Chronicle. [526 words] Copyright © 1951 by Dorothy L. Sayers

Four Sacred Plays. (*The Devil to Pay* [973 words], *The Just Vengeance* [1,059 words], *He That Should Come* [364 words]) Copyright 1948 by Dorothy L. Sayers.

Great Short Stories of Detection, Mystery, and Horror, Third Series, edited by Dorothy L. Sayers [173 words]

"Letter Addressed to 'Average People.'" *The City Temple Tidings,* July, 1946, p. 166. [528 words]

The Lost Tools of Learning. [118 words]

The Man Born to Be King. [6,302 words] Copyright © 1943 by Dorothy L. Sayers.

"More Pantheon Papers." *Punch,* January 13, 1954, p. 84. [165 words]

"The Psychology of Advertising." *The Spectator,* November 19, 1937, pp. 24–26. And "The Wimsey Papers – IV." *The Spectator,* December 8, 1939, 809–10. [1,751 words together]

Unpopular Opinions. [8,727 words] Copyright © 1946 by Dorothy L. Sayers.

The Zeal of Thy House. [1,476 words] Copyright © 1937 by Dorothy L. Sayers.

The Letters of Dorothy L. Sayers: Volume Two. [1,663 words] Letters Copyright © 1997 by The Trustees of Anthony Fleming deceased.

The Letters of Dorothy L. Sayers: Volume Three. [411 words] Letters Copyright © 1998 by The Trustees of Anthony Fleming deceased.

The Mind of the Maker. [4,449 words] Copyright © 1941 by Dorothy L. Sayers. Copyright renewed 1968 by Anthony Fleming. (print rights only)

The Documents in the Case. [1,741 words] Copyright © 1930 by Dorothy L. Sayers Fleming and Robert Eustace. Copyright renewed © 1958 by Lloyds Bank, Ltd. (ebook rights only)

Extracts from the following works published in ebook editions by permission of Open Road Integrated Media:

Whose Body? [3235 words] Copyright © 1923 by Dorothy Leigh Sayers Fleming.

Unnatural Death. [996 words] Copyright © 1927 by Dorothy Leigh Sayers Fleming. Copyright renewed © 1955 by Dorothy Leigh Sayers Fleming.

The Unpleasantness at the Bellona Club. [1,209 words] Copyright © 1928 by Dorothy Leigh Sayers Fleming. Copyright renewed © 1956 by Dorothy Leigh Sayers Fleming.

Strong Poison. [1,139 words] Copyright © 1930 by Dorothy L. Sayers Fleming. Copyright renewed © 1958 by Lloyd's Bank, Ltd., Executor of the Estate of Dorothy L. Sayers.

The Five Red Herrings. [645 words] Copyright © 1931 by Dorothy Leigh Sayers Fleming.

Have His Carcase. [433 words] Copyright © 1932 by Dorothy Leigh Sayers Fleming. Copyright renewed © 1960 by Lloyd's Bank Ltd.

Murder Must Advertise. [1,531 words] Copyright © 1933 by Dorothy Leigh Sayers Fleming. Copyright renewed © 1961 by Lloyd's Bank Ltd., Executor of the Estate of Dorothy L. Sayers.

The Nine Tailors. [5,048 words] Copyright © 1934 by Dorothy L. Sayers. Copyright renewed © 1962 by Lloyd's Bank Limited.

Gaudy Night. [3,168 words] Copyright © 1936 by Dorothy Leigh Sayers Fleming. Copyright renewed © 1964 by Anthony Fleming.

Busman's Honeymoon. [1,158 words] Copyright © 1937 by Dorothy Leigh Sayers Fleming. Copyright renewed © 1965 by Anthony Fleming.

Mind of the Maker. [4,449 words] Copyright © 1941 by Dorothy L. Sayers. Copyright renewed 1968 by Anthony Fleming.

"A Panegyric for Dorothy L. Sayers" from *On Stories and Other Essays* by C. S. Lewis copyright © 1982, 1966 by C. S. Lewis Pte. Ltd. Extract reprinted by permission.

The Gospel in Great Writers

The Gospel in Dorothy L. Sayers: Selections from Her Novels, Plays, Letters, and Essays. A master of the detective story delves into mysteries of faith, doubt, human nature, feminism, art, and more.

The Gospel in Dostoyevsky: Selections from His Works. Passages from Dostoyevsky's greatest novels explore the devastating, yet ultimately healing, implications of the Gospels.

The Gospel in George MacDonald: Selections from His Novels, Fairy Tales, and Spiritual Writings. Discover the spiritual vision of the great Scottish storyteller who inspired C. S. Lewis and J. R. R. Tolkien.

The Gospel in Gerard Manley Hopkins: Selections from His Poems, Letters, Journals, and Spiritual Writings. Discover in his own words the struggle for faith that gave birth to some of the best poetry of all time.

The Gospel in Tolstoy: Selections from His Short Stories, Spiritual Writings, and Novels. A rich, accessible introduction to one of the world's greatest novelists, this anthology shows how the life and teachings of Jesus inspired some of Tolstoy's best literary work.

Plough Publishing House
151 Bowne Drive, PO BOX 398, Walden, NY 12586, USA
Brightling Road, Robertsbridge, East Sussex TN32 5DR, UK
4188 Gwydir Highway, Elsmore, NSW 2360, Australia
845-572-3455 • info@plough.com • www.plough.com